M000286363

By KAREN BOVENMYER

Swift for the Sun

Published by DREAMSPINNER PRESS
www.dreamspinnerpress.com

SWIFT
FOR THE
SUN

Karen Bovenmyer

Published by

DREAMSPINNER PRESS

5032 Capital Circle SW, Suite 2, PMB# 279, Tallahassee, FL 32305-7886 USA
www.dreamspinnerpress.com

Swift for the Sun
© 2017 Karen Bovenmyer.

Cover Art
© 2017 Anna Sikorska.
Cover content is for illustrative purposes only and any person depicted on the cover is a model.

ISBN: 978-1-63477-763-6
Digital ISBN: 978-1-63477-764-3
Library of Congress Control Number: 2016914554
Published March 2017
v. 1.0

Printed in the United States of America
∞
This paper meets the requirements of
ANSI/NISO Z39.48-1992 (Permanence of Paper).

This book is for Troy, Craig, Sean, Chaz, and Pete, who let me into their lives and hearts. I love you, friends.

ACKNOWLEDGMENTS

FIRST AND foremost, thank you to my editor, Desi Chapman, without whom this book would not exist. A champion from the beginning, I deeply enjoyed and valued Desi's ability to challenge me to write at my very best, provide pinpoint advice and suggestions, and demonstrate sheer grit through multiple drafts. Thank you also to editor Paul Genesse for critical advice and crucial encouragement that launched my professional career.

Thank you to a vast crew of personal friends and family: Sean, David, Sarah, Jeff, Heather S., Audrey, Austin, John, Heather E., Joan, Jeremy, Beth, Joe, Marilynn, and Ellery Jude for everything from politely listening to story ideas to reading early drafts to feeding and walking me during deadline/crunch times.

Props to members of my critique groups—the OddStones (Shawna, Renee, Cecelia, Olivia, Brigitte, Dave), Stonecoasters (Mike, Cortney, John, and Richard), and Wonder Woman Dumpster Fire (AJ, Peter, Kaitlin, Jen, Erin, Paul, Kate, and Cameron) for unflagging emotional support and stupendous edits. My eternal gratitude to the MFA faculty in the University of Southern Maine's Stonecoast program and also all of my creative writing students at Iowa State. You inspire me so much!

Lastly, I would like to thank Rodrigo y Gabriela for the beautiful acoustic guitar music that sustained me while creating this manuscript.

KAREN BOVENMYER'S NOTE

WORDS AND phrases from French, Icelandic, Italian, Latin, Louisiana Creole, Portuguese, and Spanish used in this story are translated in a Glossary of Foreign Terms and Proverbs at the end of this book.

CHAPTER 1.
DREAD ISLAND

THE STORM billowed across the evening sky, a dark bank of clouds coming fast from the southeast, as if God were drawing a curtain between us and Brazil.

"Captain."

The *Sea Swift* jumped forward under an enormous press of sail, and I held tight to the gunnel to keep my feet on deck. The deep blue Caribbean waters rose quickly and swelled, tinged with the gray rage of a tempest sea.

When I didn't answer, the first mate, Black Miguel, repeated himself sharply. I abruptly remembered I was, in fact, his captain—a man the crew thought was Benjamin Swift, infamous smuggler and gunrunner—and no longer the boy I'd been when I left New Orleans.

"Furl the sails," I said, hoping that sounded wise as I studied the full-bellied canvas. I'd been captain of the *Sea Swift* for three weeks, and apart from sharing a first name, mulatto coloring, and general good looks with the real Captain Benji, I still barely knew a halyard from a hawsehole.

"Clap on, both of you! You heard Captain Benji. Close-reef the topsails and furl the rest," Black Miguel shouted my modified order at the jolly lads amidships. The two sailors, Carlos the Whistler and Joaquim One-Leg, brothers, both as skilled with rope and tackle as they were with song and jest, hauled hard on the lines to raise the mainsail.

"*Um, dois, três,*" Carlos sang out the rope, Joaquim echoing him, and I was delighted when they followed with the opening lines of "Marujo Português," a sea song about the joy a Portuguese sailor has for his profession. Yards of canvas folded up, neat as bed linens, and more men climbed high in the rigging to fold back a corner of the topsails—a precaution that nevertheless kept some wind in the canvas as we ran before the gale.

There was no sign of the *Sea Fury*, our sister ship, but she'd put in for repairs and was a few days behind us. Black sheets of rain fell across the horizon behind the roiling cloud bank. It was easily the largest storm I'd seen during this, my first, short voyage at sea.

"Is there anywhere nearby we can safely berth and take shelter from the storm?" I asked, the last line of Carlos's song—*ameaça de carinhosas marés*, the threat of loving seas—echoing across the deck.

Black Miguel shook his head. "We're too far south of Barbados and too far north of Trinidad…." He pinched his chin in the way I recognized from many nights of cards together in the captain's—my—cabin that meant he was considering a risky wager.

"Go on," I urged him.

He ran both hands through his close-clipped curly, black hair. All the men wore their hair short aboard ship to discourage lice—no gentleman's ribboned queue on either of us, not that I was any more of a true gentleman than I was a smuggler. Miguel pulled me aside and lowered his voice. "We're not far from Dread Island, but… well, you asked for a safe port. There's nothing safe about that skull-and-bones stretch of sand."

I laughed. "Skull and bones? As in a Jolly Roger? Miguel, we're gunrunners. What do we have to fear from a pirate island? Likely we'd meet fellows in arms." Some of the associates I'd met before we left port I was certain were other gunrunners and malefactors—as was the chief smuggler I met over a game of billiards, a Scotsman named Edwin James, who swore he'd make me a rich man for my investment.

"No, in a literal sense. Dread Island is a place where men die. No man who sets foot on her sands returns to his ship. Dark spirits haunt that place."

"This is the age of reason, s—Miguel." I had to stop myself from adding his gentleman's honorific. Aboard ship he was first mate, and no gentleman, and even though we were having a private conversation, it was best not to fall out of the habit. "Superstition does not become lettered men."

Miguel gestured to include the seamen climbing through the rigging, hauling ropes, binding the sails tight against the storm. Sailors were as famous for their superstitions as they were for whoring and gambling.

"Well, yes. But we don't have to tell them where we are mooring," I said.

"Because they are not learned, do not take them for fools. Every man who sails the Caribbean knows to steer clear of Dread Island. And, moreover, even I have heard the stories. Pirates, merchants, and navy men alike avoid the place, even when in need of freshwater and food. Cursed or not, all die who set foot there."

I stared at the forbidding storm, and my instincts, what few I had, urged me to make for the island with haste. "Miguel, look at how fast those clouds are moving. We need to make berth."

Miguel shook his head, loosed a juicy curse in his native Portuguese, and then dashed off for the sextant to take our latitude using the last of the setting sun. We argued fiercely about it under our breaths so the men wouldn't notice dissention between us, nor where we were making a heading. I felt something pulling me to Dread Island, the strains of Cowper's hymn sounding in my head:

God moves in a mysterious way
His wonders to perform;
He plants His footsteps in the sea
And rides upon the storm.

"Look here." Miguel pointed to a small arc on the chart, northeast of a speck of an island in the Lesser Antilles. *Here be shoals.* "We'd need gentle or no winds on a clear day to navigate those. Our best hope now is out to sea."

I looked again at the clouds, which had thickened into a solid wall of wisp and fury.

"So be it," I relented as thick drops of rain slapped against my face and shoulders. "Sail on." Yet I could not help but feel the island was where the *Swift* needed to go.

"Yessir." Miguel hopped to, shouting orders to furl the close-reefed topsails to ride out the storm.

The wind had been blowing us south by southeast, away from the Lesser Antilles and out into heavy seas in the wide Atlantic, which would make dodging the powerful and fast French marines easier. Considering the devastating shipwreck of the *Medusa* and Napoleon recently in his grave, the *capitaines* had something to prove about France as a naval power and were particularly vicious to anyone they suspected of illegal activity. With a southeastern wind, we'd reach the coast of South America in two days, but the storm threatened to push us back the way we'd come, amid the volcanic once-islands the sea was slowly grinding down into shoals. Only luck and a skilled hand would keep us safe, so I left the command of our crew chiefly in Black Miguel's capable hands, lest I reveal myself as a lubber.

"Get below, *Captain*," Miguel said as rain started to drum the planks. Men were still in the rigging, struggling to let out the reef and furl the too-full topsail. The sea had slowly become more violent, but, much to my surprise, my uneasy stomach made no answering rumble. It seemed I'd finally adapted to the rolling of the ship. I watched the frantic activity around me and realized for the first time in my life, I was part of something bigger than myself. I had always wanted to be a sailor, and now, in truth, I was. I was a man of the *Sea Swift* and, ultimately, as captain, she and every rough, unlettered, jolly soul aboard was my responsibility.

"No. The men need their captain. I'll stay above decks."

Black Miguel rose one elegant black eyebrow—his hair was the only thing dark about him. In every way, he had looked and spoken like a well-bred, if well-tanned, Portuguese gentleman in New Orleans, and Edwin James, the handsome Scotsman who had brought me into this adventure, had failed to explain the reason behind the nickname when he introduced us. It really wasn't fair; from the moment Miguel Maria's feet touched the deck of the *Swift* and he introduced me to the crew, he'd moved through rigging and hauled ropes like a man born to it. Miguel did everything like a man born to it—dancing jig, sawing the fiddle, playing a brilliant hand of cards, fixing the bungled orders during my first few weeks and preserving my identity for the men. He was my right hand, and I knew well I would not long have managed this farce without him.

Miguel nodded, his lips twitching upward in a habit I'd come to associate not only with amusement but approval. "As you say, Captain. Hold fast, and keep your wits ready."

A shout drew our attention. The mizzenmast topsail had broken free of the reef and flapped wildly in the gale. Rain came down in sheets, and I held tight to the mainstay to keep my feet as the deck pitched on an angry sea. Miguel shouted, and more men climbed the rigging, Carlos among them, to wrestle the sail back under control and furl all the reefed sails, which even I could see were now taking on far too much wind. The storm grew fiercer, and I was needed to retie lines for the bowsprit—a feat I accomplished with a line wound around one arm to keep me aboard despite the waves crashing over the gunnel and washing across the deck.

I lost track of time in the work, and then a resounding crack drew every eye to the mizzenmast. The still-flapping topsail pitched overboard with twelve foot of spar, and Carlos, holding tight to the lines, disappeared under the heaving waves.

"Man overboard!" Miguel's commands thundered through the racket of storm and sea, and the crew dashed to stations, but then the ropes ran out of give.

The ship groaned alarmingly and yawed hard to starboard, pulling against the broken topsail, which was now acting as a massive rudder, and I slammed hard into another man assigned to the bowsprit, Big Swede Erik, who knew even less English than Portuguese, every word of it a viler curse than the last. He held fast to me with one thick arm. Then Miguel was on hand with an ax, chopping at the ropes that attached us to Carlos's doom, Joaquim screaming for his brother.

The storm and the wreckage pulled against each other, near capsizing the ship, and another man fell past me to splash into the sea. Shouts and thrown ropes followed him. The *Swift* gave another mighty pull against the fallen topsail, and the deck tilted so sharply I thought we were done for certain. Then, with a splintering crack, another topsail tore free, this time from the mainmast, sweeping men and wood overboard as it fell. A line snapped tight, caught Miguel in the chest, and slammed him hard against the mainmast. Blood ran red from his mouth and over his chin.

I picked up Miguel's ax. There was nothing to do except chop the lines that anchored us to the wreckage spinning the *Swift* in churning seas. I am not ashamed to admit I cried as I cut the lines, pervaded by a bone-deep feeling that Miguel and all hands were doomed regardless. I had delayed too long in making the decision to ride out the storm rather than make for Dread Island. Every dead man was my fault. When I cut the line holding him against the mainmast, Miguel slumped to the deck and slid into me.

"What do we do?" I screamed at him over the storm and splintering wood, the shouts of drowning men and a loud grinding coming from the hold beneath us.

"Pray, preacher's son." He coughed a splash of red into his fist and looped a rope around my waist, then tied it fast to a barrel on the deck. "You were never much of a sailor, even if you are the spitting image of Captain Benji," Miguel said, snugging a bowling knot under my arms, "but I damn well hope you can at least swim." Then he cut the barrel free, as a scream of splintering wood growled up from below decks, a jolting crash that even I knew meant we had run up on shoals, and then I was overboard and falling through a chaos of rain and sea and splinters.

I DO not clearly remember the passage of that awful night—a tumult of wave and wind and the yells of drowning men and the splintering *Swift*. My body was battered and buffeted by water and shattered wood and other bodies. The sea tossed and turned me; I did not know up from down. Taking a breath meant water as often as air. I hauled myself along the rope until I wrapped both arms around the barrel, and then all was darkness and aching hands and fingers.

The storm seemed to last an eternity, until I thought I had drowned and this was, in fact, hell. There came a sudden calm in the storm, and I looped my rope tighter around the barrel, tying my body to it as best as I could, because I did not know how much longer I could hold on. Other wreckage bobbed in the chop around me, but I could not make out if any of the shapes were survivors. Then the rage of the storm returned, tossing me with such ferocity I lost all sense of the man I was. I was naught but an animal striving to live until the struggle abated with death's embrace.

I floated in darkness, nigh insensible, praying for an end, praying for the other sailors of the *Swift*, until I felt something solid against my feet and, kicking out, discovered it was sand. Thanking God, I struggled through the surf, forcing my tired body away from the sea and up onto a beach, until I couldn't haul both myself and the barrel farther. My hands were too weak and battered to untie the ropes, so I stayed where I was and gave myself over to exhaustion.

I woke in dawn's first light—the false dawn that turned the sea beautiful shades of silver-gray—and took in my surroundings. White sand stretched in a crescent to either side, lapped gently by glittering waves. Pieces of the *Swift* littered the shore and the water, drifting closer, then back.

I did not see another man, living or dead.

My hands were chafed and torn from holding the rope and barrel that had been my salvation. I thought of Miguel and his last act, saving me, a man who knew nothing and was nothing, while Miguel and the crew of the *Swift*—men I believed good and true, despite being smugglers—faced destruction and death. And yet I, the son of a white preacher and a mixed schoolmarm with no claim to fame other than a striking resemblance to a famous smuggler, lived. Despair crashed over me, ill-fitting the beauty of my surroundings and the gentle susurrus of the sea. Deep loss pulled at my heart and soul. My first voyage, my first real responsibility, had ended in horror, as Father had always said it would.

The sun was somewhat higher in the sky as I mastered my feelings, gathered my wits, and untied myself from the barrel. I took stock of my surroundings. Coconut palms arched over a white beach, a thick forest of mangrove and fern dark shadowed behind them, with the great indistinct cone of a mountain shrouded in wisps of fog beyond that. I had the clothes on my back and nothing else; my saber and pistol were gone, belt and all, as was my coat and hat. I had only my battered shirt and britches, not even shoes. I sifted through the smithereens of the *Swift*, the command that had cost me everything, and found nothing of value except the wood, as kindling.

Not even kindling was useful, because I had no flint and tinder, but I pulled each piece up onto the beach, regardless, as if by doing so, I could conjure up Miguel and Carlos and Joaquim and the rest of the hearty, gambling, laughing seamen I'd known.

I had a vague feeling someone was watching me, and thought perhaps it was God.

As the sun rose in the sky, so did my want of drink, and I realized that, though I'd been spared from the sea, I was not spared from the dangers of thirst, nor hunger, nor exposure. My skin was lighter than first-generation mixed but darker than a white man's, no matter what my father claimed to avoid paying North Carolina's mulatto tax on me. Any man, whatever color his skin, burns in the sun of the tropics. I needed shelter, food, water. I had the barrel to which I'd been tied, but nothing to open it with. In any case, it did not feel heavy enough to contain water—not even the green, scummy water aboard ship—so a source of freshwater was my chief concern. It was time to leave my small camp of wood and barrel, and explore the island. I used a large, round leaf from a sea grape to keep the sun off my shorn head and out of my eyes and set off in search of salvation.

As I walked the curve of the beach, staying mostly in the shade of the palms to stop the sand burning my feet, I saw more wreckage scattered along the shore—pieces of spar and rigging, sailcloth, other unrecognizable things—then a shallow impression in the sand, as if a man had lain there. I ran forward, swearing as I scorched my feet and apologizing to the Almighty as I did so, to find that there had, indeed, been another survivor. The shape of his hip where he'd rested, the sweep of his thigh, the impression of knees as he rose were clear imprints in the sand, as were his footsteps leading away. I ran after his prints and struggled up a low dune cresting in a rock formation, but the trail ended at a dark pool of wet sand. I felt the wetness, and my hand came away red.

Blood.

Climbing the dune and rocks elevated me above the beach as the last of the fog dissipated. A great volcanic cone rose from the island's center, pitted and sunken at the rim, giving the mountain the faint look of the empty eye sockets and gaping jaw of a human skull, the braincase truncated and open to the heavens.

Confronted with this ghastly vision and the evidence at my very feet, I could not doubt that I was marooned on the isle Black Miguel had mentioned. The beach of skull and bone.

Dread Island.

CHAPTER 2.
THE HUNTER

I CROUCHED, hiding among the rocks, as if the skull peak could see me and by seeing me, inflict its curse upon me. When Satan himself failed to come and gather me to his bosom, I regained my wits and applied logic to my predicament. No matter how much blood, a body, alive or dead, did not simply disappear. I slowed my breathing, calmed my mind, and looked carefully for tracks. There were, in fact, drag marks, which I followed cautiously down the slope on the other side. The trail led off into the mangroves. A rational man I was, but not an armed one. Following whomever or whatever had taken my shipmate away into the dark forest seemed foolhardy at best, suicidal at worst, so I returned to the beach and rooted among the smithereens for a likely weapon.

My thirst only grew as I searched for a weapon in the sun. So, finally armed with a belaying pin, I made my way back up the beach to hunt for freshwater, looking before and behind, keeping a careful eye on the dark edges of the forest, prepared to defend myself if anyone attacked.

The feeling of being watched by a silent observer intensified—from time to time, a faint sound echoed from the forest, as though something as large as a man was moving through the undergrowth.

Now and then, I walked through the surf to cool my burning feet. Miles of wreckage lay scattered along the sand, and by standing atop another rocky dune, I spotted a large piece of what looked like a forecastle far out to sea, spearing up from the water. I thought I made out what was left of the figurehead on the broken prow—a battered swift, missing one wing. My ship. Nothing moved on the wreckage, so my brief hope for survivors was dashed. The prow, perched on the crest of some unseen shoal, rocked with the waves. It was too far to swim, especially in my thirsty, hungry, rapidly weakening state, so I continued on.

I found nothing but more rocks and sand as I walked. It was afternoon by the time I rounded the north shore and started following the west, Dread Island's mountain skull a far less threatening green-and-brown cone from this side. Yet the feeling I was being watched lingered. At times the shore had no beach but only sheer mountainside, and that was when I swam against an alarming undertow, past mysterious rents and fissures in the stone—partially submerged caves that echoed with pounding surf—until I was once again on the beach. There was no undertow in the lakes and streams of North Carolina, where I'd learned to swim. I cursed myself for not deciding to walk the other way round the island, because the sun followed me down the western shore, and for relief, I had to walk closer than I liked under the shade of the trees, where I was now convinced the lurking watcher waited.

I found no freshwater, not a river, not a stream, not even a small runoff from the recent storm. I dared not go too far under the canopy, but at last I could not resist the relative cool the shade offered. I managed to gain some freshwater from pools collected in wide leaves of undergrowth, but it was barely enough to wet my lips and did little to quench my thirst.

Something moved in the jungle, sending ferns and a wide-leafed plant I could not name swaying. I readied the belaying pin and put my back to the sea, in case it was the watcher. A bright green anole scurried across the leaf I'd drunk from a moment before and leaped onto the neighboring mangrove, disturbed by whatever moved deeper in the shadows.

"Who goes there?" I shouted. The rustling grew louder, but it moved fast away from me, lost in the gloom. I felt a little better having frightened it away, whatever it was, but clutched my makeshift weapon nevertheless, despite my battered hands.

When nothing else happened, I continued my circuit of the island. By dusk, I was back at my camp of piled wreckage, and none the wiser. I'd flushed birds and lizards from the trees, watched a speckled turtle glide through the clear blue water, taken note of several varieties of fish, but saw no other men nor a source of freshwater. I was too weak to put together any defenses, not even a small perimeter of standing boards, but I did wrap a piece of torn sailcloth over myself as my bed—the sand still held the heat of the day, but the wind coming off the sea was cold after my exertions. I fell into a fitful sleep, my belaying pin ready, and I woke for every small sound, shivering as the night slowly stole all warmth from the sand.

I WOKE suddenly, pulled from dreams of sea and storm by a fearful sound—a horrible squealing growl, like a rusty hinged porthole forced open. I scrambled to my feet, confused, sailcloth tangling round my ankles, the sky bright with predawn around me. The sound came from the tree line, but no one else was on the beach, only me. A victim of sudden vertigo, I fell to my knees. My head felt only vaguely attached to my body, and my heart thudded wildly in my chest. A vicious rustling of ferns accompanied the terrible sound again, and I pushed the sailcloth away, snatching up a shattered plank.

Nothing came out of the forest, which was just as well, because I was too weak to hold the plank up for long. I waited, but nothing happened, so I moved cautiously to the tree line. I felt certain something other than the volcano was watching me. Perhaps this time it was whoever or whatever had taken away my fellow survivor. I fervently wished for my trusty flintlock pistols. I strove to break my fast on what water remained in the leaves, but finding very little indeed, I chewed up the bitter, curled ends of ferns in hope they would be enough to sustain me.

I spent the early morning trying to catch some food—a lizard, or bird, or fish—but I lacked both tools and skills. I failed entirely to fashion a net from a piece of sailcloth, and had nothing to hone a point of wood to make a spear. I knew my situation was dire and growing more so. I worked to create a small shelter with the barrel, sailcloth, and wood from the ship, but it collapsed partway through; I was no better a carpenter than a sailor. However, this gave me the idea to build a signal fire made from the bones of the *Swift*. If I could signal some other smuggler or merchant marine, they might chance Dread Island, superstition or not, to see who had lit it. A long shot, but likely the only one I had with no source of freshwater but the rain, and no clouds on the horizon.

By the end of the second day, I had the best pyre I could build with the materials on hand, but no way to light it. My attempts striking rocks together to make a spark were not only fruitless but exhausting. My skin crawled with the eyes of the watcher, and for long periods of time, I found myself looking into the forest or at the volcano above the trees.

As the third day dawned, I woke aching and almost too weak to move; I knew if the watcher were God, this was the day He would collect me. I felt insulated and distant from the passage of time. I marked that the sun traveled across the sky, but a sense of the unreal blanketed my thoughts and feelings. My dread of the forest seemed inconsequential now—death on the beach was certain, so death under the canopy seemed the lesser evil. Still, when I entered and felt the forest closing around me, I had to push through more than vegetation; I had to push past fear. I grabbed for lizards that escaped me, scared small birds I could not catch, and found a mass of fiddlehead ferns I ate greedily. I dug for roots, tried them with my teeth, and found them too tough to chew. I ate bugs and the small crawling things that lived in the earth, then paid for it with violent retching and watery bowels back at my camp.

When night fell, so did I. I lay on the hot sand and thought, *This is it. This is death.* And I laughed weakly, because I'd never expected it to end this way. My father had always said I'd be found hanging from a tree because of my "unnatural lusts," and when I announced my intention to become a sailor, he'd said they'd make do with dangling me from a yardarm as a sodomite. I'd tried to explain to Father on many occasions that I simply preferred the company of men, and none of the women in the village held any particular interest for me. He'd scoffed and continued to beat me whenever he caught me spending more time than was necessary watching our boy chop wood or too much time standing up for drinks with the village men at the tavern.

"It's for your own protection, boy," he'd say as he raised the belt. "Without me, you'd be dead in a fortnight." Afterward we would pray together for God to forgive us for our sins and help us find the right path. I prayed now. Though Father was dead and gone, it seemed he was right. My end was nigh.

"Help me. Please," I called, with what life I had left in me, to God, to the watcher, to anyone, as darkness cooled the sand and my body. "Forgive me." I did not have the energy left to shiver, only to lie there and feel my body become cold, like a stone, calling out for I knew not who or what.

He came for me in the deepest part of the night, and with him, my fear returned in a final, instinctual rush.

I was too weak to fight the sudden shadow that blocked out the stars above. I tried to yell, but my parched throat only produced grunts and moans. He lifted me from the cold sands—his hold strong and his body warm against my skin. He hoisted me across his shoulders, my head and arms dangling down one side, legs the other. He was a small man but sure of foot, and he neither stumbled nor slipped as he carried me up the beach, my head bouncing. His oiled skin shone with reflected moonlight. We entered the darkness of the woods, which had come to represent fear and death to me. I lost sensibility for a while then, feebly trying to slide free of his hold, but did not even manage to unbalance him. My head and feet brushed leaf and fern, but I saw nothing in the night-dark forest, not the man who carried me, the unseen path he followed, nor our eventual destination when we reached it.

I felt it, though, when we entered a cave, the deeper cold and echoed sounds of rock revealing its nature. I came to and faded out and came to again. He lowered me carefully from his shoulders onto something soft, a pile of half-haired leathers that smelled strongly of gristle and faintly of mold. I was only partially aware of the application of a soft, wet cloth to my face and lips—freshwater—which I sucked at greedily. He dribbled it into my mouth in the darkness and spoke quietly in a language with hard consonants I did not recognize. His hands were gentle on my cold skin, and he covered me with another hide that lay stiff across my body.

Throughout the black of the night, he nursed me. I passed out or slept, then regained my sensibilities, calling out, and he gave me water and kind words. At last I fell into a fitful sleep filled with images of sea and storm and a puddle of red, red blood.

FOR THE first time in three days, I woke without sand crusting my mouth. My lips were painful and cracked, and bright light streamed in through the cave opening—a yawning hole facing the rising sun. My eyes were sore, and my head hurt mightily. Rock walls surrounded my bed of half-cured hides, and as I tried to rise, I found my wrists and ankles bound with cords. I called out, but I was in the cave alone.

It smelled of leather, smoke, and old meat. Personal effects littered the ground—I recognized an empty snuff box, a battered kettle, a brass pocket watch, a horsehair brush but no shaving knife, and a tattered red flag bearing a white cross among the jumble. A few barrels nestled along the wall and seemed to serve as rude tables. Next to them was a woodpile with an ax laid neatly atop. I crawled toward it. I'd read about the *canibales*, island natives who ate human flesh. Although my captor had brought me here and saved my life rather than staining the white sands with my blood, I still did not know who my rescuer was, and I'd rather starve or die of exposure than be eaten. My weakness necessitated short rests as I struggled across the floor, each a fearful interlude waiting for my captor to return. I managed to knock the ax to the ground and laboriously cut, with careful sawing, my ankles free, only gouging myself once, but I had great difficulty bracing the ax so I could free my wrists.

I didn't hear him come, so intent was I, but I noticed when his shadow blocked the cave mouth. I rose unsteadily to my feet, the ax held awkwardly in my bound hands. He crouched in the entrance and stared at me, unmoving. His hands were full of round green fruits that looked somewhat like small limes. He was naked except for a scrap of leather he wore around his hips like a loincloth.

The sun rising behind him lit his hair with tints of shining gold, sunlight streaming past a mass of tangled blond braids. His eyes surprised me, not the brown of a native, but smoke-blue like an angry sea, dark and hidden, set deep in the sharp angles of his face. Not a *canibal*, then... a European alone—another shipwreck survivor like myself? He wasn't smiling. He entered the cave slowly, his eyes tracking the ax trembling in my hands.

He stopped before me, out of reach, and spoke. It was his gentle voice that had carried me through the night, though I did not recognize the language. He thrust his tanned and scarred arms toward me, peeling a green rind in a long coil, showing me the yellow flesh inside. He held it up.

"*Aldin.*" His voice was high, a young man's, but cracked, like he wasn't used to speaking. He turned the fruit slowly and took a bite. Juice ran down his chin.

I studied him as he ate, hunger roiling in my belly. We were of an age. Despite his many scars, he looked as though he were in his late teens or early twenties. I was bigger, but his slender body was packed with strong, wiry muscles, and I was weak. I could barely stand, and if I didn't eat what he offered, I wasn't likely to live much longer to lament the fact. I didn't know why he was saving me, why he'd tied me up, who he was, or where he was from, but I decided I wanted to live long enough to find out. I lowered the ax and let it slide to the ground.

"*Aldin.*" I nodded. He smirked and held one for me until I carefully took it. He watched me bring it, double-handed and restricted by my bonds, to my mouth. It was tart but delicious and mostly pit. His eyes tracked my movements, and a tension in his body showed he was ready to defend himself. He needn't have worried. Now that I had satisfied my curiosity about his appearance, I turned my attention fully to the food he'd brought me. In fact, it and he, were my only hope of surviving the island.

I ate every morsel, even sucking the juice from the pit, and when I looked back at him, he smiled widely. His teeth were white, straight, even, like what God dreamed of when he made men, and the harsh planes of his face were softened by the appearance of a dimple.

"*Aldin,*" he said again, and licked juice from his fingers. I saw now he was very fair under the dirt and tan. His eyebrows and eyelashes were white-blond, his bone structure fine, but the scars heavy across his shoulders told the tale that someone had whipped him savagely, not only once, but many times.

I flinched as he rose, but he only fetched a covered basket from atop one of the barrels, then opened it to reveal more food. I knelt before him, sharing a meal of fruits, nuts, and what I supposed was dried lizard, and I hoped I was right to trust him, even though I knew I had no other choice. Clearly he'd survived for some time on this island, and I wanted to do the same, so I reasoned it best to learn from him and do as he did. If there was one thing I was good at doing, it was following better men. Except, unlike Black Miguel, I hoped I didn't get this one killed.

CHAPTER 3.
THE HUNT

HE UNTIED my wrists after we finished sharing our meal and brought more water, but then he stopped me from gulping it, motioning that I should take small sips. Between sips I asked him questions—chiefly if he'd seen any other men who survived the *Swift*, and if he knew the reputation of this place and what happened to those marooned here—but he didn't have the English to answer. He asked me questions as well, in his language, then a few other tongues, but none I knew, and I couldn't answer him any better than he answered me. I had a reasonable command of French from Mother and some Latin from Father, as well as a smattering of curse words from half-a-dozen other languages, but no formal training in anything else.

Still, he was companionable enough, if a bit abrupt in his movements. He had no qualms about pushing me down when I tried to get up and follow him out of the cave that evening, pressing me into the leathers and covering me with them. His gentle care as well as food, water, and rest were working wonders, but I was still weak, so I stayed and listened to the sounds of birds calling in the jungle outside. He returned some time later with a woven basket, smelling of brine, holding a spear split at the end into a cluster of four spikes.

He removed a fish from the basket and brought me a board and a small knife, clearly indicating I should clean the fish. While I set to work, glad for something to do, he built up a fire by a method I had never seen before. He carefully selected logs from his collection of firewood—larger ones on the bottom, then successive layers of smaller and smaller kindling until he topped the pile with a handful of shaved bark, opposite of how I'd been taught. Then he wrapped his hands in heavy sailcloth and retrieved what looked like a tea strainer from the ash bed of the fire pit. He carefully dropped a live, red-orange coal from the strainer on top of his kindling. It lit quickly, with almost no smoke, and burned down, not up. What little smoke came from the fire went up and out the high door leading into this place, which served as both an entryway and a natural chimney. As the fire burned down to a more consistent temperature, he wrapped the fish I'd cleaned in broad leaves and put them directly in the coals. Before long, we were peeling back the leaves and charred skin to the delicious, flaky meat inside.

He spoke to me in his language again, but I only stared at him, feeling more and more idiotic.

"Sóli," he said, tapping his chest.

Finally, a word I recognized—it sounded like sol, the Latin word for sun.

"Sun? Your name is Sun?"

He shrugged, then nodded. He tapped his chest again. "Sun."

I felt myself grinning stupidly but didn't care. "I'm Benjamin." I tapped my chest. "Benjamin." I didn't know what last name to give him—should I be myself, Benjamin Lector from North Carolina? Or was it better to pretend to be Captain Benji Swift?

"Benjamin." He pronounced it with a hard *ja* sound, but it was close enough. I decided a last name could wait.

"Yes, Benjamin." I thumped my chest again.

He grinned back, pointed to the fish, and said, *"Fiskur."*

"Yes. Fish."

"Fisk," he said back, nodding, twining one of his many blond braids between his fingers.

We went on like that, naming the things in the cave to each other, knife was *hnífur*, which made sense to me, ax was very close to the same word, brush was something like *bursti*, leaf was *lauf*. I tried to keep the new words in my mind, but, while I love to read, I was never a hand at languages apart from French, and also I was still recovering from my ordeal. Sun learned my words faster than I his, so mostly we spoke in a pidgin made up of simple, slightly mispronounced English.

I tried asking him how he'd come to be here, but he only shook his head, sending his blond braids flying, and repeated his name. So I told him that my ship had run aground on the shoals, but I had managed to survive. It took a long time for me to explain what I wanted to know using our limited language. Were there any other survivors?

"Annað folk? No. Benjamin." He pointed at himself. "Sun. *Einn.* One." He pointed at me. *"Tveir.* Two." I hadn't taught him my counting

words. His expression was inward and focused, and I understood he must have learned some English long ago and was trying to remember.

"Yes. We two. Benjamin and Sun," I said encouragingly.

He grinned again. "Two. Good." He pronounced the *d* with his tongue between his teeth, but the meaning was clear to me.

My stomach was full, I was safe, for now, and we'd had another long day—my eyelids drifted down.

"*Farðu að sofa*, Benjamin."

Then he pulled the musty leathers over me, and I gave myself to sleep.

I WOKE from a dream of fear and blood. I didn't know where I was. The cave was dark except for a faint orange glow from Sun's ember-catcher in the fire pit.

"Sun?"

He knelt by my side in a moment. "Benjamin. *Allt í lagi? Allt*… good?"

"Yes." I nodded, but to my shame, I trembled. Sun's hand found mine and squeezed.

"Only we two, Sun? No other folk?"

"*Nei*. Benjamin. And Sun." He patted the back of my hand.

I tried to explain about the blood in the sand, but he didn't seem to understand. He did seem to listen to me, told me *allt* good, and squeezed my hand until the fear of the dream faded and I went back to sleep.

I WOKE in the first light of day feeling almost like myself again. Sun and I peeled the *aldin* fruit and spoke back and forth—his English was even better, saying words I hadn't taught him and putting them together in new ways. His intelligence surprised me, coming from someone who looked so very unkempt, but he seemed to absorb everything I said with reasonable understanding and said it back to me.

Again I asked him who he was and where he came from, but he would only say his name was Sun. I gathered he had been shipwrecked here like me. He didn't need to say it had been a long, long time since he'd had company. There was something savage and wild about him and a hesitation in speech and action that bespoke many months alone.

I could not help staring at his body—he had a considerable number of scars that could not be explained by whip marks. They looked like someone had sliced him with knives on more than one occasion. Where his people were or how he came to survive what had happened to them was a mystery.

I felt stronger that day, and when I tried to follow Sun out of the cave midmorning, he didn't stop me. It was muggy and warm under the canopy of trees compared to the cool rock underground, but it felt good to stretch my legs. I was taller than Sun, topping him by six inches or more, but there was something in the confident, ready way he held himself that reinforced the sense that he would easily be able to defend himself in a fight.

With Sun by my side, the shadowed forest was not intimidating in the least. I smiled at my remembered fear, both the nightmare and when I was first marooned. Someday I'd stop being a silly lubber and a boy fresh out of home. An idea seized me—perhaps I could make myself understood if I showed Sun the evidence I'd found of another survivor.

"Sun, which way is the beach?"

He shook his head, white-blond braids brushing across his shoulders.

"Sand. The beach. Where you found me."

"*Strönd*?" He pointed down a well-worn path through the trees. "*Strönd* this way."

I started off at a jog, Sun running behind me, then ahead. He was so quick, and watching him run was a joy. I did my best to keep up and was pleased when I didn't fall behind.

My pyre was still a mess of planks and barrels and sailcloth, but instead of leading Sun back there, I went the other way, up the low dune and rock formation where I'd seen the blood. Sun came with me, looking up and down the beach, as if searching for others from the *Swift*.

I topped the small rise and marked my place by the aspect of the skull in the volcano above us, but there was nothing but white sand and rock around our feet.

"It was right here." I knelt, feeling the ground. Had I imagined it?

"*Komdu*, Benjamin. This way." Sun pulled my arm.

"No, Sun. This is where I saw the blood." But there was nothing here to show him. Perhaps the sun and heat had conjured the illusion; I had been through quite an ordeal. I allowed Sun to pull me back to my camp.

He slapped a barrel with a grin and said something that sounded like *braudth*.

I shrugged, because I didn't know what was inside. He pushed it on its broad staves and started rolling it back the way we'd come. I followed, and we spent the rest of the day salvaging what was useful from the beach camp and taking it back to Sun's cave, stopping only for a meal of the browned crispy fish skin from the night before and *aldin*, which I was coming to understand meant any kind of fruit. Sun kept three buckets full of freshwater in his cave, which we drank from using a dented tin ladle.

Sun used the ax on my barrel, and we broke our evening fast on the sailor's hardtack we found inside and a root-mash porridge Sun made from crushed tubers.

"What other animals live on the island? What else is there to hunt?" I asked, thinking of a nice roast.

He looked puzzled.

"What else is there to eat?" I asked. As we moved through the forest, I'd noticed bent stems and scraped bark—signs of other creatures, larger animals, apart from men moving carelessly through the undergrowth.

We shared words back and forth, but it seemed *fiskur* was one of the few animal words close enough for our languages. I pantomimed a bird to make myself understood, and Sun capered about like a monkey. However, I'd seen no signs of the primates, who, in my previous experiences during this voyage, made their presence loudly known whenever men came near. I named his monkey, and he told me the word in his language, *api*, which was close enough to ape for me to understand. Then I tried for lizard, and we passed an amusing evening with pantomime learning words for animals from each other. Sun had a fine comic sense, and his agility allowed him to play the animals quite well. I laughed heartily several times.

When Sun snorted, squealed, and pawed the ground with an imaginary hoof, I realized where I'd seen the same kind of bark scrapings before. Wild boar.

"Pig?"

"*Svín.*"

"Swine, yes!" My mind conjured memories of bacon, and my mouth began to water. "I know what we'll do tomorrow." I would show Sun how we hunt wild boar in the Carolinas.

That night I woke with the same dream, calling out in my sleep, but Sun held my hand until I fell asleep again. When I woke, he was still there, sleeping next to me, curled around himself. His scars crisscrossed his back, white through his tan. He looked so very small and vulnerable

I did not want to disturb him, but when I moved, he was quickly awake and on his feet. He nodded good morning to me, his expression rather grim, and then went outside to make water before I could say ought else, nor sort out my own feelings about having spent the night sleeping so close together. The inconvenient truth was that I woke with stiff muscles and a throb in my unmentionables.

Fortunately we had many preparations to make for the hunt to take my mind off such musings, the likes of which were no doubt causing my father to turn in his grave.

"MORE?" SUN dropped the sticks onto the growing pile on the floor of the cave. The dimpled smile on his face said he was humoring me.

"No. That should do it." I dropped my own pile. "Now I'll show you how we eat in the Carolinas." I was determined to prove I was more than a mouth to feed, though I wasn't sure if I was showing him or myself. "Tonight we feast on wild boar."

Sun watched me carefully as I sharpened a sapling with the small knife I'd used to clean the fish.

"Pig." He grinned and grunted, pawing at the ground.

"Yes. Pig." I couldn't help smiling. He was scarred, half-savage, and the dirt on his person would have caused half the ladies of my acquaintance to faint. But he was funny, warmhearted, and so intelligent we'd more or less only used English all day. He was picking up the language so quickly it was clear he'd once used it in more than a passing way. I imagined him in a suit with a gentleman's queue and a full hand of cards, sitting across the table from Edwin, and I had to laugh. That Sun was so farfetched he would not materialize fully to my mind's eye.

Thinking of Edwin reminded me of Miguel, and the sorrow for my lost shipmates returned. Sun had a means to make fire. Now that I had seen to my immediate survival, I should turn my energies to rescue. However, I'd lost the *Swift* and all the goods she carried, primarily guns bound for Brazilian colonists. A man should have the right to protect himself, and by all reports, huge hunting cats wandered the Amazon. So, despite the restrictions on bringing guns into South America, Portuguese merchants-turned-opportunists ran guns right under the noses of the crumbling empire, and sloops like mine and Edwin's *Sea Fury* were essential to the operation. Trouble was, the *Sea Swift* wasn't really my ship. The loan I'd taken out to lease her from Edwin was half what the guns would have brought me. I would have come out ahead, if both guns and ship weren't currently at the bottom of the sea. What would Edwin do? Would he charge me for those losses? It was easy to remember his broad smile and firm handshake, because those memories had kept me busy many a lonely night in the captain's cabin of the *Swift*, but even I, in my innocence and inexperience, had problems believing the friendly gambler would take the losses lightly.

I put those thoughts aside. At the moment, I was living the grand adventures I'd read about as a boy. Sun and I set out into the forest. I smiled at my hunting partner as he moved soundlessly through the woods. Sun might have been equipped with a lithe body and quick reflexes, but I hadn't misspent my childhood rereading *The Life and Strange Surprising Adventures of Robinson Crusoe* and *The Swiss Family Robinson* for nothing. I was finally having an adventure of my own. It didn't matter that I hadn't actually been on a feral-pig hunt but only heard the tavern men speaking of it. It was a simple matter to apply my educated mind to this task. I was quite convinced those pigs were in trouble.

SUN LED me on a circuitous path around the volcano. There was one well-beaten track that ran around the base of the mountain, sometimes higher, sometimes lower, following the slope of the ground, with occasional side tracks joining up with it. I found hoofmarks in the soft mud of the forest floor now that we were farther away from Sun's cave. Definitely pig—I was at least enough of a naturalist, if not a hunter or farmer, to recognize the splayed hoof.

As we went, we found more signs—torn earth from rooting, a dirty puddle surrounded by tracks and hairy impressions in the mud that must have been a wallow, and more signs of boars rubbing their tusks on the trees, which, as we entered a low coastal plain, were festooned with long dark bean pods that caused the foliage to resemble old men with grasping fingers.

I motioned to Sun to be quiet, which was entirely unnecessary because he made no sounds I could detect. If anything, I was the loud one. I held my whittled javelins lightly in one hand and a bag of the small green fruits in the other as I scouted around the outside edge of the plain, where it sloped gradually away into the sea, changing from grasses to rocky grasses to rocky sands, to beach. An escarpment clearly defined the northern edge of the plain, falling sharply from one of the shoulders of the mountain, making a shallow bowl under the volcano skull's face. I decided that was where we would herd the pigs once we found them, and trap our prey in the small canyon formed by mountain slope and shoulder.

I looked for Sun, who had been my silent shadow as I scouted, and spotted him gracefully climbing down from one of the wide-trunked bean trees. He approached softly and motioned back the way we had come. I tried to quietly explain my plan, pointing out the canyon, and he listened, asking clarifying questions until we were both thoroughly confused. Then he signaled I should wait for him.

"Stay here? Why?"

But he was already gone. I waited, and he was back very quickly with wide, dark green, waxy leaves. He scratched one with a pointed stick, and it left very clear marks, almost as good as parchment would have been. I used it to draw the canyon and a few pigs and to show him my plan. Among my limited talents, I do admit to some modest artistic skill, and was able to make myself understood. Sun scratched an *X* in the place where he intended to wait for me as I herded the pigs into the canyon. Then it was my turn to show Sun what a Carolina man was made of.

I carefully circumnavigated the plain, listening for all I was worth. I found the sounder rooting in the skirts of the volcano. About thirty animals were grazing a small yellow star-shaped flower from the sides of the mountain. They were a mix of males and females, some with young, all different shades—some pink with spots of white or brown, others darker browns. Among them was the dominant boar—the largest pig I had ever seen. He was huge and covered with so much hair he looked more like a small bear than a hog.

He lifted his head as I approached, so I stopped and waited in the undergrowth until he lowered it again. I picked my target carefully and readied one of the *aldin*. Then I threw it into a tree trunk behind a group of young sows so it exploded messily and sent the pit flying. I threw six more as fast as I could, each splatting loudly against the tree. The sows spooked and ran away from the disturbance. I waved my arms and hooted, and fortunately, the boar was more interested in following his sows than chasing me down, and the whole sounder thundered across the plain, dodging trees and plowing through undergrowth. It was not difficult to run along with them, isolating a young sow as we neared my trap, hooting and chasing her away from the rest of the sounder and into the blind canyon.

Sun waited on the slopes of the canyon, his spear ready, but didn't move, giving me the courtesy of first strike. I chased her in, running past him, and readied a javelin. Then I heard a loud, grinding squeal behind me, the same I'd heard during my explorations my first day on the island—deep, terrifying, and insistent.

The dominant boar charged out of the forest, directly at me.

I managed to get mostly out of the way, but his tusk caught the edge of my thigh and sent me spinning. I hit the ground hard, and then Sun was there. He yelled, and the boar charged him. He dodged and danced back out of the way, performing a leap worthy of an acrobat into a gnarled bean tree. The boar savaged the trunk, squealing in rage. My thigh throbbed, blood flooding a tear in my britches just below my groin and darkening my leg. I clapped both hands over it to slow the bleeding and looked back to Sun. From the tree, he threw his spear with perfect accuracy and so much force that the sow went down without a squeal. In his impotence, the boar tore the tree, rearing up to the lower branches in his furious attempts to get at Sun. I tried to get to my feet, but a pulse of blood pushed through my fingers, and I felt light-headed. I lay back, the canopy of the bean forest spinning around me, the pod fingers reaching for me from the end of a dark tunnel.

I CAME to slowly. "That could have gone better," I said. I was on the beach by the plain, wounded thigh wrapped in a leaf bandage tied with a cord, the sow next to me, cleaned and trussed. There was no sign of the boar. Sun crouched beside me, frowning with concern.

"Hurt." Sun gently touched my knee with his fingertips.

I examined myself. Ordinarily I would have been annoyed by the fact Sun was not only an excellent hunter but also good at binding wounds, but as a beneficiary of his skill, I was glad. I moved my leg and found it didn't hurt too much, but a throbbing pain and weakness told me the wound was deep and I'd lost no small amount of blood. I felt a little faint and lay back.

Sun leaned over me.

"I'm *allt* good, Sun. All good. I'm fine."

Watching my face carefully, Sun rested his hands lightly on my thighs. He blinked his big eyes slowly, their storm-tossed depths holding the mystery of his untold story. He was breathless, as if waiting for me to do or say something. When I didn't, he slid his hand farther up my leg, fingers slipping over the hem of my britches, which were becoming quite ragged round the edges, until he reached the waistband. He then unbuttoned them, one button at a time, and even though I thought he must be doing so to check me for further injury, I felt the old stirring my father had desperately tried to beat out of me come alive with each tug. The pull of Sun's hands and fingers sent tiny shocks of lightning up my spine, and despite my light-headedness, I hardened painfully, with a rush of heat, and wanted nothing more than for him to grasp me and hold me.

"Stop." I grabbed his wrist. I watched the open expression on his face vanish, and then he was gone, running into the woods, back the way we'd come.

"Wait," I said to the empty beach, want and shame and guilt coursing through me. Sun was a good man, kind and brave, and he had saved my life. Why had I stopped him? What had I stopped him from doing? And why was he running away now?

I thudded my head back into the sand, with no one to speak to but the sow next to me, whose accusing, empty glare did nothing to assuage my guilt.

CHAPTER 4.
THE STORM

I WAITED, but Sun didn't come back.

I wasn't able to carry the sow with my injury. When I tried to lift her, pain shot through my groin with an intensity I knew I couldn't ignore all the way back to the cave, so I regretfully left her on the beach.

I was starting to learn the geography of the island, and it was not difficult to find my way back to the cave. Sun wasn't there. I refreshed with a few ladles of water from the bucket and realized I didn't know where the source of freshwater was. The cave was stocked with fruit, some dried fish, and the barrel of hardtack, which I lunched upon, but the water would need replenishing.

I spent some time cursing myself soundly for scaring away my only friend. The feel of his hands unbuttoning me lingered as well as the vision of his face, so full of curiosity and... something else. I rubbed my temples. This line of thinking was not taking me anywhere productive.

I returned to the beach, calling for Sun as I walked, and when I arrived, the sow was gone.

Quite suddenly I remembered my dreams of blood. Fears of the forest crested within me, as if Sun had been a talisman protecting me from them. Death seemed to hover close—the drowned sailors of the *Swift*, the pool of blood I was now quite certain I had seen, whatever my earlier supposition that it was hallucinatory, and my own near brushes with death by sea, storm, exposure, and boar.

I had to get off this island. I'd left North Carolina after Father died because it was not safe for a mulatto like me with tensions between freed men and slave owners rising, but I could go somewhere else, back to New Orleans—no. Edwin would find me there. Mother had relations in New York and Ohio. But no, I would not want to lead trouble to them either. The territories of the Louisiana Purchase perhaps, somewhere north of President Monroe's abolition 36°30' line from the newly minted Missouri Compromise ought to be out of Edwin's reach. Except I had no useful skills. I'd make a fair teacher or preacher; I could read and write, sing and play a number of instruments Mother had a passion for, but those talents were not of much value to men and women carving out homesteads.

But those were problems for later. Right now my primary need was to survive long enough to solve them, and without Sun, that meant getting myself off this island. I had to focus on my predicament.

I returned to my pyre and rebuilt it carefully from what the tides had not yet washed away. I enlarged it with driftwood and wood that I dared the edges of the forest to find. As evening approached, I returned with an armload of sticks to find a bucket of freshwater there and a hunk of roast pork. Footprints—smaller than mine, with a shorter stride—led from the forest to my pyre and back again.

"Sun!"

I ran to the edge of the woods, calling for him, but could not bring myself to enter the trees. There was no sign of him, and he did not join me on the beach.

"Sun. I'm sorry. Please come back and…." But what I wanted him to do, I didn't know and couldn't say, so I went back to my dinner and my work. When night fell, I wrapped myself in the sailcloth again and readied the belaying pin, but my exertions of the day and my full stomach sent me soundly to sleep.

I WOKE from a dreamless sleep in the morning light with my mouth dusted with sand again. A small pile of *aldin* waited by the refilled bucket, Sun's footprints leading to the edge of the forest and back, but also around where I had slept. There were two dimples in the sand where he'd rested on his heels for a time, watching me sleep. Perhaps protecting me from nightmares, because I'd had none.

"Sun?" I called, quietly, not really believing he was near enough to hear me.

Perhaps he was avoiding me because he had decided taking care of me was enough of a burden and did not want the added trouble of interacting with me. Perhaps he had simply been on the island alone too long and no longer desired the company of men. Perhaps he was completely mad. I sighed and cleaned the sand from my body in the sea and refreshed myself with the water, calling for Sun, but he neither answered nor appeared.

I headed for the escarpment that thrust out across the beach and into the water. It would be the easiest high place to access and watch for ships. Not that anyone but Edwin would come looking for me, per se. My ship and my manifest wasn't on any docket, and I'd seen no sign of our sister ship, *Sea Fury*. I assumed they'd gone down with all hands like the *Swift*. There was only one group who would miss the delivery—our Brazilian contacts—and I knew if they came looking for me, I wouldn't want to be found. My hopes rested in a random mercantile ship desperate enough for freshwater to put ashore on the fabled Dread Island.

It was a hard climb to the top with my injured leg. A trickle of blood rolled down the inside of my calf by the time I reached the crest, so I rested there for a time. From here, the mountaintop looked less ominous. The sides were very sheer, but I briefly wondered what was inside the caldera, regardless. Even with ropes and crampons, it would be a perilous journey to go and have a look. I wondered if Sun had tried it. Then I could not help but imagine his lithe form climbing up the volcano, mastering it, discovering its secrets. I scratched the stubble of my chin and shook my head. Was it the volcano I wanted him to explore or something else? I slapped my cheeks hard and shook my head to clear it. I told myself to focus on the merits of getting off this island, not on those of staying here.

From the escarpment, I could see far out to sea. The remains of the *Swift*'s forecastle had dislodged from the shoal and sunk beneath the waves. The only evidence of my captaincy now were the oddments in Sun's cave and the refuse I'd piled on the beach.

I could see for miles, and then, upon spotting a ship, I'd need to get back down to the beach quickly and light the—

I realized I had nothing to light the pyre with. I needed to chance the forest to get to Sun's cave and retrieve his ember.

I swore from the top of the escarpment and heard an answering rustling where the forest encroached—was it Sun? The dominant boar? Some other predator, a panther or leopard? A hunting cat would certainly explain the blood I'd found my first day, if I hadn't imagined it.

I carefully climbed down the escarpment, favoring my leg, and keeping a weather eye out for the mad boar, who I very much respected and so had named Ernest. The forest loomed ominously as I climbed down. As fearful as I was, I was going to have to brave it and get Sun's hot coal so I would be ready to light my signal when a ship passed. I fetched my belaying pin and found myself at the edge of the palms.

Taking those first few steps alone into the dense vegetation were some of the bravest I had yet taken in my life. As I walked, I stopped and listened every few feet, but nothing happened. The deeper I traveled, I began to feel as though something was watching me somewhere in the shadows—Sun? Ernest? The killer? By the time I reached Sun's cave, my muscles were in knots and sweat flowed down behind my shoulder blades.

The cave was empty of Sun but full of his presence, nevertheless. It was his, and I was the stranger here. I suddenly felt the need to make my own place on the island. I gathered some food, hoped Sun would forgive me for borrowing the ax and his kindling coal, and found myself back on the dappled path.

The ax was a much better source of daring than the belaying pin. With considerably more bravado than I felt, I limped down the path away from the cave. But I stopped and turned around halfway back to the beach. Sun's source of freshwater had to be somewhat near the cave, or at least there was a trodden path to it from the cave, and I didn't want to count on him bringing me buckets of water as I waited on the escarpment, looking for ships. A man takes care of himself. If I ever hoped to win back Sun's friendship, I told myself I'd need to win his respect.

I walked carefully down the beaten path leading the other way from the cave. The cave, the state of the path, and the state of Sun's person indicated he'd been here a long, long time. Months, if not years. Was that my fate? I shuddered, not knowing how much humanity would be left of me after that much time alone on the island. Then I realized the point was moot, because I probably wouldn't have survived on my own.

I at last found the water hole Sun had been using—an almost perfectly round, dark pool in a small clearing in the jungle. Nothing fed it, so I assumed a natural spring must burble in the depths. An enormous mangrove tree loomed over the basin, shading it and dwarfing the surrounding flora. The undergrowth was particularly thick and lush here. Animal tracks decorated the mud all around, not only pig, but I didn't recognize the ones that weren't birds and lizards. I remembered what fun our game of charades had been, and the image of Sun crouching like he did, kneeling with hands on the ground, came to mind. I imagined he would probe the prints with his quick fingers, maybe taste them, tell me what they were in his hard-consonant language, while at the same time, looking ready to leap into battle with any of them. He was wild, yes, dangerous, most certainly, but something about him attracted the eye.

Damn. Given too much time to think, my thoughts had strayed into dangerous territory once more. I focused on the situation.

The watering hole really was too far from the escarpment for frequent resupplies, even with Sun's bucket, but the mangrove towered over the forest here, so I climbed its broad branches, favoring my injured leg, until I was above the rest of the canopy. The leaves of the mangrove itself blocked my view, so I climbed yet higher, and when I came out, I saw clearly over the jungle, across the swine plain, even over the escarpment and to the small, dark mass that was my pyre. Beyond that, stretched the open, empty sea.

It would be a run from here to the beach to light the fire, but not too far to get it burning in time if I spotted a distant ship from the tree's high branches. Also, up here I was safe from Ernest and most other things, and less exposed.

I decided this was as good a place as any to build my own house—near water, by a tree with a good view of the sea, but close enough to Sun's cave that, should I need to return there for any reason, I could do so.

I climbed painfully back down—my thigh hurt fiercely by this time—but I wanted shelter before dark, so I set to chopping down the tall stalks I could not name growing all around the watering hole.

I found another rock sharp enough to mash the thick fibers of the woody, knobby plants, then stripped one into strings and used those to bind the others. Unlike my earlier attempt during my first days on the island, I employed nearly every knot I'd learned aboard ship. The idea it might fall apart was preposterous. I was convinced it would still be standing during the second coming.

"This is how you make a proper dwelling," I told the watching trees, and Sun, if he were listening.

I built three walls and a scaffold for a thatch, using the wide trunk of the tree as the fourth wall, completing all faster than I'd hoped. I put a window in one wall, because I liked them, and even made a leaf shutter and door that opened and closed. I thatched the whole thing with the same wide leaves, overlapping and lacing them together. Dusk seemed to be coming on rather fast—the time had passed without me noticing.

"Grandfather was a tailor," I said, imagining Sun was out there somewhere, watching me. "He taught me some of his trade." I didn't add that it was after it became apparent that I was not going to follow my father's footsteps as a preacher. I was a godly man, but one without much inclination to persuade others to follow the righteous path. I would make a serviceable preacher if I set my mind to it, but never an inspirational one. I had too many other interests, and an unhealthy obsession with science and the rational mind.

"Father didn't have much use for a son who loved books and music. There was only one book he loved, and it had a black leather cover with gold lettering. The good book."

Could Sun understand all I was saying? I didn't know. I also didn't know if he was even listening. Or if he cared. But I couldn't seem to stop babbling. I told him all about Mother, how she would read to me, and how we often sang together. How important teaching the village children was to her. I told him about losing her. I told him about Father's discipline. And I told him what being mixed blood meant in North Carolina. The flood of words kept my rhythm going as the sky darkened.

"And the final touches of civilization." I found a load of soft dry grasses I made into a bed in the middle of the floor. I was going to have to spend a night covered in grass, because dark was coming on and the beach was too far to fetch my sailcloth. The ax didn't give me enough bravery to traipse through the night-dark forest. No fire—I was reasonably sure that my house would light up fast and burn long if I tried that. I kept Sun's kindling coal well away from it, propped safely on a stick in the mud by the watering hole.

Night fell fast, and I knew a storm was coming. I smelled it on the wind. After the storm at sea, I would never forget that smell so long as I live. I believed God smiled on me, because I'd no sooner finished making my bed when the first rain started to fall. I huddled inside and listened to the drops splat on my leaf roof.

"See, Sun?" I spoke from my safe little house into the gloaming darkness. "Much better than a cave."

I was quite proud. God must have been watching me in my hubris, because sometime in the middle of the night, the storm caved in my roof.

I woke to massive thunderclaps and rumbles that shivered up through the sand and into my bones. The hut creaked alarmingly, and my thatch started to blow away one leaf at a time. Then the whole roof collapsed, and the walls fell in on top of me. I fought my way free of the sodden mass of leaves and sticks, using every choice word I'd ever heard, and found myself pummeled and slashed by rain and wind in the dark. My thigh throbbed, but I seemed otherwise undamaged. The night forest raged around me—ferns and palms whipped in the ferocity of the storm, flying debris pelting my body.

"Sun!"

I went through the trees then, yelling his name, panic rising. When I started, I knew approximately where the cave was, but with the storm buffeting all around me, I was lost in short order and stumbled off the path. I felt the stinging cuts of a hundred tiny wounds, huge razor-edged leaves lashing me. I screamed his name as though it were my last gasp.

Then Sun's gentle hands were just as suddenly on me, pulling me away. Calm and sanity returned as Sun's sturdy, warm grasp led me firmly back to the path. His arm around my waist, he held me up, helping me as I limped along. His voice spoke the same gentle words from our first night together. Safety—he was my safety. By the time we reached the cave, the terror of the woods had faded, and it was only Sun and me climbing down through the rocks to shelter.

The cave was warm and dry compared to outside, where the storm raged. A rivulet of water poured in through the opening, but he had a leather flap across the entryway that let smoke out but saved us from the worst of the driving rain. He had a blaze going—a charred spindle and plank nearby showed Sun knew how to make a friction fire—and it was merry, bright, and welcoming. I sat as close to it as I could, shaking the rain out of my hair. I was so damn happy to see him I couldn't stop grinning.

He watched me from the other end of the cave. He was as far away from me as he could get but still be inside and watching. His expression was closed and guarded.

"Sun. Come here." I patted a rock next to me.

He didn't move, only watched. I shook my head, frustration getting the better of me, and pulled off my shirt in one angry tug, which ripped part of the collar. I swore and wrung it out, feeling Sun's eyes on my body.

Living aboard ship and on the island had changed me. I was now dark with tan, darker than I'd ever been in a sheltered home with a father who wanted me to stay lighter skinned so he didn't have to pay the mulatto tax, and I knew I was putting on more bulk and muscle mass from activity—no books and constant study now, which had been my previous life. I was starting to look wild, my hair growing out into the thick, dark curls my mother complained of taming while still refusing to cut them. When she died, Father demanded my head be shorn close every fortnight. My growing hair felt strange, like some lost child I had been was pushing his way out through my skin.

I stretched my shoulders and spread my shirt over the woodpile to dry.

"Sun." I patted the rock next to me again.

He still watched, but it was as though he were watching against his will, his lithe body and golden braids dappled with firelight. The storm throbbed and moaned outside, thunder vibrating through my soles and up my legs, pulling at something primal that lived behind my belly button. Father would have a thing or two to say about my thoughts just then, but he was dead and gone.

I pushed my hands through my drying hair and leaned back on my rock, then hissed as the motion pulled against the gouge from Ernest, my first and newly forming battle scar.

"Hurt?" Sun asked, his eyes darting to my torn britches. He still didn't move.

"Aye." I lied. All was well. I had checked the wound before bedding down in my little hut and noticed it had stopped seeping and was starting to scab over. "Come, look at it for me?" I patted the rock again.

This time he did come, slowly, on all fours, as if ready to dash out into the storm if I were to yell. I kept still to avoid startling him. His gentle fingers—so much more slender than mine, but crisscrossed with fine, white scars—unwound the bandage and probed the wound. I was lucky; the boar could have killed me, or worse, unmanned me. Instead I had a long, deep cut with a hook on one end. Sun rummaged together a fresh leaf and some white stuff to bind my hurt once more. While he readied the bandage, I unbuttoned my wet britches and eased them off, noting my wet and threadbare smallclothes concealed rather less than they once had.

His hands were gentle and quick. He was very close to me, touching me like that, closer, I think, than any other person ever had been. Well, any person not giving me a whipping. Heat rushed to my face, and to other parts, embarrassment disappearing in the feel of his hands on my body. My manhood stiffened, and I could do nothing to conceal how much I desired him, even if I cared to try.

He looked at my arousal, and then his eyes met mine. I didn't dare breathe or look away; the tension in his body meant he was ready to run, and I didn't want to be without him again. His hands moved from my thigh to rest on my hips.

His storm-dark eyes were wide, surprised, his mouth open slightly, his expression framed with creases caused by sun and sea and the harder road he must have traveled. He didn't have much in the way of a beard, only a few blond, wispy hairs on his upper lip. I envied him that. My hair was thick and coarse. I likely looked a bit like a bear by now, black beard grown out a half inch.

My lack of a barber didn't seem to bother him, and his eyes traveled from my face to my hips and back again. There wasn't anything soft on my body anymore. Weeks of hauling ropes and chasing Sun on the island had toughened me, hardened my stomach, broadened my shoulders.

His fingers moved across my abdomen and up my ribs, leaving a trail of tingling, forbidden fire behind them. His nails were short but not bitten, dirty but with no hangnails, and I wondered why in the hell I was noticing that while his fingertips were moving through my chest hair, and my nipples were so hard they hurt.

I studied his eyes. They were uncertain. I didn't know why, but I felt that, in that moment, everything hung in the balance.

I put my hand awkwardly on his shoulder to tell him without words it was all right, to tell him I wanted him—devil may care how my father spun in his grave. A balance tipped at my touch, and he slid his arms around me, pressing our bodies together. I was excited and afraid at the same time. He held me tight to him, his face against my chest, his hold so firm it was hard for me to breathe. My desire for him burned hot until I felt his tears trickle down my skin. I put my arms around him and held him as he cried. He clung to me and sobbed like I was his last hope, great, heartbroken sobs that shook his small body. Maybe I was. The tears didn't make me think any less of him—my quick, brave, kind savior. Maybe he needed me as much as I needed him. So I held him to me, like he was my last hope, while the storm raged outside and within.

CHAPTER 5.
SCARS

I WOKE up with a crick in my neck. I hadn't wanted to scare Sun off again, so we'd fallen asleep while he cried himself out. Now the cave was empty except for me. I put my britches back on, skipping the shirt, and promised myself when they gave out, I'd make a loincloth like his. It seemed simpler—and, well, they were more, ah, visually interesting.

I found him at the watering hole, the mound of refuse that had been my attempt at a dwelling scattered all around.

"House." He held up a piece of one of my walls and grinned, showing another flash of white teeth and that dimple I found so disarming. I smiled back.

"Not much of one," I said, but I was glad he wasn't running from me and relieved to have something to do apart from talk about the night before, which had left me feeling strange, like my head was somehow floating six feet above the ground rather than connected to my body. I'd shown him I wanted him, and yet, we'd done nothing but hold each other last night.

He was shy and skittish as we worked. I held very still whenever we accidentally touched while binding the stalks back together, like he was a deer I might spook. He slowly calmed, became surer of me. I think I finally convinced him I wanted him around, or his desperation for human contact overcame whatever had caused him to run away from me after the hunt. I certainly wasn't a man to be feared, least of all by Sun, so his reaction was a mystery. I silently vowed to allow him to touch me any way he wanted. I told myself my main reason was because I didn't like being alone. I felt a deeper revelation looming, but I ignored it. I'd found out a long time ago that self-discovery usually revealed things I didn't want to know.

When we finished lashing together what the storm had destroyed, Sun carried the supports back away from the watering hole and climbed the wide-trunked, leggy mangrove. After a few misunderstandings while he pantomimed, I eventually understood what he had in mind and handed up sections and bundles. We took breaks by the watering hole, eating *aldin*, coconut, and cool, flavorless root mash in a pair of tin cups Sun produced. By the end of the day, we had a serviceable tree platform.

Over the next several days, we built a tree house—far sturdier than I could have managed on my own—and Sun wove enough living branches into it that it was well hidden. Not that we had anyone to hide from in this desolate place. It was as though we were the only two men in the world. However, the tree was easy to climb, so my lookout for a ship, if any ever came, was nearby.

ANOTHER WEEK or so passed, and life on the island settled into a pattern. We hunted in the forest, cooked meat in the cave, and lived in our tree. Sun and I settled into a truce about touching. Well, not a truce, really. I let him touch me as much as he wanted, afraid to scare him off again, but I didn't know how I should touch him back. Hell, I didn't understand why and how much I wanted to touch him. The main thing he required from me was to be held, well, him holding me, at night while we slept.

I admit, after a while, I started to feel rather pent-up about this arrangement.

Every night he slept with me, I was hard as a rock, dusk to dawn. The smell of his skin, the feel of his braids against my chest, his warm, muscular body against mine. I couldn't deny my attraction for him, and I came damn close to wondering if I even cared to resist it anymore. Grandfather blamed my bachelor status on the fact nobody would marry a preacher's son. The truth was I'd never been the least interested in women, and my father had beaten me plenty of times for "an impertinent mind." I never could tell how the old bastard knew what I was thinking. My lessons master, the stable hand who broke the horses, the young fellow who built the scaffold in front of the church, and pretty well countless others.... Father always gave me a whipping before I had time to puzzle it out. Maybe that had been his point.

Maybe he was protecting me from my own dangerous passion, because I felt like I was going to explode like a cannon every time Sun locked his arms around me. That couldn't be good for a person's health. I shouldn't want him. According to Father, wanting him was sending my soul to damnation. Acting on my desire for him would send his soul to hell too, and I couldn't do that to him.

"RAIN IS coming." Sun stretched to hang a bag of fruit from one of our branches. Night came on with the storm, and our tree house was full of the soft blue-gray glow of a cloud-laden sunset.

"I can smell it." I came up behind him and put my hands on his hips. Now he stilled. I had been somewhat shy about initiating touching until now.

"It will shake the house." His voice was so quiet it was almost a whisper. I lowered my face to his neck and inhaled. He smelled like coconut and, inexplicably, like the sun tea Mother used to make, sweetened and kissed with lemon.

"Good," I mumbled. I admit I wasn't really listening. I slid my hands up Sun's back, tracing some of the longer scars there, but didn't stop at his shoulders. His arms felt good in my bigger hands, and because I wanted to, I stretched until I circled my fingers around his wrists.

His breath came out in a gasp, and he pressed against me, our bodies connecting in one solid line. He was warm and firm, and my arousal throbbed between us. There was no way he could help but notice it, because I was pressed against his lower back. He moaned.

I stopped, uncertain. I could tell he wanted me to do more, to keep going, but I wasn't sure what I thought about that or even what to do next.

He seemed to know something churned through my slow mind, because he held very still. I felt him shaking a little, a tremor across his shoulders. It reminded me of a deer I'd surprised on a trail once, checking for danger.

That fear decided me.

I laid a kiss on his neck. He tasted like coconut too. His breath came out in a soft sigh, but he still didn't move. I decided I liked that.

I put his wrists together so I could hold them both in one hand, pinned against the branch where he'd hung the fruit. With the other hand, I stroked down his arm, over his ribs, and across his stomach. He was breathing pretty hard now.

"Say my name." I pulled him tighter against me.

"Benjamin." He'd gotten a lot better at saying it like that. His accent still flowed around it like he had a caramel in his mouth, but it sounded good to me. Very good.

"Turn around." I loosened my grip and slid my hand over his hip to his buttock as he turned to face me.

His eyes were shut tight, his mouth open.

"Sun." As I said his name, I yanked at the knot on the side of his loincloth. The damn thing was stubborn, as happens with leather when it's been wet and worn until it's dry. I tugged on it, then gave it a fearsome yank, and the fatigued knot finally slipped free with a rasp.

He gasped again, and I think whimpered a little, but it wasn't the kind of sound someone makes when they don't like what's happening. And I liked the sound. I liked it a lot. I tossed the frustrating scrap of leather into a corner and had my first look at all of him.

A nasty purple scar started at his hip, leaving a puckered ridge that disappeared into his dark blond pubic hair. It was not a surface scar like the others on his back and arms, but the kind of thing that had been deep, that could have killed him. Someone had laid him open like a fillet. The pucker made a crescent around his staff, which stood at attention, as excited as I was. Below, the wound had taken one of his balls, leaving him lopsided and bunched with scars.

Whatever I'd expected, it hadn't been that. I let go of him and stepped back. He watched me with his mouth slightly open, his eyes dark and unreadable. I couldn't do anything about it; my own enthusiasm visibly flagged as my arousal fled, and I looked away. My father, when he was whipping me, talked about *castrati*—that was what was done to boys who liked other boys in the Carolinas, if I didn't want to be hanged or sent to prison or made a slave—and if I couldn't keep my eyes in my head when the stableboy was around, I could expect the same. I'd dreamed about it, had nightmares about someone doing it to me. It had been one of the few threats I'd actually listened to, and something that had cooled my lusts until the day Father died.

Sun stood unmoving, his arms hanging by his sides, where they'd fallen when I let go of his wrists. He didn't run, though I thought he would. Or maybe I would.

"I'm going for a walk," I heard myself say. I suddenly needed out of the tree house, the close confines and muggy pressure of the oncoming rain, and my father's ghost around us.

Sun bowed his head. He didn't say anything as I left.

CHAPTER 6.
SAVAGE

THE NIGHT air was cool and fresh in the forest, and the rain started as I left the tree house. It was a gentle shower that fell somewhere high above the canopy and trickled down slowly. I knew it was raining, but I was not soaked. The darkness and the music of the drops kept me company while I walked, sorting out my feelings. I started with the same questions I'd been asking since I was old enough to notice the differences between men and women.

Why did I want men? What was it that drew me to an easy smile, wide shoulders, and a flat chest? Was I in truth a woman? One of the gentler sex, except born with man parts?

What I felt for Sun wasn't anything like what I imagined women felt. There wasn't anything gentle or tender about what I wanted to do to Sun's body. I wanted to hold him down and put my mouth on him. I wanted his mouth on me. I wanted my skin against his. I wanted nothing my father's God would condone. Tonight I'd been thinking like an animal, doing what I wanted to do because I wanted to do it. Animal instinct, nothing civilized about it. Had a month on the island turned me into an unthinking beast, responding only to the Devil's will for my flesh?

Rain trickled down my naked back. I hadn't worn real clothes in more than a week now, like a savage. Was that my fate? Was I going to be on the island so long that I lost my mind, my language, my humanity entirely?

I remembered how Sun had looked as I left him, standing, head bowed. I remembered how his cheeks had reddened with blush and a drop had trembled from the tip of his nose. I remembered him standing naked, shaking, and I still wanted him, and I was ashamed. Was I ashamed for wanting him? Or ashamed for running away after I saw his scar? Or perhaps both. That wound… that horrible wound haunted me, present in my thoughts. Who had done that to him? How had he survived such horrors?

I ran then; I don't know for how long. It felt good to run, to not think about anything but avoiding that hole, this tree. My leg was sound enough now it didn't hurt. Wet leaves slapped my body, and I felt as though they wiped something off me. They were cold, cleansing slaps from giant hands as I ran through the body of the forest, making my way I knew not where. It felt a little like being born must feel. The trees thinned, and I found myself on the sand. The moon's bright face hid behind a hazy wash of rain clouds, but there was enough light to see the gentle waves washing in and out from the shore, pebbled by the rain.

I ran along the beach, wondering where my legs had brought me. Then a shape loomed suddenly from the deeper darkness, and I recognized it as the tower of wood I'd built during my first days on the island. The signal fire for the ships I hadn't been looking for and for some reason had stopped caring about. The tower had been scattered to hell and back by storms and neglect. All of it was damp with rain.

I started gathering up the wood. It was something to do while I sorted my thoughts. Big pieces, small pieces—all of it flotsam and jetsam from the *Sea Swift,* my previous life. Before I really knew what I was doing, I had collected every scrap into a huge, haphazard pile. It looked like a funeral pyre built by an incompetent child or someone bereft of his senses. Both applied.

When the pyre held every ragged shard from the beach, I waded along the shallows, looking for anything else that could burn. Everything was wet from the rain, so something brined with seawater hardly differed, and it was then I found the prize. A small, water-tight keg bumped against my shin. Gunpowder for the *Swift*'s cannons. I carried it to my pyre, sprinkled half of it in wide arcs over the mess and tucked the rest in the heart of the jumble of wood. My past. My present. My future.

The rain slackened, the clouds drifted away, and the moon blazed so brightly across the sands it was as if she were trying to light the pyre herself. Sun had shown me how to make fire by spinning a stick against a hollow with some tinder, though I had yet to be successful at it. I searched along the forest's edge until I found coconut shells and husks that had been sheltered from the rain by huge leaves. I brought them back to the pyre with half a cracked coconut shell, which I filled with small filaments of coconut husk. I found a stick that wasn't too damp, fitted the tip into a depression in the shell, and worked at it like a demon. I felt I couldn't stop. If I stopped moving, something awful would happen to me.

It lit faster than I would have guessed, and I found some dry leaves and coaxed the smoldering husk fibers into a flame. I carried the half shell gingerly to my pyre, like a supplicant, and set it inside the heart, not far from where I'd placed the gunpowder keg, feeding the fire more grass and husk and leaves until it was crackling closer to the keg than I liked. Then I backed away and fast, putting a few thick trunks between me and the pyre.

The fire burned sluggishly at first, but there was plenty of air to feed it, and before long I knew I would see it crackling merrily like a small star in the tangle. Just as I was beginning to wonder if the gunpowder had gotten wet and wasn't going to work, a bright blossom opened, a loud boom sounded, and I heard shrapnel rip through the foliage around me. The fire went up high and hot then, catching more of the pockets of gunpowder I'd sprinkled in the wreckage. I ran to it and threw in pieces of wood the explosion had thrown clear, until everything I could find from my former life was burning.

I ran along the beach yelling—nothing like words, but dancing and jumping, looking out into the night sea. Would there be a passing ship? Would they see a fire? Would they see a man waving for help? It occurred to me they would see a naked animal, cavorting around his fire god.

I spent my vigor long before the blaze burned down. I lay on the beach near the destruction and looked up into the night sky. It was clearing to show the pinpricks of white, as though some realm of pure light was hidden from us by a blanket stretched taut overhead, like a child who does not want to get up a' morning. I turned away and watched the black sea, thinking of Sun's golden skin and the way he'd trembled when I held his wrists, until sleep took me and I thought no more.

CHAPTER 7.
LADRÕES DO MAR

I WOKE at first light with sand crusted on my lips and thick in my hair. The fire was done, except for a column of dirty gray smoke smearing the sky north by northeast. The finger of smoke seemed to be pointing home, which I thought was a cruel jape, because I had no means to get there and had stupidly burned my massive signal fire with no rescue in sight. And why? I combed my hands through my hair, dislodging a rain of sand across my shoulders. Because I was afraid of how I felt about a certain blond savage. Had I burned what was left of the *Sea Swift* because I hoped some ship passing in the night would see it and come for me? Or had I burned it to rid myself of the hope of rescue because I wanted to stay here, relaxing in the shade of the tree house and eating *aldin* with Sun? Watching juice run down his chin. Enjoying the way he'd shake his head and his blond braids would fly out from him like rays. My desire for him stirred again, deep in my belly, and I crouched, holding my knees against my chest until I mastered myself.

The pyre was naught but bones and ashes now, a black smear on white sand. Nothing was left of the *Sea Swift* and the plans I'd made for the man I would become. I was reasonably certain Sun wanted me. He ran away from me, but he came back. I wanted him. Now I had run from him and who I was and every violent end my father had threatened me with.

I sat on the beach while the sun climbed higher, and my stomach growled. If I had Sun's strength, I would run through the jungle for days like he had, avoiding him to give him a taste of what being alone felt like, as if he didn't know. But I didn't have his strength, and God only knew how long he'd lived on this island alone, surviving on his own. But *I* didn't want to be alone. I couldn't survive like this anymore—not in the sense that I was by myself on the island, but alone in a grander sense, the way I'd been all my life. Sun was someone I could be with, as I truly was. It was time to stop fighting that like the fool I was, and embrace it and everything it meant for myself, for God, for my father's ghost.

Sun's scar came vividly to mind. What had happened to him? How did he live through that? Who had done that to him, and was it in punishment for what he was? What we both were? Was there no world out there for us—no world we could be together and safe in? No world but here, it seemed, and it was time I started appreciating what I had, what we had. I stood, brushed the sand from my knees, and left the burning beach for the cool shadows of the forest.

My journey back to the tree house was nothing like my night flight. Shadows dappled the path, and a gentle breeze set the treetops swaying, the leaves chuckling against each other as I walked. Then a mounting desire to see Sun, to tell him what I'd learned and decided, rose inside me. I realized I knew every root and trunk. My feet were sure and quick, and I ran as though I were in the Carolina woodland. I stopped only for a quick swim in the watering hole to wash the sand from my face and drink deep before I pulled myself up into our tree house.

Sun lay on the floor, not far from where I'd left him, curled in a ball, with his arms locked across his shins. Fear burst from the center of my chest, and in my haste to reach him, I slipped on the scattered sand and slammed my knee painfully into the floor behind him. He didn't move while I employed some of the more choice blasphemous phrases the sailors had taught me.

"Sun." I put my hand on his shoulder. He cringed away from me, only a little, as though he barely had the strength for it. I didn't know what to say, so I lay down next to him instead. He tensed and held his body away from me. I put my arms around him and pulled him close to my chest.

"I'm sorry," I whispered, and held him until he stopped resisting. "I'm sorry for leaving. I'm sorry... for what happened to you."

He relaxed against me and let out a breath, like he'd been holding it a long time.

"Tell me about it?" I asked. His head was tucked under my chin. It felt good to hold him against me like that, to protect him. He was quiet for a long while, and I listened to him breathe until our breaths synchronized in a steady in and out, like the beating of a single heart. Eventually he spoke.

"They took me from my house. I was a boy." He started haltingly, his voice thick with a sleepless night. He stopped and breathed a while, gathering himself.

"Go on." I waited, and his voice grew in strength.

"They took me to the sea, took me far from my house. The ship was big. I work hard. Years come, years go." As he spoke, his words came faster, tumbling out of him, his limited English working hard to keep up. I gathered he'd been crimped, pressed into service. Or maybe his parents sold him to sailors. That happened sometimes too.

"There was a big hunt on the sea. I was not a boy. A new man. A newly man. Then they came. They killed the big men. They took the small men." He stopped, frustrated because he couldn't find the words he wanted.

"They... *ladrões do mar*." He spoke the words in a whisper, as though forcing himself to speak them.

Most of the men of the *Swift* had spoken Portuguese, and I had learned the seamen's language to better communicate with them as their captain. I was especially familiar with that phrase. Pirates, thieves of the sea. A creeping tingle crawled up my back and across my neck. I'd heard stories, awful stories about pirates. They weren't smugglers or gunrunners like me. They were vicious predators who rarely left anyone alive when they took a vessel, and it was said those who lived to be ransomed after a long, cruel captivity usually wished they hadn't survived.

"They took me out of the sea. I learn to fight." His voice was quiet again. I wouldn't have heard him if I weren't so close. Water and sand mingled on our bodies and tickled my chest hair, but I dared not let him go now that he felt safe enough to share his story with me.

"The fight hurt me many times. I fight until I hurt, then fight more." He ran out of words and stopped, frustration silencing him, so I rubbed the top of his head with my chin in what I hoped was a soothing way.

"*Você fala Português?*" I asked him. If he knew I spoke Portuguese reasonably well, he might be able to find what he wanted to say. Instead, he stiffened in my arms and trembled from head to toe. I realized speaking the language of his old masters was not going to help him feel safe. "No, Sun. It's all right," I said. "We don't have to speak in.... We can use English." I stroked his arm, but it was a long time before he calmed down. I think if he'd had the spirit, he might have run away, but he stayed where he was, in my arms. "No *ladro*, Sun. No *ladro*. You're safe." I said it again and again, not really knowing what else to do. After a while, he stopped trembling. I nuzzled his braids and kissed the top of his head.

"Tell me." I held him tight against me. I didn't know where the emotion came from, but I felt a wave of rage rise up. If the man who was responsible for damaging Sun so deeply were here, he would be in trouble. The wrath was new and strange. I'd never been much of a fighter, and revenge was a sin, but right then, I didn't care.

"I fight many times." He shuddered, as though shaking something off, and then turned in my arms. I propped myself up on an elbow so I could see his face. Dark circles shadowed his gray-blue eyes. He looked like hell. "Gone now. All gone," he said. He looked lost.

"Yes, Sun. They're gone. They can't hurt you anymore." I felt a rush of shame for leaving the night before. I guessed the hurting of him was in my power now. And I was going to try damn hard not to do it anymore.

He watched me, his eyes bright. "You want home."

"We have a great home right here." I patted the bound stalks that made our tree house.

He got up and looked out the window facing the beach, where last night's signal fire still smoldered, the smoke still clearly visible across the blue sky, then back at me.

"Well, I don't want to stay here forever." As I said the words, I wondered. Didn't I? Hadn't I decided on the beach this was the place for us? But I kept talking. "Don't you want to get out of here too?" My stomach gave a mighty grumble. I missed bread. And cheese. God, I missed cheese.

He stubbornly shook his head, and a few braids fell over one eye.

I would have continued arguing, but I didn't really care about escape anymore, so I stopped. "All right, be willful, then."

He frowned. I missed playful Sun. I wanted him close again.

"Come here." I patted the floor next to me and beckoned him over.

He shook his head again, but a slight smile curled his lips.

"Sun," I growled. "Come here." I patted the floor again.

His dimple appeared as he smiled wider and moved farther away.

"I'll chase you." I folded into a crouch. Damn it all if I wasn't grinning like he was.

A wild yell burst from him, and he swung out the window onto a branch. The game was on.

CHAPTER 8.
CATCHING SUN

HE STARTED running as soon as his feet touched the ground, and I was right behind him, tearing down the forest path toward the beach. He must have been tired from his sleepless night, but he knew the forest far better than I did and kept his lead. I paused a moment to admire the way the shadows dappled his tawny body as he ran, the play of his muscles under the network of scars. The distance between us lengthened, and I nearly lost him when I leaped over a fallen log and tripped, but he slowed and waited for me to catch up so he could stay a few strides ahead. He let me catch him at the edge of the beach, where it was still cool under the shade of the trees this time of day. I wrapped my arms around him and overbalanced so we both tumbled over onto the sand.

He laughed. I hadn't heard him do that before. It was nice, very nice, and I was laughing too, but then it wasn't funny anymore—it was something more. I held him down with my chest, my hands on his wrists. He wriggled under me, and that did things to my insides I didn't know anyone could.

"Hold still."

He held his breath, watching me. I pulled both of his arms together so I could hold his wrists with one hand. His eyes half closed, and I kissed a white scar across the top of his pectoral. My attentions brought a quiet moan from his lips. I kissed across his chest and the inside of his arm. I had never done anything like this before, had no idea what I was doing, but he didn't seem to mind my inexperience.

I stroked his side and stomach with my other hand, wandered down to his thigh, then traced my fingers upward firmly. He arched his back, so I kissed down his stomach, but I didn't know what to do next. I thought I understood how it worked with women—they closed their eyes and prayed for God and country until it was over. I'd heard enough jokes to understand what "it" must be, but I was completely lost when it came to him.

So I improvised.

I reached inside his loincloth, and my fingertips found his staff. I took my time exploring him with my hand. His manhood was smaller than mine, but so was he, and it fit him, and my hand, perfectly. I rubbed my thumb across the underside, and he seemed to like that as much as I did, because he was soon panting and thrusting against my palm and fingers. This did interesting things for me also, because of the way my own manhood pressed against his thighs.

I played with him until he cried out.

"Benjamin. Benjamin." He mixed my name with other words from his hard-consonant language. They weren't Portuguese. They sounded more like German or one of the north men. We'd had Big Swede Erik on our ship, who liked nothing more than oaths in every language he knew. So I finally recognized a few of Sun's words that were Erik's swear words, and then I had my answer to where he was from.

He begged and cussed me at the same time.

"Sun, let go for me," I growled into his ear, my beard probably rough against his neck. I was too far gone to whisper or be gentle.

It was enough. He shuddered under me and released all those weeks of pent-up frustration into my hand. Bringing him over like that was almost enough to set me off too, but I managed to control the rising tide. I let his wrists go as his breathing slowed, but I stayed over him, keeping him pinned and framing his body with my arms.

His eyes blazed when he opened them, and he looked up at me and blinked slowly, as if he were seeing me for the first time. He slid his hands up the insides of my arms, where the muscles were tight from keeping myself above him, and trailed them across my chest, then raked them down my ribs.

I couldn't help it—I grunted. My control wavered.

I felt his lips on my neck, collarbone, and then he licked down my chest. He tried to wriggle lower, so I lifted my hips and let him.

"Stop." It was his first command to me. "Hold still." I held myself above him while he worked his body lower, leaving gentle sucking kisses down my chest and stomach. I felt the tug of him pulling open the buttons on my britches, which he then pushed down so my manhood sprang out and hung between us. He found my mast with his hands and slid the skin back and forth.

"Sun." I wasn't going to last very long. I felt the heat and wet of his mouth close over the tip of me, and I forgot what words were.

I wondered if this was what it was like to be inside a woman, but unless there are things people hadn't told me, women don't have a maddening tongue down there that swirls and licks.

I couldn't stop it; he sucked me and stroked me, and in no time at all, I filled his mouth with sin. I was too gone in the sensation to feel guilty. I was too gone to feel anything but a hot flood of release that rolled through my body from feet to scalp.

I fell to my side in the sand and scrubby plants that grew here at the edge of the forest. Then Sun was there, inside the circle of my arms, cuddling against my chest.

"Sun." I kissed the top of his amazing head. I felt quite dead, or newly alive, or at least like life wasn't going to ever be the same for me from this moment on. All these years of touching myself in the dark, and I must have been doing it wrong, because it had never filled me with the tickling fire that now lived in my belly.

"Benjamin," he murmured, his lips brushing against the hair on my chest. A wave of tired came, and I slept a while. Perhaps I dreamed, because I woke afraid this hadn't happened. But Sun nestled in my arms, watching me, a smile on his lips. I tried to feel guilty or outraged or something, but I only felt warm. His face filled my field of vision, and I knew my smile mirrored his.

I stroked his dimpled cheek, laced my fingers through his braids, and pulled him close to kiss him on the mouth. His response was warm, wet, and enthusiastic. We rubbed against each other like two fish caught in a net, and then I started learning what my mouth could do to him.

We made up for the first time's speed by sinning carnally four more times before dark—once slowly in the warm, sunlit sea while washing the sand from our skin, then again on our way back to the tree house when we stopped at the pond for a drink, then inside the tree house after Sun insisted on feeding me slices of *aldin* fruit one by one, and again while we bedded down as lengthening shadows overtook the forest and our home.

Sun snored softly in the circle of my arms, and I thought about everything and nothing—how much better he was at everything and how much I didn't really care about that, how we both had to cross half the world and nearly die to find each other and paradise, how stupid it was that feeling this way for someone meant my soul was damned. Everything about Sun fit so perfectly, except that one piece. How could this be wrong? My father's beatings for my own good, the laws of the Carolinas, the cruel jokes men told—all of it to stop something so beautiful from happening. And why? I couldn't puzzle it out. Because we were both men, we could not become one flesh. Was not Jesus kind and loving? Could not I live as one with Sun and still be a man of God? I didn't know, and in my uncertainty, my arms tightened reflexively around Sun, who turned in his sleep, pulled a couple of braids out from under my arm, kissed the inside of my elbow, and went back to sleep.

It wasn't fair. Sun was right and good. He'd done what any godly man would have done; he'd saved my life. Except for a bit of smuggling, which was really breaking only the laws of men not God, I wasn't so bad. I'd tried to live right and do right by people. And, by God, I was going to do right by Sun too.

CHAPTER 9.
VOICES

THE NEXT day we were both so chafed we could barely walk, and I didn't care. I felt tender, yes, but awake, alive, truly like a man for the first time in my life. I was restless and full of energy. I cut down thirty new stalks while Sun slept, making up for his sleepless night, but instead of building something with them, I dug a fire pit so we could roast pig here by the tree instead of going back to Sun's cave. It was hard work, and my parts were sensitive, so I had to move with care. Afterward I went straight to the waterhole to cool off. Sun must have heard me splashing, because he joined me there.

"Morning." I stroked through the water to where he sat cross-legged, breaking his fast with coconut and some of that root paste he made. "Ugh. I'm not kissing you if you're eating that." I pulled a face, so he put a blob of paste on my nose. I grabbed one ankle and yanked him into the water. After much splashing, he made me a liar, because I kissed him longer and more passionately than the day before. I was learning how to use my lips and tongue more creatively, and I showed him what a good and fast learner I was.

Later we went to the south lagoon and speared fish in the clear blue waters. The yellow-and-brown honeycomb-patterned small fry were easy to see against the bright sand under a gently rippling sea, so easy even I was able to spear a few. Though I got half as many as Sun, I felt quite proud of myself for doing so well. We roasted them right there off the shore, wrapped in leaves from a fruit Sun called *plátanos*, which were bitter when green but sweeter once they yellowed. I felt quite full and happy as Sun tried to explain the rules of a game he called *tafl* that he'd played in his childhood, and which sounded like chess but had different rules. We had an enjoyable argument about the merits of each, both of which he'd played, and even more fun drawing out a few playing boards and creating pieces out of rocks and shells. A kiss became the toll paid each time a piece was lost. After winning six times in a row, I began to suspect that Sun was losing on purpose.

We made our way back to the tree house to drink and swim, then to the cave, where Sun showed me how to smoke and salt what was left of our fishing so we would have some variety laid by to add to other meals. Ham was still curing in the cave, hanging from the roof in salted or jerk bundles, and I was quite glad we'd built the tree house, because the cave smelled strongly of char.

Sun called the dried fish jerk *harðfiskur*, and we used the last of Sun's salt on the fish, which was quite sensibly called *saltfiskur*. When I asked what we were going to do with our extra meat now that we were out of salt, Sun said we'd have to make more. Not having learned any survival skills to speak of, I was very curious how this was done. Sun explained the process his grandfather had taught him to boil salt from sea water, and having nothing else in particular to do, we gathered a bucket, sail cloth to filter the water, a very precious metal pot, and Sun's kindling coal and headed for the north shore.

On the way, I quizzed Sun about the process. He said we could start by scraping salt deposits from the rocks in the north shore's shallow rock pools, where the tropical sun evaporated the water and left salt behind. I was asking how efficient that was compared to the boiling method, when Sun suddenly stepped off the path and pulled me down into the undergrowth with him. I smiled, thinking he had a romantic interlude in mind, but he only took the bucket and pot from my hands and pressed his fingers to my mouth to stop the question I was about to voice. When I saw the look on Sun's face, fear stiffened my spine and clutched my heart. He listened intently, his eyes wide and breath quick, looking out into the jungle. I had never asked him if there were panthers on the island, and I scanned the underbrush fearfully for a predator.

What I finally heard was the most fearsome predator of the Caribbean—the low sound of men's voices echoing up from the beach. Sun pushed me down almost flat to the ground, then pressed against my shoulder twice, pointed to himself, then down to the shore, and pushed my shoulder down with one hand while he pressed his fingers to his lips with the other. His meaning was clear. I was to stay here, hiding and quiet, while he went scouting. I couldn't fault him that plan, since he was silent as a shadow and I was louder than Ernest.

A voice sounded clearly from below.

"*Encontrei onde estava o sinal de fogo.*" It was Portuguese. They were discussing my signal fire. I looked over my shoulder to find Sun, but he was gone, leaving no trace of his passage.

"Son of a bitch." I swore quietly, crouching in the undergrowth with no idea what to do next.

I waited for Sun, hearing the distant sounds of the men, flinching at every bird or lizard that traveled through the foliage, until I decided I was at least quiet enough and far away enough from the beach to climb a tree unseen and unheard. I assured myself that Sun's kindling coal was resting safely in the pot, then pulled myself up into the canopy. Real as daylight, a square-rigged Portuguese caravel, her masts high with white sails, was at anchor in the bay. My heart soared for a brief moment while I considered our rescue. That ship could take us out of here and back to civilization. But the caravel wasn't flying a flag. If that meant what I thought it did, these men represented no kind of rescue we'd want. Pirates. Portuguese-speaking pirates. No wonder Sun had disappeared. He was afraid of nothing, except *ladrões do mar*.

I climbed down from the tree and slunk into the darkest part of the forest. I had to get a glimpse of them. I didn't have control over the impulse. I had to see them, so I went, as quietly as possible.

I CREPT through the forest underbrush, my mind busy, my ears straining to hear the intruders. Why had I lit that pyre? Stupid, stupid impulse. I used cursing myself as a mantra while I closed in on the strangers.

"*Onde estão os homens?*" They wondered who lit the fire and where he was. I heard a grunt nearby. They'd disturbed the feral pigs. I pulled myself up a tree and fast before Ernest decided to try to gut me again. It was a good thing I had. Mere moments after I was up, gunshots and squealing thundered through the wood, but I could only think about Sun and whether he was safe.

I heard more sounds in the underbrush—the pirates hauling away their kill. Long after everything was silent, I climbed back down and crawled on my belly until I could see the beach.

There were four men, all of them with hats or kerchiefs tied tight over shorn heads. Most sailors I'd met shaved to ward off fleas and lice. Never seemed to work for me; I always had red bites all over me aboard ship, but I'd never had any bother with them on the island. I figured the fleas drowned along with everyone else, except me.

The men had killed a pig. A tall, full-bearded mulatto in a red kerchief skinned it. The others, Europeans and mestizos by their coloring, took turns watching the trees while the hunters reloaded. One fellow kicked the ashes of my signal fire.

I spotted two long boats on the shore and noticed tracks going down the beach. Another group was probably searching the island for water. They'd be disappointed walking the shore—Sun's spring-fed waterhole was the only freshwater source I knew. Hopefully they wouldn't strike inland, because then it wouldn't be hard to follow all the pig paths to the watering hole, and to our home.

The men looked more or less like every sailor I'd seen before, but they watched the woods with a readiness that belied them. These were fighting men, and they were ready for trouble. I watched as they dug a fire pit in the sand and the bearded man butchered the pig. The shore stank of blood—the sounder the gunshots had scared away was likely not coming back anytime soon with that smell around. The four hunters gathered what wood was still burnable from my pyre and used axes on jungle deadwood that had been too large for me to drag out to the beach when I first made my signal fire. They made quick work of it and soon had a handsome pile of wood at the ready. While the flames licked up the first logs, they sharpened stakes and set up a spit, which they mounted over the fire once it died down to cooking height.

The water-scouting party came back and took some meat, no doubt to be salted aboard ship, and both boats rowed out to the caravel, likely to retrieve more crew, because the four hunters stayed on the shore. The pirates would eat and drink and make merry in the sand. This would mean more men on our beach, dangerous men, for who knew how long. When my anxiety and fear for Sun grew too great, I left.

I CREPT back to the tree house. When I was far enough away, I started calling out for Sun in a voice barely above a whisper. If he heard me, he wasn't answering. The tree house was empty. I walked around the outside and assured myself the branches and shrubs Sun had woven into it kept it hidden. They would serve if someone getting water didn't look up or too closely. With full light of day, the Portuguese would see it, but dusk or storm and no one would be the wiser. It was too much to hope that, once they discovered a source of freshwater, they'd keep their eyes down and only come when the lighting was convenient for us.

I paced in front of the watering hole, alternately praying for and cursing at Sun.

When he came out of the brush at last, I couldn't read his eyes; they were lost in darkness under his brow. He looked at the ground before him. His knuckles were white where he gripped his fishing spear.

"Benjamin." His voice sounded empty. Hollow.

"Don't you disappear like that." Everything about the way he stood told me to stay away, but I couldn't keep myself from coming to him, putting my arms around him, because I couldn't stand the thought of not touching him. For a minute, it was like hugging a tree, but then he softened in my arms. He dropped the spear and grabbed ahold of me so tight I thought he was trying to crush the two of us together until we became one person.

"Shh, Sun. It'll be all right." I stroked his hair and held on to him too. He nuzzled my neck and then let me go.

"No." His tone was sad, and he crouched to retrieve his makeshift trident.

I watched him pick some grass off the tines. Then he scrambled up the tree and came back with his new pig spear. I admired that one—he'd shaped black volcanic rock into a perfect spearhead, wide and tapered. The obsidian was fragile, but I wagered it would take the fight right out of a pig in one thrust, though we had yet to try it.

"What are we going to do?" I wanted to find out more about the visitors, but not without Sun. I didn't want to let him out of my sight.

He shrugged and wouldn't meet my gaze. He turned the spear slowly, looking over the blade for flaws.

"We could hide. They'll come to the water hole, fill up their barrels, wonder why someone built a tree house, get tired of the place, and then go."

Sun shook his head.

"*Ladro* will not go. *Ladro* will come here. There is pig. There is water, shade, fruit. They will use this place. Not go." His voice still sounded flat.

"What about the superstition? This is Dread Island, after all."

Sun gave me a blank look.

"The stories? The sailors on my ship said that no one goes to Dread Island. This island. It's cursed or bedeviled somehow. They won't want to stay here."

Sun looked down at his toes, where he slowly dug a hole in the sand. A frown creased the corners of his mouth. He shrugged and, without looking up, said, "I have not heard these stories."

Anger prickled the back of my neck. Anger at myself for sending up my stupid signal fire, anger at Sun for not having more hope that everything could return to the way it was.

"They're not going to set up camp here, Sun. Don't worry." I said it, but the words were empty until I remembered my fear of the forest and the mystery I'd discovered when I first arrived here and still didn't know the answer to. Then I had an idea. "They won't ever come here again, Sun. Not after we get through with them. They're going to find out what it means to beach on Dread Island, and they're going to leave here telling that story to every other sailor."

He looked at me then, smoke-blue eyes doubtful, but the ghost of a smile played at the edges of his mouth. I'd do anything to keep the dead sound out of his voice. Anything at all.

CHAPTER 10.
PIRATES

AS THE sun set, dusk closed in around us, protective and sheltering. Twenty men, probably most of the small, fast caravel's complement, were on our beach. They had roasted the pig, shot another, and gathered every ripe *aldin* in the area. Their fire was right on top of where mine had been, as if daring me to step into the wavering light and expose myself.

We crawled close enough to hear them speak and see their faces in the firelight. I kept Sun near, made him stay where I could touch him. I still wasn't sure what he might do, but I knew he had reason to fear them, and I believed the proverb that fear makes a man do funny things. Fine trembling ran through his entire body when we were settled right at the edge of the forest, but he made no sound.

I squeezed his shoulder and settled in to find out what we needed to know.

Most of the talk was the usual—glad to be off the ship, complaining and comparing the food they'd found here to what they ate aboard, bawdy jokes about women and the lack thereof.

"Did you see anyone?" the butcher, the tall, black-bearded mulatto who prepared the pigs, asked the patrol returning from down the beach. He spoke Portuguese but with an American accent. I was somewhat surprised by how fast the language came back to me, considering the circumstances. I understood most of their talk.

"No. Nor water either." The head of the patrol was a skinny bloke in a striped stocking cap.

"If he's still alive, he'll come out, Vasco." A short, stick-armed sailor with a French lilt—who reminded me of a rodent—spoke to the patrol leader and then laughed a high-pitched chuckle.

"As you say, Weasel." The butcher nodded at them both and looked into the forest thoughtfully, scratching his black beard.

"You think he's our man?" Vasco watched Butcher as he spoke. He seemed to look for a signal or direction from the other man.

"He is." He held up a charred piece of wood. It was from the bow of the *Sea Swift*. They'd recognized the carved feathers that had made up the figurehead's wing. "I know this figurehead." A rueful smile curved his lips.

I cursed myself. I should have burned that part first. They'd marked me, and worse, it sounded like these men knew what cargo I'd been carrying.

I felt our chances at rescue evaporate. *Goddamn it.* And if they set up a supply camp here, our peaceful life together was over. They'd find us eventually. It didn't help that my calculations put this island along the best path for smuggling to and from Brazil, somewhere in the eastern archipelago. If they found out Dread Island had nothing to fear, they would make this a convenient stopover. There was nothing for it. It was time to execute my plan. I patted Sun on the arm and left him there.

I crept through the underbrush slowly, as silently as possible. The plan hinged on the right sounds at the right time. I remembered my first days on the island, the strange barks and grunts from the woods that fed my fear. Well, now I lived with the pigs, I understood those sounds had been turf battles and wars for dominance. Wars Ernest always won.

Finding where the pirates had thrown the waste from the two pigs they'd slaughtered wasn't difficult. I crept close and, looking over my shoulder nervously, cut free the scent glands. I made off with them into the deeper undergrowth. I knew this part of the forest belonged to Ernest. If I'd learned one thing on this island, it was Ernest didn't like interlopers. I made sure to put different scents on trees near each other, mingling the smells. I stank too. Poor Ernest would think there wasn't only one interloper, there was a full-scale invasion.

And, to be honest, there was.

I thought for certain the pirates would hear the crack of a twig as I moved around the perimeter of their camp, the shuffle of sand as I rubbed the musky stink on the trees, but they continued merrymaking. Someone had brought several bottles of what must be liquor from the caravel. By now everyone was full of roast pig and having quite a good time.

Twice I heard a night bird call. It was Sun, drawing attention away from me. He was to make the call to distract anyone looking away from the fire. I finished my work, cleaned my hands as best as I could, and made my way back to him.

Tension sang through his muscles. He hadn't moved from where I'd left him.

"Sun, what's wrong?" I crouched close and put my mouth to his ear.

He shook his head slightly and pointed with his spear.

There was a giant in the camp.

He had to be seven feet tall, if he was an inch, with mestizo coloring and a broad face with a great beak of a nose. He wore nothing but a pair of britches without hose. His entire body was covered in thick muscles, scars, and tattoos. He wore a huge whip coiled at his belt, and I saw a glimmer when he laughed that meant some of his teeth were gold.

I looked at Sun. His eyes were bright in the reflected firelight, but there were shadows across his face that made them look as though they were floating in his head. He followed every movement the giant made, not sparing any attention for the others.

"Sun, it's time to go." I had to pull on his arm to get his attention, but at last, he followed me.

Our plan was only going to work if we could get Ernest to the scene of the crime.

CHAPTER 11.
THE MATTER WITH THE PIGS

WE STRUCK in the wee hour just before dawn and drove the pigs hard. It wasn't difficult to find them; we'd learned the sounder's habits. Once we surprised them at their nighttime feeding place, it was an easy thing to herd them back to where the pirates were.

We stayed clear, out of gunshot range, but I wanted to be close enough to enjoy the commotion.

Their fire had died down, but I could make out the shapes of sleeping men from my treetop. The underbrush moved as though many hands were stroking it. The pigs passed through at an agitated gallop. They didn't like going this way; this way smelled of fire and burnt flesh.

My ears picked up an enraged grunt. Ernest had found the scent rubbings soiling his territory. With a mighty squeal, he cantered around trying to find out who had violated him while simultaneously trying to replace the scents with his own.

The other pigs were well riled by this, and Ernest's rage drove them out of the forest and across the beach. The alarmed sounds of the guards and gunshots roused some of the lesser drunks, and the pigs stomped with their sharp little hooves and gored with pointed tusks anyone who wasn't fast enough to get out of the way.

Ah, it was glorious. Chaos. Drunk pirates stumbling everywhere, guns going off in every direction.

But, alas, my fun couldn't last forever. The giant was roused, and he shouted down all the rest into a semblance of order. I had the feeling he was probably first mate. Everyone more or less gathered around the fire, a bleary-eyed troop with wavering guns pointed out, toward the threatening woods. The giant left them there and waded through milling pigs toward the sounds Ernest made in the woods.

I never thought I'd feel sorry for a pig, but the way this giant moved with purpose, I did. A loud squeal echoed, the trees shook, and then there was silence. The giant came out. Ernest didn't.

This display didn't do much for the rest of the men, who looked like they weren't sure what to do, half of them pointing their guns at the giant, the rest out at the forest. He roared at them, his Portuguese accented by some native language of Brazil, and several broke ranks and went, cringing, into the woods. I didn't know what he, or they, thought they'd find, but I decided it was time to meet back at the tree house.

SUN CLIMBED down from the treetop lookout and met me on the ground.

"They are not leaving." He looked petulant.

"Give it a day." I grinned, remembering the drunks stumbling away from the boars, but Sun glowered and twirled his spear in his hand slowly. I decided to be blunt. "You know that great giant of a man, don't you?"

He nodded but didn't speak.

"Were you a pirate?" I wasn't sure if I wanted the answer.

"No." His voice was quiet. "I fight." He showed me the scars on his arms. "They took money from the fights, many fights." Seeing my confused expression, he sank into a crouch and made the unmistakable motions of a *gaucho* with a *facón*, a knife fighter, fleet and swift. I suddenly realized where the other scars were from, the ones on his arms, thighs, chest... and down there. All from knife fighting, from surviving many battles. For the second time in as many days, I felt my blood turn to ice. The hair on my arms stood at attention.

If he wasn't a pirate, that meant he'd been a slave. I'd heard of trading and betting on slave fights. It was, naturally, completely illegal, and thus of course practiced all over the Caribbean. Pirates and merchants alike would join together for the quick, bloody battles that almost always resulted in the death of one or another of the combatants. To have scars like those, Sun must have killed dozens, if not scores of men.

He watched the slow realization dawn on my face, straightened, and held his ground, as if waiting for my judgment.

"So. You're good with a knife, then?" I asked.

He nodded.

"And the big fellow?"

"Martio." He clenched his jaw and slapped his shoulder and the thick whip marks there.

"You're not, I mean to say, you didn't belong to these pirates in particular, did you?" My scalp crawled.

He nodded. I sat on the ground and took long, shallow breaths. I'd lost my ship and my illicit cargo, so my life was forfeit anyway, but now I was involved with aiding and abetting the escape of extremely valuable property—a slave trained in knife fighting. No wonder Sun didn't want to tell me where he was from or how he'd come to be on the island. He was a runaway, and I knew exactly what happened to runaway slaves in North Carolina. My day was not improving.

Sun watched me carefully, waiting to see what I would do. He continued to finger his spearhead. I felt tired all over. My filthy lucre cargo run had turned into something far more perilous for my immortal soul. Loving Sun was one thing, murder quite another. I didn't agree with Father's interpretation of what Jesus thought of my being drawn toward men, but I couldn't argue that murder wasn't evil. Killing a man in battle, in self-defense, was foul enough, but murder to keep our hiding place secret? That was something else entirely.

"Sun, you can't kill them." I looked directly into his eyes as I said this so he would know how important it was to me.

"They are not leaving." He avoided my eyes as he spoke. "One, two. Here, there. Twenty men will go quickly. We can fight them. Win." He made a snatch and twist motion with his arms. He wanted to stalk them, thin out their numbers, murder them one by one in cold blood. I felt dizzy.

"No, Sun. We're not doing that." Whatever I was, I wasn't a murderer. I smuggled questionable goods, I was an arms trader, and I'd spent the last several days violating Leviticus 18:22 in every delicious way I could imagine, but I wasn't a killer. And I didn't intend to become one.

"Benjamin." He came to me and crouched, taking my hands. I looked into his eyes. He looked worried. "We must do this."

"No killing." I stood and stepped away from him. He crouched by the edge of the watering hole, watching me. I paced. There had to be another way, there had to.

But if there were, it remained hidden.

CHAPTER 12.
SACRIFICE

WE SLEPT in the tree house that day, making up for a sleepless night. My thinking was that the pirates were also recovering from the night before, and, in any case, whatever we settled on doing, we'd need to do it at night.

I woke in the late afternoon. I heard Sun in the branches high overhead. I saw him in a new light now. I'd thought of him as innocent, a victim, but his wanting to murder those men helped me realize I was living with a killer. His skill at hunting, hell, his skill at everything, made perfect sense now. He'd spent years as a fighting slave, being honed into a weapon, and he still was one. In fact, being a deadly weapon was nearly all he had left now.

The whole argument over man versus beast, giving in to my urges, seemed pretty moot. In fact, everything I'd been through up until now seemed moot. The Portuguese weren't going to leave. Not without finding what they'd come for, and what they'd come for was me.

I heard Sun climb back down from the lookout, but I didn't turn to look at him as he lay next to me. He must have seen something in my eyes, because he spoke.

"You will go to them?" His voice was carefully neutral.

"No," I lied. I was surprised to find I'd made up my mind. I would go to them, and I had to do it soon, before they found Sun and took him away, made him kill for them again. My going to them would save him.

"I love you, Benjamin." He sighed softly and stroked my arm, kissed my cheek.

I turned to him and took in the sincere look in his too-blue eyes. The way I felt about him surprised me too.

"I love you, Sun," I whispered, and saying it made it both real and true. Suddenly I didn't care about pirates or sin anymore. Everything I cared about was right here in front of me, in the dappled afternoon light of the home we'd built together.

My hands found his face, and I pulled him to me, meeting him halfway. We wrapped our bodies around each other, kissing, touching, taking off clothing when it got in our way. I felt the need for him burning through me, so hot it hurt my chest.

"Sun." I whispered his name again and again. It was my prayer and my salvation. His mouth found my staff, and he worked me over until I trembled and shook. I resisted as long as I could, but as usual, I couldn't hold off very long when Sun was involved. I came hard, and I was desperate to have my mouth on him too.

He cried my name as I brought him over, and then we lay, spent, holding each other.

"Benjamin." He looked into my eyes, my favorite smile curving his lips. The sunlight fell across his braids, making them glow golden in the light. He looked like an angel to me. I let sleep come to take me then, knowing we were together, and, at least for the moment, safe.

HOURS LATER I woke in the dark alone, and a terrible feeling of foreboding made breathing hard. I felt my way over to the corner. Sun's spear was still there. I felt better for a moment, until I thought things through, and the realization made my skin prickle. He was gone. And he'd left his weapon behind.

Oh no. Oh God no.

I don't remember the trip from the tree house to the beach. I only remember the bottom dropping out of my world as I stood holding his spear, then the utter blackness of the night jungle, and then crouching where the tree line ended at the band of sand surrounding our island like a shackle.

The Portuguese had a fire going again.

The smell of roast pig filled the night. I felt nauseated when I realized the source must be Ernest.

The big man, Martio, loomed by the fire. He stood looking into the night while everyone else ate and drank.

I almost yelled a warning when I saw what Martio was staring at.

Sun stepped out of the forest shadows, his lean body bathed in the flickering light of the fire. He looked naked in his loincloth compared to the pirates, and the fire lit up his golden skin and braids like the Greek's Helios or Rome's Sol Invictus. His hands were empty, arms at his sides with palms facing out to show he had no weapons.

Two sentries at the edge of the light pointed their guns at him, but Martio held up his hand.

"Come," the big man said in his native tongue, and Sun walked with fluid grace into the camp. There was no trace of the trembling fear I'd seen in him when we'd hidden in the bushes together. It was as though making up his mind to go to the fireside had also banished his terror.

The other pirates gathered around, the more drunk glaring through squinted eyes, as if working hard to figure out who the newcomer was.

"Sóli," Martio said. I watched open surprise and recognition mingle on his face. It was quickly replaced by a narrowing that spoke of both greed and desire. Clearly Sun was someone, something, he valued.

Martio sunk into a fighter's crouch as Sun approached, and Sun mirrored him. The big man was more than twice Sun's bulk, but he moved with a grace that looked just as deadly. I held my breath and imagined them fighting, Sun would be quicker, but I had the feeling Martio would be tireless as well as stronger.

"You remember well." Martio stopped circling, straightened, and laughed, the sound booming across the beach. Sun straightened too, but he didn't laugh. He watched Martio like a snake watches a boot, ready to strike if a man steps too close. This didn't escape Martio's notice. In fact, he seemed to expect it, like it, a smile curving his full, cruel lips. He stepped away from the roast hog with a chuckle, leaving a wide space.

"Join us." He sat and indicated a place by the fire next to him—I didn't like how long his reach was. Sun's eyes flicked to the sentries, who still stared, mouths gaping. Martio waved their muskets down. The men obeyed without argument, but I noticed they didn't sling their weapons. Everyone in the camp watched Sun as he crossed the short distance and crouched by the fire.

Martio gave him a generous piece of hog off the spit, and Sun took the steaming meat from him and tore into it with his straight, white teeth. For reasons unknown to me, Martio found this gladsome and laughed again. He touched one of the braids tailing down Sun's back and ran it through his fingers. It reminded me of someone inspecting a horse for soundness. There was a look in Martio's eyes I didn't like, and for a while, I fantasized about skewering him with Sun's spear.

Sun casually took his braid back and rotated on the balls of his feet so he faced Martio directly. I couldn't see the expression on his face from where I was, but Martio stopped laughing and instead watched him eat for long moments.

"Why are you here?" Martio's voice was low but rumbled through the clearing.

"I want you to leave." Sun's voice was steady, easy to hear. His Portuguese was perfect, his accent very slight.

"Why would we do that?" Martio grinned at him like Sun was a child asking for an indulgence.

Sun chewed and didn't answer him.

"We're looking for a man," Martio said as he held up the charred wing from the *Sea Swift*'s prow. "Have you seen him?"

"*Já.* I have seen him." Again, Sun's voice was clear. I tensed. Had I been wrong to trust him? Had he only been waiting for the right moment to turn me in? No, I would not believe that.

To a man, the pirates looked out into the night past the circle of light. I felt eyes raking the darkness where I lay.

"Where is he?"

"If I take you to him, will you leave my island?"

Martio's eyes narrowed as he searched Sun's face. What he looked for, I couldn't say.

"This is not your island." Martio's voice deepened with the ring of command.

Sun shrugged and tore another piece off the meat. Martio no longer thought this was so amusing.

"He belongs to us. He owes us."

Sun shrugged again.

"Show us this man." Martio stood.

"It's dark." Sun stood too and reached down to pull a piece of flaming wood from the fire. He turned it slowly in his hands, considering it.

"Torches," Martio ordered.

I kept as low as I could in the undergrowth. All the men on the beach gathered into a scouting party. The atmosphere turned festive, and the bottles of liquor were brought as well. The men seemed to regard the outing as a hunt. There was no other choice—when they passed, Sun leading them into the forest, I followed.

CHAPTER 13.
THE GRAVE

I MOVED as quickly and quietly as I could. Fortunately they were making enough racket I doubted they would have noticed if I simply blundered through. As it was, I crept through the darkest shadows and followed them carefully, keeping Sun and Martio in sight. Vasco and Weasel were sent to scout ahead, and Butcher brought up the rear with the drunks. The others spread out in a ragged line between.

"Where is he?" Martio looked down at Sun as he walked next to him. I noticed the heat in his glance as he took in how Sun's muscles moved in the half-light of the torches. I ground my teeth.

"Not far." Sun looked straight ahead into the night. He led them up the steep slope of the mountain that took up most of the center of the island. He'd never taken me up here, and I hadn't wandered on my own. The rocks were sharp and cruel without shoes, even with all the toughening my feet had been subjected to these last few weeks.

Sun led the men along a narrow path skirting the slope, and I had to work hard to keep out of sight in the undergrowth to one side, but I was unwilling to be any farther away from Sun than I had to be. The line of pirates thinned out behind us as they clambered over occasional rocks. Martio took the chance to talk to Sun alone.

"I looked for you a long time." He stroked one of Sun's shoulder scars with a thick finger.

Sun shuddered with revulsion before he could stop himself. Martio laughed.

"You did not always feel this way." He seized Sun's upper arm and pulled him close, disguising the motion as groping for balance and using Sun as a post. However, they both moved like tigers, and I was certain they'd easily leave the entire troop of pirates behind if they didn't have to wait for them to keep up. Which was good, because then I could keep up as well.

"No," Sun answered quietly. I heard the strain in his voice as he fought to remain calm.

"God gave you to me, Sóli." Martio kept moving, pulling Sun with him.

"You do not own me." As Sun spoke, he twisted and dropped, breaking the larger man's grip on him. He darted out of reach, but didn't run up the path and away like I hoped he would. He stood on a rock and watched Martio. The big man laughed again, and I couldn't help but wonder when he'd get tired of playing games and do something violent, or sexual, or both.

"I have, and I will again. I did not want to lose you."

"No. You sold me. I do not belong to you anymore. I will show you the man. Then you will leave." He stepped down from the rock, purposefully turning his back on Martio. Martio glowered at Sun's backside but kept moving, still following him as he strode ahead, just out of reach.

"What happened to your new owners?" The big man's growl was so low I knew only Sun and I could hear it.

"You will see." Sun didn't stop moving. Martio considered this silently as he walked. By the frown on his face, he liked Sun's answer even less than I did.

It wasn't long before we came to a big hole in the side of the mountain. The mouth was jagged, and Vasco and Weasel stood on either side of it, torches casting weird shadows.

"*Caraca*! It stinks in there," Vasco called down to Martio.

"Go in." Martio ordered his men as he levered his bulk up onto the ledge, a swinging, graceful jump that echoed Sun, who was already striding into the cave. Martio had no choice but to follow close after him. The two scouts exchanged a glance and plunged into the darkness as well.

I swore softly and circled wide, looking for another entrance into the mountain. There was no way for me to keep Sun in sight without also being seen if I followed them within. My last glimpse of the cave mouth included Butcher helping a few still-tipsy pirates onto the ledge.

I scrambled carefully, trying not to tear my hands or feet on the rough rock that draped like a sloping sheet from the cone above. Either erosion or a long-past eruption had left fissures of various widths and lengths in the rock wall around the cave mouth, so I had many handholds as I climbed more than crawled, looking for a way in, a way to follow them. I stopped when I heard pirate voices echoing up from the depths of a particularly wide fissure. I tried to wedge myself within, but only managed to painfully scrape my back. I swore and climbed back out, following the echoes of the men's voices as I scramble-climbed farther. Thanking God I at least had the voices to guide me, I followed them until I found a large opening crusted with years of guano, which I crawled quickly through. The pirates' flickering torchlight bounced off the walls in the depths. I was ahead of them. The mouth opened onto a ledge, then dropped off sharply below me into darkness.

I didn't expect the hole to smell sweet, with the years of guano coating it thickly, but something worse than feces wafted up from the depths, like carrion and rotten eggs. But Sun was through this deeper hole, so down I must go. I held my breath and lowered myself into the dark.

"Stay close. There are dangers. Long drops." Sun's voice echoed up from what I decided was the main tunnel. I backed up to keep from being seen and cut my head on a sharp rock. I had to bite my lip to keep from swearing. The pirates could easily hear any noise I made in the echoing tunnels. My scalp bled like the dickens, but there wasn't anything I could do about it except try not to drip loudly and continue blinking blood out of my eyes.

"What is that horrible smell?" Weasel's high voice chased Sun's around the main tunnel. The tunnel I stooped through ran parallel to the main passage's ceiling, so I moved slowly to keep stray rocks and dirt from giving away my position.

"We find him soon, Sóli, or I will make you tell." Martio patted the whip at his belt meaningfully. Sun moved with skill and care ahead of the three men, stepping around sharp rocks the others bumped into or tripped over.

"We are here." Sun stopped on a ledge under me. I stopped moving and lay down, wishing I had some way to communicate with him.

"He is there. Below." Sun pointed to the hole under him, which was concealed in shadow. He sidestepped out of the way as Martio, Vasco, and Weasel carefully approached the ledge and cast torchlight down.

The hole was full of bodies.

I felt sick as I counted nine... ten... fourteen. They were in layers, carefully arranged, each in different stages of decay. I recognized Big Swede Erik and Joaquim One-Leg. Each body, well, the ones with enough skin on, showed a gaping cut across the neck. The urge to vomit burned my throat.

Vasco swore. Weasel retched. Martio looked mildly impressed.

"Now. You leave my island," Sun said. I tore my eyes from the pirates and looked for where Sun had gone. He'd climbed halfway up the wall, and I could barely see his face from the corner of my eye. If I moved or made any noise or signal, the pirates would see me. The shadow I hid behind shrank in the torchlight from below as more pirates arrived.

Sun put something in his mouth, a nine-inch blade he held between his teeth as he climbed higher up the sloping wall, closer to my hiding spot. He pulled himself onto my ledge without any sign of seeing me crouched in the deep shadows and turned to face them. He held two knives, wicked and curved—fighting knives—one in each fist. I had no idea where he'd gotten them. I'd never seen them before.

Martio's laughter filled the cave, startling both of his companions. More pirates stumbled forward in the dark.

"You stuck them." Martio's voice boomed in mirth. The other pirates looked over the ledge at the bodies now, retching or crying out.

"You stuck your masters, slave." It was probably only the light from the torches, but Martio looked like the devil himself as he grinned over the open grave. "Slaves who stick their masters face justice." He pulled the whip off his belt, and I calculated the distance. The whip was easily long enough to reach Sun. I nearly grabbed him to pull him back, but he was too fast for me.

The whip whistled through the air, cracking into the ledge, but Sun wasn't there when it struck. He was already flying. He'd launched himself at Martio, both knives poised to strike. His leap was a thing of perfect beauty and deadly precision.

A man I hadn't noticed before, a redhead with blackening teeth, snapped his flintlock pistol up, aiming at Sun.

Everything froze in that moment. Without thinking I stood and screamed, the wordless howl of an animal, but it got the redhead's attention.

The gun went off, filling the air with gunpowder smoke. Sun landed below, twisting awkwardly toward the sound of my scream as he did so.

"My Benjamin! My Benjamin!" Sun's heartbroken screams penetrated the dull buzz the gunshot left echoing in my ears. He reached toward me, as if he would fly up to me, knives still clenched in his fists. I didn't understand what he was doing, or why.

Martio didn't pause to find out. A heavy fist caught Sun on the side of the head, and he fell, tumbling down among the corpses.

"Sun!" I screamed. Martio's arm flicked out, and I felt the searing pain of his whip lash my chest. I yelled wordlessly and tried to duck away from it, but the next time the whip curled around my thigh. Flexing his huge arms, Martio pulled me off the ledge with one fierce jerk.

I landed in the bodies with a dull thud, cracking my head on a rock with a force that rattled my teeth. The bodies were rubbery, sliding under my bare feet. The fall forced the air out of my chest, and I swooned and hacked as the stench of the fetid hole invaded my body. My bile rose, and I gagged and vomited, scrambling among the corpses to find a way to stand even while my stomach emptied. I felt darkness close in around me, the buzzing in my ears grew worse, and then I couldn't hear or see anything anymore.

CHAPTER 14.
SLAVE

I WOKE with something scratchy pressed into my face. I blinked, and my eyelashes brushed straw aside. I took a breath and coughed, because my mouth and throat burned.

Coughing hurt like hell.

Firstly, I had a deep lash mark across my chest burning with each heave of my lungs, and secondly, my wrists and arms were tied painfully tight behind me. My hands tingled, and I could scarcely wiggle my fingers. I managed to get my legs under my body and rise to my knees. My head ached.

I knelt in straw. It was dark, but light filtered faintly in through the seams of a hatch overhead. I heard a squealing sound. There were cages, a fat pig here, a few chickens there. From the rocking of the deck, I realized I was in the hold of a ship.

I tried to struggle to my feet but fell. I'd been shackled with leg irons, and the links were bolted to the main beam. If I was careful, I could stand, but I found lying down in the straw was much easier at the moment. My head pounded, and light had a fuzzy quality to it that didn't feel right.

"Sun," I whispered into the decking. I didn't really expect an answer, but I got one anyway. Someone moaned from across the hold.

I strained forward, trying to make out the shapes in the gloom. A large iron cage lurked against the farthest end; a shape huddled on the bottom.

"Sun?" I strained against the chain, forcing my hoarse voice to make sound.

The shape turned over, and I saw him, but he didn't look much like my Sun. The left side of his face was one big bruise, his eye swollen shut. The trailing edges of fresh whip marks snaked across his shoulders. He rolled onto his back and hissed, then turned to his side reflexively.

His back was cut to ribbons. So many lashes I stopped counting them.

"Sun." I felt something rush up inside me and press against the back of my eyes, spill over, and race down my cheeks. I crawled forward as far as I could, pulling my chain tight, and lay on my belly so I could be as close to him as possible—about an arm's length away from the bars. The straw ground into my chest wound and burned, but I had to get close to him.

He painfully lifted himself on shaky arms, then crawled toward me and lay down carefully on his stomach so we could look at each other.

"Benjamin." His voice was hoarse, barely above a whisper.

"Are you all right?" It was the most stupid question anyone had ever asked in the history of questions, but I'd never wanted to know anything more badly in my life.

Sun smiled faintly, the horrible swelling of his face obliterated his dimple and made the smile lopsided.

"I live." His smile faded, and he tried to reach through the bars. The move cost him, and he gasped quietly as he stretched to brush my hair with his fingertips. My hair was stiff with blood under his touch, and I remembered my scalp wound.

"I thought he killed you." His swollen lips struggled with English. He looked rueful, maybe. I remembered him standing before Martio, calling out my name. I recalled the gunshot. I took a quick inventory of my hurts. Aside from the pain in my chest, the stiffness in my arms and hands, my only other complaint was a stinging tingle on my scalp where I'd gashed my head open in the cave. No bullet had pierced me, I was sure.

"I'm *allt* good, Sun." It occurred to me my face and chest had been a mask of blood last night—nothing bleeds like a scalp wound. He must have thought the redhead's shot, the one meant for him, had pierced me instead. I realized, as usual, it was my own damn fault I was here. And now my terrible luck had taken Sun too, because he loved me.

"*Fukka.*" I used Big Swede's favorite curse, one I suspected he invented himself. I was the one who deserved the lashes, not Sun. And now he faced a life of slavery, and I would, very shortly, either be thrown overboard or tortured to death, because I had nothing to give the pirates.

I prayed then, for a bit. I prayed for Sun's freedom. I prayed he would get to live out the rest of his years. I prayed he'd find the family he was taken from. I prayed my death would be quick and Sun would get over me.

CHAPTER 15.
THE SPY

BOOTS SOUNDED on the deck overhead. Sun tensed as someone came down into the hold.

The small figure lit a lantern hanging on the wall, and I suddenly felt vulnerable stretched out on my stomach. I curled onto my side to protect myself. I heard Sun making pained sounds as he tried to do the same inside the cage.

"Well, well." The voice belonged to Weasel. "You wouldn't be Benjamin Swift, would you?" The English was slightly accented, but Weasel spoke it clearly and well in his thin, high voice.

"Who wants to know?" My bravado was halfhearted, considering my condition, but I had to try anyway, especially if I were still playing the infamous smuggler. Keeping up the farce that I was Swift and might have a vengeful crew of fellow smugglers out there somewhere seemed more survivable than being Benjamin Lector, preacher's boy with no family or dangerous friends not presently caged.

"Where are the guns?" The diminutive sailor put the lantern down, adjusted the cutlass in his belt, and sat on a crate.

"That depends. Who wants to know?" I repeated.

Weasel got up, sauntered over, and went down on one knee so I could more properly see the hard look on his pointed face.

"Listen, stupid. They are going to kill you. You understand? You are going to die, and there is nothing I can do to stop it."

"Why would you?"

"Tell me where the guns are."

I glared at him from the floor and decided this conversation wasn't going to improve with my face near his boots. I twisted to the side and sat upright. The leg irons made it hard to do anything but sit awkwardly on my hip, but I managed it without whimpering, although my head threatened to explode off my shoulders.

"Tell me why I should tell you," I managed to say after the briefest moment of prayer for my splitting head.

"I'm not your enemy, Swift. You tell me where those guns are, and I'll keep them out of the Brazilian's hands." Weasel raised an eyebrow, inviting a confidence and wholly failing to convince me his offer of friendship was genuine.

"Still not seeing how this helps me." It was hard to concentrate on his face. He seemed to slide sideways across the deck. I finally had to close my eyes and trust my ears to keep working. Was it Brazil he mentioned? That seemed important.

"You're a dead man walking. Even I can't change that. If he doesn't kill you today, it means the *capitaine* is waiting for another, more entertaining fate." Weasel's voice was a low whisper. I realized it was because he didn't want to be overheard above decks. "If he allows the big one, Martio, to take you as a slave, you might live long enough for us to get to Georgetown, but no promises."

"Georgetown?"

I had never heard someone sigh with frustration so quietly. "In Guiana. I'll try. No promises. You tell me something I want to hear, and I'll do what I can for you."

I nodded, and my headache made me regret the motion. "And my companion?"

I managed the best glare I could. Weasel looked at Sun with barely disguised contempt.

"Do you have any idea how many deaths he's responsible for?" Weasel's voice sunk even lower so I could barely hear. He swore softly in what sounded like French. "Martio will avenge himself by prizefighting Sólmundur until he dies. That is, if they don't hang him in the next port as an example to escapees."

"We go together or not at all," I insisted. Sólmundur, of course. Sóli was short for Sólmundur—a Norse name? Sun wasn't his name at all. But regardless, my name for him fit, because he was my sun and moon so much so that I wasn't taking what Weasel offered without Sun too.

"You're a fool, Swift." The Frenchman evaluated me with beady eyes.

"So they tell me."

Weasel nodded, not taking his eyes off me, and I knew we had an agreement concerning Sun.

"Where are the guns?" His question was softer this time.

"They're at the bottom of the sea." I felt desperation rise again as I decided to tell him the truth. It wasn't much to bargain with. "The *Sea Swift* was caught in a storm just east of the Antilles. We'd have made it to Guiana in two days."

Thinking of my crew summoned them before my eyes again. The way Black Miguel pinched his chin, Carlos's sweet fiddle, Big Swede's swearing. They were laughing in my memory, and I recalled the mass grave in the cave. Slit throats. A realization tried to batter its way to the surface of my brain, but I ignored it.

"Good." Weasel sighed in apparent relief. He stood, his eyes cold as he measured me once more.

"We have a deal, yes? You'll help us?"

He didn't speak, only turned to leave. I couldn't quell a sudden sinking feeling in my chest.

"Wait," Sun spoke. Weasel turned as Sun settled into a crouch in his cage with a quiet, painful gasp. The look on his face bespoke that movement made his back hurt like hell, but I supposed there wasn't anything we could do about that.

"You ask about guns?" His eyes narrowed, watching Weasel's reactions. The rodent-like little man looked surprised to be addressed by an escaped slave.

"If you know anything about the guns, you tell me now." Weasel switched from English to Portuguese.

"I do not know you." Again, Sun was fluent, better with Portuguese than I was.

"No, but I know who you are." Weasel nodded at Sun. "You're a slave in a cage. Soon you will be a dead slave in a cage."

"And you are a spy." Sun rose carefully to his feet so he could look down at Weasel. Weasel crossed his spindly arms, and his eyes grew even beadier as he studied Sun with new respect.

He's not only handsome, strong, and deadly; he's also smart as hell, I wanted to warn Weasel. But Sun did just fine by himself, so I kept my mouth shut.

"I know where the guns are," Sun continued. "They are not underwater. Help us escape, and I will take you to them. Fail us, and Martio will know what you are before we die." He leveled his best ruthless expression at Weasel, who regarded us both.

Sun possessed an excellent ruthless expression. I tried to do my part and look tough, but I probably managed something not unlike a kicked dog. From the way his hand stroked the hilt of the cutlass in his waistband, Weasel was considering finishing us off right now and making up a story about it for the others. He glared at us both, his mouth set into a fine line.

"No guarantees, but if the opportunity arises, I will honor our deal." He threw a flask to Sun, who caught it with quick hands. A quiet hiss told me how much his sharp reflexes cost him. Then Weasel the Spy went up the stairs and was gone.

CHAPTER 16.
CONFESSIONS

THE FLASK was full of water. Sun managed to press himself against the bars so he could reach far enough for me to drink, since, with my hands tied, I couldn't hold it myself. I was parched. Never in my life had tinny, lukewarm backwash tasted so sweet.

"What was that about? Why was it so important to him that the guns were lost?" I asked Sun after we'd emptied the flask. He shook his head, looking at the deck with thoughtful concentration.

I knew who and what Sun was, so Weasel's little revelation about his escapee-prizefighter status hadn't come as much of a surprise. There were more important things I wanted answers to. I spoke Sun's name softly until he looked at me and I could hold his eyes with my own as I asked the next question.

"My crew, Sun. I saw them in the cave. How did they die?"

"All gone." He looked away. "Dead." A muscle twitched in his jaw as he waited for my reaction.

"Yes. How?" It seemed like too much of a breach for me to ask him directly. *Pardon me, gent, by the way, do you murder defenseless men?*

He turned around, and I found myself facing the livid bruises on his bloody back as he spoke. When he switched to Portuguese, the language he hated, I knew it was important to him that I understand what he had to say.

"The north shoal founders ships in a storm, sometimes." He spoke slowly, his voice distant, but steady. "I go there to watch. It was too dark. I did not see your ship, but I heard the crack of wood and stone. When the sea calmed, I dove. I looked for what your ship had held."

"You found the guns?"

"*Já*, and boxes, many boxes. Some were broken, and I could feel what was inside."

"How did you move all those boxes from the bottom of the sea, Sun? No one could do that without a winch." Not even my amazing Sun.

"They were in the forecastle, and scattered on the shoal and sandbar. It is very shallow there, for a man on foot with a raft, not so *erfitt*. I lifted them onto the raft and took them away in twos and threes."

"But I would have seen you. I saw the forecastle on the sandbar." Even so, what Sun was describing would have taken considerable strength and single-minded focus—both of which I knew he had.

"I moved them the day you walked around the island. Once you passed the northern shore, I knew you would make the circuit. Walking around a thing makes it smaller. Everyone who comes here does the same. So I took the chance to raft the boxes away then. It is not my custom to waste what washes ashore on my island."

I shook my head. Clever, so clever. But if he was set on not being seen, and he knew I was the only one around to see him....

"And my crew?" I asked.

Sun was silent for so long I thought he wasn't going to answer. "Washed up, on the shore."

"Like me."

"Benjamin." He stopped speaking, gathering his strength. His hands curled into fists. "I dream every night. Every night Martio comes in my dream. He finds my island. He takes me back. He makes me...." Sun shuddered and stopped talking.

"Go on." I worked hard to keep my voice level.

"I did not want him to find me, Benjamin." His voice thickened. "I could not risk anyone telling him about this place."

I felt the skin on the back of my neck prickle. "You've killed everyone who has come to your island?"

Sun nodded. "I could not bury your crew, or burn them. I am sorry. Someone would see the smoke and come."

There wasn't anything I could say to that, so I clenched my teeth. Sun had single-handedly created the superstition of Dread Island. "Go on."

"Through the night, I found your men, one by one, as they came onto the beach." His voice grew quieter as he spoke. "I made it quick. I dragged men away, one at a time. I did it all night, through the storm, so the rain would take the blood away."

And I thought I was a walking miracle for surviving the storm and the shipwreck. What had been waiting for me on the shore was just as merciless.

"Some still walked the next day, so I hunted them." He paused, and I could tell he was sparing me some gory details. At least now I knew what had been the source of the pool of blood that had so haunted me. I wondered who it had been. "You were the last one. You came ashore farther away from the others."

"Why was that, do you think?" I said, to say something, anything. My voice was so faint even I could barely hear it.

He shrugged, then made a pained sound. I didn't feel sorry for him. "You are young. Strong. You swim farther. I do not know."

"So why isn't my body lying in the cave?"

He took a few deep breaths. "I watched you explore, fetch parts of your ship from the sea." He shook his head. "I tried, but I could not hunt you. I did not want to. A man like you was… kind to me once." He looked down, studied the bottom of the cage. "I was alone for a long time. I liked watching you."

"Why didn't you come out?" I whispered.

"I did not know what to do. I wanted you to die, but I did not want to kill you myself. You were too smart. You ate leaves, grass. You stayed alive. You wandered. I watched."

"Until I couldn't walk anymore." I finished for him.

"*Já.* Then I came to finish you quickly, as I should have in the beginning, but I took you to the fire cave instead." He put his face in his hands.

It seemed like another man's memories, remembering waking up in Sun's cave that first morning. I couldn't absorb what he told me. I couldn't understand the twists of fate that had kept me alive this long, from shipwreck to murderer's island to pirate ship's hold. The King of Terrors was apparently trying to make up his mind when to claim my soul.

"I knew, even as I fed you, kept you, that you would bring Martio. Somehow, by allowing myself to keep you, he would come." Sun turned around. He glanced at me, but I found I couldn't look him in the eye. It wasn't being spoken about like a stray dog that bothered me. Sun had murdered people—people I knew. People I'd shared grog with, and laughter and cards and sweat-blooming hard work. My crew.

"Now I have killed us both. He will kill us both." His voice broke, and he covered his face with his hands again. I don't know how long I waited in numb silence, staring. I barely registered when Sun sank to his knees and curled into an unresponsive ball on the bottom of the cage.

I'd thought him a young castaway-turned-savage. At worse, I'd thought him an ill-used slave. But these deaths weren't because he was forced to fight for survival. He'd come in the night and killed helpless men, my friends, and dumped their bodies in an open communal grave. He was absolutely ruthless. He was a murderer.

He also happened to be the man I loved.

CHAPTER 17.
PUNISHMENT

I DIDN'T know how much time passed. Sun lay unmoving on the floor of his cage, and I leaned carefully on my side and stared at the wall. There was a salty crust on my skin, so I supposed I'd been dunked in the sea a few times when they brought me to the ship. They probably had to wash the remains of my crew off me.

I was too numb to shudder at the thought. Brought lower than ever before, I considered our situation from the floor as the ship rocked on the sea swell. The world kept turning around me. Greed brought me here—a way to invest Father's meager inheritance and launch my career as a smuggler. A whim of God was all that stood between me and death, and I couldn't seem to find the strength to care.

[handwritten margin notes: Not much lower to go. literally or metaphorical. The ship floor]

I heard someone walk down the stairs again. I didn't bother to look up. Vasco passed into my field of vision. He held the lantern and sneered. His long gun rested under his arm, pointed lazily in my direction.

"Get up." Martio's voice cut through my numb haze like a slap, but he wasn't talking to me. He stood at Sun's cage. Sun didn't answer, didn't move, still curled up in misery.

"Get up or Vasco will shoot this one." He pointed at me.

Vasco steadied his gun, and I found myself looking down the barrel. I glanced at Sun. Our eyes locked, but I felt paralyzed. Sun didn't stop looking at me as he got slowly up off the floor.

"Look at me." Martio's voice was low and husky. Sun closed his eyes. His fists curled, and the muscle in his jaw jumped like mad. Vasco poked me with the long gun.

"Vasco," Martio barked. Vasco kicked me hard in the ribs. If I thought I wasn't capable of feeling anything anymore, he proved me wrong. The pain was sharp and immediate. I tried to curl up as the air whooshed out of my lungs. I risked a quick look at Sun.

His glare was blazing lightning, blue eyes throbbing with threat like a hurricane sky.

"That's better." I heard the laughter in the big man's voice. "So much spirit. That is what made you brilliant in a fight, Sóli."

Sun's lips pressed into a tight line.

"Vasco, turn around."

Vasco's eyes flicked to Martio, then back to me. He maneuvered himself so his back was to Martio and Sun, but his gun was on me. His eyes hardened over a cruel sneer.

"Now, my slave." Martio unknotted the rope around his waist as he talked. "Remind me why I shouldn't kill you." Bile rose in my throat. Sun closed his eyes. His fists clenched and unclenched. Martio dropped his britches and cupped himself.

"Get to work, slave. If I feel teeth, Vasco will put a bullet in Mr. Swift here." Martio's voice purred. Vasco grinned at me. His smile was yellow and not all there.

I closed my eyes. I didn't want to see this. Nothing could keep me from hearing it, though. Martio enjoyed himself loudly.

Afterward, he spoke again, his voice low and breathless. "You have earned your dinner and another day." Vasco gave me a parting sneer, and then they were both up the stairs and gone.

I blinked the tears out of my eyes and looked for Sun. He retched in the corner.

"Sun," I moaned. Then I heard someone open the hatch again and come down the stairs. *Oh God. What now?* I couldn't look. Bare feet walked into sight. It was the tall mulatto I'd seen cutting up pigs on the shore. The Butcher crouched. He put two bowls on the ground and unsheathed a knife. I shrank away from him.

"Hold still or you'll get a slice." His voice was gruff. He pulled me over onto my stomach. I felt the blade saw at the ropes around my arms and wrists.

The sound I made as they gave way was somewhere between a surprised grunt and a yelp. My hands burned as the blood rushed back into them. They felt like swollen sacks. My shoulders popped and ground in their sockets as I brought my arms forward, slapping my deadened hands against the floor to regain my balance.

That turned out to be a bad idea. I swooned from the pain crawling over the surface of my skin and deep in my shoulders.

"It'll pass." Butcher's voice was quiet. "Sit up, do it slow."

I took his advice mainly because my head spun again and I couldn't do much else. He steadied me with a hand on my shoulder—the face under the bushy beard was slightly older than Sun's and mine, but his hard, brown eyes were experienced and savvy.

"Breathe, son. In. Out." Slowly the pain became bearable, but my hands were freezing cold as the burning sensation subsided.

"This'll help." He sheathed his knife and handed me one of the bowls he'd brought. I thought food was the furthest thing from my mind, but when the smell of stew wafted up, I managed to summon hunger from somewhere. I vaguely remembered I'd hardly eaten anything the day before.

He handed me a spoon and went to Sun's cage. I fumbled with the spoon and almost dumped the bowl before I decided to simply eat with it sitting on the floor. I crouched and drank out of it like an animal.

"Come on, lad. You need your strength." I heard Butcher coaxing Sun. Sun pushed himself upright and gasped, but his braids hid his face. Butcher pushed the bowl of stew within Sun's reach and shook his head, sighing as he stood but keeping his distance.

He sat on a barrel, watching me until I was done. "Let's have a look at that cut," he said, taking my empty bowl.

I sat up. My arms and hands had calmed to a dull ache. One good thing about having a tourniquet suddenly cut loose, I forgot about all my other pains. I barely remembered the gash on my chest until Butcher poured water on it.

The stinging pain of it came back with startling clarity.

A lash mark is an odd kind of wound to have. It was like having a bruise with burst seams. The cut was deeper on one end, where the end of the whip had slit a curling tail above my right nipple. The rest of it was a diagonal stripe of split skin over a deep purple bruise across my sternum and ribs. It bled from Vasco's kick. I closed my eyes to block out the memory of his sneering face.

"This won't feel nice," Butcher warned me.

I opened my eyes as he smeared something across the wound. He was right, it didn't feel nice, but it wasn't awful either. I managed not to flinch and was rather proud of myself.

"What about Sun?" I asked this without looking at the cage. Butcher poured more water over my head.

"Worry about yourself." Butcher finished his brisk and ungentle treatment of my scalp wound and stood. He stared at me. "Uncanny likeness indeed," he muttered.

I didn't know what he was talking about, but I wanted Sun cared for. "Look at his back. Give him some of that." I pointed to the tin Butcher held. I could smell now it was honey.

Butcher turned and, scratching his bushy beard, looked at Sun. "You want him patched up, it'll be you doing it." He tapped the corner of his eyes. "I'm too fond of my peepers."

"Your eyes?"

"If you'd seen him fight, you'd have a care with any part of you near that cage." He stood, taking my empty stew bowl with him and went up the stairs. He left Sun's dinner, water, and the tin of honey.

Moving around was much easier now my hands were free. I gave the chain of my leg irons an experimental tug, but I was locked tight to a ring in the post behind me. However, I could get closer to Sun's cage, so I did. He didn't look up.

"Sun," I started. His gasping had calmed, and he'd sunk to the floor again. I didn't know what to say. I knelt.

"You need to eat." I pushed the stew bowl closer to the bars. He didn't move. "It's not the best, really."

He didn't respond.

"Sun." I felt my anger rise. If I was going to live with what we'd been dealt, he was going to damn well do it too. "Eat the damn stew."

He raised his head. His eyes were still streaming, whether from retching or from trauma, I couldn't tell. The side of his face was so swollen that what Martio had made him do had to have hurt more than his dignity.

"You are going to eat this," I told him. "Then I am going to clean you up and put honey on you." He blinked and stared at me. The wounds on his back were ugly and seeping. "I am going to fix you up." My voice broke a little as the severity of his injuries became clear. "And then we are going to get out of here."

"How?" His voice was the smallest whisper.

"I don't know." The anger ran out of me as quickly as it had come. "But we will. I've been praying." Whatever good that would do us. "I killed them, Benjamin. I killed your men so this wouldn't happen. And it happened anyway." His blue eyes were full of pain.

"If I can forgive you, so can God," I said. I pushed the spoon through the bars. Sun closed his eyes again and cried, but he let me feed him the stew.

CHAPTER 18.
THE CAPTAIN

THEY CAME for me in the morning.

Sun was resting. His wounds weren't as bad as I'd feared. The water washed off the worst of the blood, and I found the whipping had mostly left him black-and-blue. There were five gashes where the skin had broken, and these cleaned up well. I'd used the rest of the honey on him, and it managed to cover all of his back.

It had taken me past sunset to treat him, and the hold was black as the devil's ass by the time I was done. After that, there was nothing to do but wait, talk to each other softly in the dark, and try to sleep. The floor was hard, but we were both tired enough to get some rest. It helped that we could reach each other now. Being able to hold his hand gave me the strength to get through the night.

I held the hand of a killer, but I told myself I would puzzle that out later.

The sound of the bolt being drawn back on the hatch above woke me. The sudden streaming sunlight was blinding, and as I blinked, both Weasel and Vasco clomped down the stairs and pulled me up by the arms.

"On your feet, *tire-au-flanc*. I'm not dragging you up the steps." Weasel's voice was harsh in my ear.

Vasco bent and unlocked my leg irons. He looked up at me with his yellow grin. "You're to meet the captain." He chuckled evilly. "I wouldn't try any tricks either. Captain doesn't take kindly to those, does he?"

"No, he does not. This one'll meet his fate by the captain's hand, like as not." Weasel sniggered.

I thought he overplayed his role as a villain somewhat, even though I realized the necessity. If he were discovered as a traitor in their midst, I was sure his punishment would be more gruesome than whatever was in store for me. If an end could get more gruesome than being killed. I unwillingly remembered what Martio had done to Sun. Well, yes, worse than I was prepared to imagine, I reckoned.

I glanced at Sun. He stood in his cage, gripping the bars. He looked so much better than the night before, it was like he was a different person. The fire was back in him, and he looked dangerous as hell. I noticed Vasco and Weasel were careful to stay well out of his reach.

"I will see you again." Sun spoke the words in English. I nodded, despite the fact I wasn't so sure about that.

"Move," Vasco said. Without further ado, he and Weasel marched me up the steps and out of the hold. I felt Sun's anxious gaze follow us.

They let go of me on deck at the same time, and I fell to all fours, blinking madly in the sunlight. We were at anchor, and I recognized the volcano. We were still in Dread Island's cove.

"On your feet." Weasel's voice was loud in my ear. He pressed cold steel against my shoulder. He'd drawn his cutlass and had a dangerous, meaningful look in his eyes. The other men laughed as I sprang to my feet too quickly and swayed.

"Walk." Vasco pushed me forward. Jeers called down from the rigging. A sailor leaned against the rail of the crow's nest on watch, but looking down at me more than at the sea, and two more replaced frayed ropes in the mainsail's runner and tackle. The others, including Butcher, were arrayed across the deck in a line from the hatch to the captain's door.

I walked, feeling naked in my shirtlessness as I was paraded in only my britches past the men, who jeered and japed at me. Odd that my present state of undress hadn't bothered me until this moment.

Weasel pressed his cutlass at my back, as if I had anywhere to run. I could make a mad dash for the side of the boat, but I'd be shot in the clear blue waters of the Caribbean before I swam five strokes.

Vasco opened the door. "Sir, the prisoner." Vasco's leer was gleeful.

"Enter." The voice inside was cool and steady and English. The room was very much like the captain's cabin on the *Sea Swift*, and I felt a sudden nostalgia for my sunken ship. Nostalgia turned to recognition quickly. The man behind the desk, the captain of this ship, was none other than the man who had set sail from New Orleans with me in the *Sea Swift*'s sister craft, *Sea Fury*—the architect of my grand adventure on the sea, Captain Edwin James.

Edwin inclined his head for me to sit. I sank down into the chair, too stunned to do anything else. I barely registered Martio's hulking form in the small room, looming over the corner of the desk.

Before I could babble my relief at Edwin delivering me from these pirates, he spoke.

"This is not where you are supposed to *be*, Mr. Swift," he said. The quill in his hand scratched across parchment. He added the paper to a thick stack before looking up.

I could only stare at him dumbly. Gone were the easy grins, the conspiratorial glances. The handsome and smooth-talking Scotsman I'd met over a game of cards in a gin palace in the city of sin was completely absent. In his place was a cold, calculating Englishman, who skewered me with gray eyes. Father would have said I was reaping the wages of my sin, though I hadn't gotten around to much sinning before we set sail—Edwin and Black Miguel had been in a hurry to leave port.

"The question now before us"—he laced his fingers together—"is what am I to do with you?" The last time I saw him, he'd worn his hair long, a tail tied with a neat ribbon. Now his close-cropped, graying hair made him look like a retired general instead of a Scottish dandy. Tragically, he was still quite handsome.

"Let me go?" I quipped, trying to resurrect the easy repartee we'd once shared. I was still in difficulty, reconciling my memory with the man before me.

His eyebrows shot up in surprise, and he chuckled.

"Oh, no, no, Mr. Swift. I'm afraid that isn't possible." With a sharp tug, he straightened his great coat—military issue with large gold buttons. "You see, you're my insurance, *Mr. Swift.*" He emphasized my borrowed last name. He stood and paced the small office.

"Insurance?" I risked a glance at Martio. He glowered; his glare divided between me and his captain. There was bad blood there. If I could find a way to exploit it….

"Yes," Edwin continued in smooth tones, clasping his hands behind his back. "You and that randy band of blackguards I gave you for a crew were of some import. If you were captured, they were to deny knowledge of the cargo's contents and hand you over to the authorities forthwith. If the *Sea Swift* wasn't captured, they were to rid me of you after the handoff. However, as you've had the audacity to sink my ship and eliminate my loyal crew, I'm now faced with a dilemma."

I gaped at him. The silence stretched until I realized he wasn't going to speak until I did.

"And what would that be?" I stalled, glad my hands were untied. I didn't see any weapons closer than Martio's whip. I guessed he'd win the draw there. In addition, Vasco was waiting outside the door with his gun. I wondered how Edwin and the *Fury* had managed to escape the ferocity of the storm and felt stupid for not recognizing the caravel when I first saw her in the bay.

"Half of my cargo is at the bottom of the sea, Mr. Swift. It is supposed to be in Brazil. You were scheduled to be either dead by now or answering for my crimes, but you have a nasty habit of surviving."

"I intend to continue to do so." My mouth moved before my brain had time to catch up. I did, however, register that the crew of the *Sea Swift* would have betrayed me. That took some of the sting out of Sun having killed them, though I'd still be praying for his soul for a long time for murdering mostly helpless men. They weren't all bad, but knowing Black Miguel had only been waiting around to kill me darkened the memories I had of him singing in his sweet tenor while I accompanied him on a borrowed fiddle. But if he were only waiting to kill me, why tie me to the barrel in the storm and save my life? There was more to this than I knew.

"And how's that, Mr. Swift?" Edwin smiled as he regarded me. "What could you possibly have I might want or need?"

Martio leaned over the desk and seemed to hang on my words.

"I know where the guns are," I told him. Edwin raised an eyebrow. I blundered on. "They are easily retrievable."

"It's not hard to guess their location." He sat back down at his desk. "Martio tells me your new friend slaughtered the crew of the *Sea Swift*?" He picked up his pen again. "This tells me my ship sunk somewhere close by. My guess is off the north shoal."

I worked hard to keep my expression blank. Martio's dark eyes followed us both, and I wondered how much English he understood— probably enough.

"It will be a small matter for me to put these dogs to work hauling the guns off the shoal and aboard the *Fury*." He started writing, his pen scratching as loudly as before. "Tell me again, Mr. Swift, what reason I might have to keep you alive?"

I opened my mouth, then shut it, unable to think of a single reason, except—"The guns aren't on the shoal."

"Martio." He spoke the name crisply, and Martio clapped a meaty hand onto the back of my neck and pushed my face to the desk.

"I grow tired of games, Mr. Swift. Where are my guns?"

My mind raced. "Arrange to release me and my friend, and the guns are yours." I'd gambled with Edwin; he fell for bluffs. Couldn't resist the possibility of the big win.

He stared at me for what seemed like an age but then nodded at Martio, who let me up.

"You have more guile than I would have guessed, Mr. Swift." His brow arched. "And there is still the matter of the lease to charter the *Sea Swift*, an account we will settle before we part ways."

I blinked. That sounded promising for me living another day.

"On the matter of your friend, this we must discuss." He looked at Martio as he spoke. "It seems he is a slave of some monetary value."

It was abruptly clear to me that Edwin, while certainly in charge, didn't regularly travel with these pirates, all of whom seemed to know Sun, well, Sólmundur, and his deadly reputation also. Of all the islands in the Caribbean I had to shipwreck on, God picked the one a fugitive killer used as his hiding place. And I had to save us both from my former partner.

"It is clear he has no moral compunctions when it comes to killing. I'm also told he has skill as a fighter?"

"I'm sure he'd accept if you'd like to challenge him," I quipped. I imagined Sun cutting the smile from Edwin's face. It felt too good. Was it any more right for me to wish Sun would kill those who betrayed me? No. It wasn't.

"Martio." The one-word command resulted in a smack across the side of my head that rattled my teeth and caused a series of small explosions behind my eyes. I held the offending body part between my hands and concentrated hard on not retching.

"If you choose not to cooperate, Mr. Swift, I am certain Mr. de Fortaliza here would enjoy some time alone with you." I didn't have to see Martio's face clearly to confirm his leer. Yes, he would very much enjoy having me to himself.

"What do you want from me?" My voice was weak and, to my shame, quavered.

"As much as I would enjoy avenging myself by killing you, Mr. Swift, I have found revenge to be, for the most part, unprofitable." He smiled slightly at some private joke.

I waited for him to go on, very much aware Martio breathed hard with excitement, his big hands clenching and unclenching.

"Deliver the guns, Mr. Swift, and we shall call that account settled." He ticked off his demands on ink-stained fingers. "See to it that your companion, Mr. Thorvaldson, considers fighting as our representative in the slave pits at Georgetown. Mr. de Fortaliza assures me you will be able to provide adequate motivation."

So I was going to be a bargaining chip to ensure Sun's cooperation. He wasn't going to like this.

"Third, you will be my indentured servant until such time as you have repaid my losses on the *Sea Swift*." He turned the paper he'd been writing toward me and handed me the pen.

"And if I don't sign?" I scanned the document. The bastard had beautiful handwriting.

"Then, Mr. Swift, we shall have to resort to pleasure before business, as much as it pains me."

Martio laid his heavy hand on my shoulder and squeezed. Edwin looked at me, a smile on his lips, gray eyes narrowed with anticipation. In that moment, I could tell part of him wanted me to refuse. I saw in those eyes my body swinging from the yardarm, striped by Martio's lash.

I scanned the paper. Considering his original plan was me serving his prison term or dead, indentured servitude was an improvement. I didn't like the written-in clause about Sun's cooperation, and I likewise didn't know where the guns actually were, but, considering torture and death were my alternative, I signed. I ignored the acute feeling of my mother and her ancestors turning in their graves. *Well, Father*, I thought, *I didn't end up lynched, but a white man is going to have to pay taxes on me, after all.*

Edwin grinned. "Pleasure doing business with you as always."

Martio exhaled as though he'd been holding his breath. Before I could say anything, he rapped on the door sharply. Vasco and Weasel entered, took my arms, and propelled me out of there much the way they'd carried me up.

The men milled about in front of the captain's quarters, looking at me with various expressions of glee, fascination, and, at least in the case of Butcher—pity.

I pitied me too. I had no idea how I was going to break this to Sun.

CHAPTER 19.
BETRAYAL

SUN STOOD in his cage, waiting anxiously, as they brought me back down, deposited me in a heap, and left.

"Did they hurt you?" Sun's eyes followed me as I regained my feet. Vasco hadn't bothered to padlock my leg irons to the ring again, so I could, in theory, move about the hold as I pleased.

"No, I'm all right." I focused on his blue eyes. A sudden longing for open beach, sky, and freedom rose in me. Was it really only a few days ago we hadn't a care in the world? I hadn't known I'd found paradise until I'd lost it.

"What happened?" He gripped the bars.

"Well, good news first. They aren't going to kill us."

His shoulders relaxed, but he looked puzzled. "What will happen?"

"That depends on where the guns are."

He narrowed his eyes. "Why? What did the captain say?"

I looked at the floor. "He said, if he had the guns, he'd forgive my debt for them."

"And then he would let us go?" He sounded confused. And suspicious.

"Not exactly."

He waited for me to find my courage and speak.

My eyes seemed too heavy, but it would have been cowardly to tell him without looking at him, so I met his gaze. "They want you to fight for them. As their representative in Georgetown's pits."

"*Nei, nei.* I will not fight the pits again." The words rose, tumbling from his mouth. "*Nei, nei.* Never again."

"Then we're going to die." I hated myself for it, but I said it anyway. "If you don't fight for them, they're going to kill us."

"I can't, Benjamin. I won't be a slave again. I can't." His knuckles whitened on the bars.

"They want you to represent them, which might not mean being their slave. How many fights did you win?" I crossed my arms, ignoring the sting in my chest.

"Fifty." His voice was quiet but sung with tension. I had the feeling he remembered every one of them.

"And how many men were dead in that hole in the cave?"

He was silent.

"Sun, you killed them. You murdered them in the night. At least the ones you killed in slave matches had a fighting chance." Why did the higher moral ground make me feel like such a bastard?

"Benjamin, you don't know."

"Then tell me."

"You do not want to know." He sat on the floor of his cage and held his head.

"Yes. I do. I want to know what I'm in for."

"What do you mean?" He dropped his hands and looked at me, all attention.

"I'm a slave—indentured servant. Until I've paid for the *Sea Swift*, I'm signed over to Captain Edwin James."

The sound surprised me, a keening cry ending in a moan. "Benjamin, oh my Benjamin, what have you done?"

"I've saved us both, and I did rather well, considering the circumstances."

"This is not a game, not a trade. Sometimes death is the better choice."

"Death is better than being an indentured servant for a few years? Never." My anger rose like a red cloud, obscuring my worries. "There's a whole wide world out there to experience, Sun. You don't know."

He put his head in his hands and wouldn't talk to me. I vaguely felt my brown ancestors buzzing angrily in the back of my mind, but ignored them. Being a prisoner in the hold of a ship, especially one who had started out in irons, was an ancestral memory, and the voices clamored for me to get myself, and anyone I cared about, out of this arrangement.

BUTCHER CAME and went with our lunch, taking his honey tin with him. Neither Sun nor I spoke through the long afternoon. I had plenty of time to think things over, but I still couldn't see how we could have gotten out of this any other way. I held my moral indignation close to my heart, and my righteous anger even closer, to avoid grinding my teeth in frustration.

When the shadows thickened with the fall of dusk, Martio and Vasco came again. As before, Vasco pointed his gun at me, and Martio sauntered over to Sun's cage. Sun gained his feet slowly but backed into the farthest corner once he was upright.

"Good evening, slave." Martio started to unknot his britches. "Come here."

Sun's voice was steady. "No."

"Vasco, remind him." I heard the smile in Martio's voice. Vasco quickly reversed his gun and jabbed at me, but I ducked and took the butt strike on my shoulder and rolled. The leg irons tangled in my feet. Vasco was there, on his knee, and he struck me hard in the face, twice. White lights popped behind my eyes.

"Come here," Martio growled at Sun.

"No." His answer was resolute.

Vasco didn't take his eyes off me, but I could tell he wanted to look to his master for direction. I untangled my legs and readied them back under me, dizzy but prepared to fight if I needed to. Though, in a contest between me and a bullet, the bullet would win. Well, and probably a contest between me and any man aboard the ship.

"Do not anger me." Martio put his hand on his whip. "You know how I punish disobedience."

"I am not your slave," Sun said.

Martio glared at him.

"He's right," I said. "Our agreement is with Captain Edwin James. Does he know what you come down here to do, Martio?"

The big man flared his nostrils. I'd guessed Edwin hadn't known. Now I knew he didn't.

"I am the first mate." He crossed over to me, and I flinched. He grabbed my arm, yanked me forward, and pulled me to the ground, his knee in my back. I fought, but his heavy fists dazed me. He was too strong. None of my struggles to twist out of his grasp had any result. Vasco bound my arms, the ropes cutting into my skin, while Martio pinned me.

"Punishment is my responsibility," he said, holding my head up by my hair. "Vasco, you will guard the door." Vasco narrowed his eyes, turned his head, and spat. But he walked up the stairs and bolted the hatch behind him.

Martio pulled down my britches and violated me. Sun screamed from his cage.

"On this ship, I am king. You will not forget it again," he said when he was finished. He kicked me once, pounded on the hatch so Vasco would let him out, and was gone.

CHAPTER 20.
AFTER

I LOST some time that night, lying in the dark. I knew I was hurt. I thought I might be dying, I hurt so much. I couldn't bring myself to speak. Sun called my name and cried, but I couldn't answer him. It was as though Martio had damaged more than my body. He'd taken my voice also.

Somehow I lived through that night, bleeding in the pitch-black, Sun's quiet sobs my company. He spoke to me all night, sometimes talking to me, sometimes shouting for help. I didn't remember anything he said. I was numb to my very core, and I could not move my body. My mind was empty, without thoughts. I did not sleep.

When day broke, Sun's hoarse cries finally brought Butcher.

"What's all this noise about?" the tall mulatto asked as he came down the stairs with a water bucket. "Captain says I'm to gag you if you can't keep quiet." Butcher stopped just out of Sun's reach.

"Benjamin," Sun choked. "Benjamin is hurt."

"Who tied you up again?" He walked to where I lay. I curled up, flinching away from him. Butcher crouched. I heard a sound, a low animal whimper, and realized it came from me.

"Who's been at you, boy?" He looked at Sun. "Thought you'd beat him for selling you to pirates, did you?"

"It was Martio," Sun said. "He came last night. He… he hurt Benjamin." Sun didn't have a word for what Martio had done to me.

Butcher looked at me and frowned. I realized my face throbbed and couldn't understand why I hadn't noticed it before. My face felt like someone had used it to hammer the deck.

Butcher grunted and poured water over my head. I sputtered, and everything hurt worse.

"After all my work to fix you…." He looked me over, muttering to himself.

Sun watched anxiously. I was not in control of my body. No matter how often Butcher told me to hold still, I flinched from him and shivered. He washed my face, and I screamed when he straightened my broken nose.

"Not so uncanny at present. Ah well, that's for the best," he mumbled.

He left to fetch another bucket and was gone awhile. When he came back, he washed the rest of me, ignoring my cries and struggles as I tried to get away from his probing fingers.

"Stop your yelling, boy!" Butcher thundered, but his words were for Sun, who rattled his bars and screamed for Butcher to leave me alone. "He'll live. He's hurt, but he'll live."

Butcher's rough hand found my chin, and he forced me to look at him.

"You hear me? You'll live. One day soon you're going to get up and walk out of here and live your life with dignity, boy. Nobody, not Martio, not the captain, not a man of this ship is going to stop your doing that. You hear?"

I considered his thickly bearded face and too-experienced eyes. His gaze searched mine, and though I made no sound, he nodded. He grunted once and turned to leave.

"Thank you," Sun's voice rang clearly. Butcher nodded and was gone. We were alone again.

I felt a little better clean, and, as though the water had also cleared some kind of block, I felt shame boil up inside me. I had allowed Martio to do that to me. I wasn't strong enough or smart enough to stop him. I couldn't defend myself like Sun could. Martio could do whatever he wanted with me. I was powerless.

"Benjamin." Sun's voice, though quiet as a whisper, echoed in the hold. "I am sorry. You should never forgive me. When he comes, I will do whatever he wants."

Sun blamed himself. I groaned. I didn't want to have to help Sun with his guilt. I wanted to nurse my wounds and my shame.

"God damn it, Sun." My voice was a growl. "He did that to me, not you." I realized as the words left my mouth they were wrong. If Martio raped me once, he must have raped Sun hundreds of times. *He raped me.* I shook my head to clear it. "This is not your fault. I shouldn't have been flippant with him." It was my fault. He probably would have left me alone if I hadn't spoken, hadn't egged him on.

[handwritten margin notes: "People talk their own hurt at the found of" and "Blame Victim"]

"No, Benjamin. No." Sun was crying again. I was the one who had been raped, yet he was crying. "I'm sorry."

Something loosened in my chest, burned through me. Quite suddenly, I was awash with rage. As clearly as if I were doing it right that moment, I knew I had it in me to kill Martio de Fortaliza. I'd strangle him with the leg irons, attack him until I was dead, if he came into this hold again. The power and clarity of the feeling stole my strength and sent me to the floor. I'd never felt rage that strongly. I'd never wished death on another man. But, in that moment, I knew I would murder if given the chance.

CHAPTER 21.
REVELATIONS

EDWIN CAME down to visit not long after Butcher disappeared.

I heard the hatch open. I hadn't realized how quickly I'd retreated until I felt the cold bars of Sun's cage against my back. I'd crossed the hold before the first pair of boots sounded on the stairs. Sun touched my arm, and I flinched, but I stayed close to him. I could not abide the thought of anyone touching me, even Sun, but I knew the pirates feared his ferocity. I'd take any refuge I could get.

"Mr. Swift," Edwin said by way of greeting. Martio, Butcher, and Weasel accompanied him into the hold. As soon as I saw Martio, I felt again in quick succession a series of emotions—terror, shame, rage. My body shook, and I hoped it was fury rather than fear that moved me.

"We've had the occasion to search the shoals and have yet to find my guns." Edwin stared hard in Sun's direction. He emphasized the word *guns* ever so slightly. His eyes darted to Martio for the briefest of moments.

Two things became clear to me. Those crates held more than guns, and whatever else was hidden inside, Captain Edwin James did not want Martio to realize that fact.

At that moment, I understood Edwin's predicament clearly. I'd gone to New Orleans with my inheritance, looking for a ship and adventure, ripe for the plucking in my naiveté. It must have seemed like providence had answered Edwin James's prayers, because he needed some cargo gone from America and on the high seas with haste. A cargo he couldn't be caught with in the States. A cargo he loaded onto a ship full of mutinous scoundrels, each paid in gold and promises that more would be waiting after my death and their destination.

He must have survived the storm, reached his allies, and waited for the *Sea Swift*'s arrival with growing disquiet. He had been compelled to hire Martio and his pirates to accompany him in finding his missing capital, which led him here.

"Benjamin does not know where the guns are." Sun spoke, using English so Edwin would understand him.

"And you do, I assume?" Edwin narrowed his eyes as he looked at the caged savage.

"*Já*. Our freedom, and I will take you to them."

Edwin raised an eyebrow. Weasel did an excellent job of hiding his thoughts behind a wicked sneer. Martio glowered at everyone.

I didn't understand Martio's investment in this. His last name was Brazilian. I knew there was great unrest in the South American colonies; Edwin had told me as much in the port before we sailed. It was why the various governments were not allowing colonists the guns they needed to defend themselves from the wildlife. He'd told me our smuggling was really more beneficent than anything else, which made sense to me, considering the free black man's struggle for the right to bear arms in North Carolina. The guns were, of course, valuable, but why go to all this trouble?

Then I understood. Martio's men were thieves and slavers, yes, but perhaps greatly desirous for their port of call to have independence from their Portuguese overlords. All the nations kept navies in the Caribbean Sea and patrolled so vigorously that piracy was no longer a profitable venture. Perhaps they were possessed of a desperation of their own, a free Brazil to retire to. Were Martio and his men rebels and the guns meant for a Brazilian uprising?

I noticed also Weasel had not missed the silent exchange; he watched both men closely. Another piece fell into place as I remembered him swearing quietly in French. Brazil was cheek by jowl with French Guiana, one of the few bits of empire France had left after the Louisiana Purchase and reparations for Napoleon's blunders. I realized France would hold on to that tiny colony with as much force as the fallen nation could muster, one of their last footholds in the New World, now that Hispaniola had become the Republic of Haiti. Come to think of it, Edwin, being British, must have thought it amusing to select an American for this venture, sending a former colonist to his death. Even more convenient that I looked like this Captain Benji Swift fellow I was supposed to be pretending to be, to take the blame for Edwin as a famous smuggler if we'd been captured.

I remembered the British had taken a piece of Guiana from the Dutch—between the French colony and the newly independent

Venezuela—populated it with slaves and Irish, and clung to it like demons. It would be a real feather in Britain's cap if they could wrest French Guiana or Brazil out of colonial rule and incorporate them into Britain's empire.

I'd been looking for adventure, and I'd found it and a plot bigger than myself, bigger than random pirates roving the high seas, bigger than discovering who I really was with Sun on the island. My little mercantile venture had landed us in the middle of a colonial showdown between the empires of Europe. I'd thought our chances of getting out of this alive were so-so before, but I had even more serious doubts now. We were surrounded by ruthless enemies who had everything to lose by letting us go.

I stood, my mouth hanging stupidly open, while these revelations crashed against each other inside my aching head.

"You are in no position to make demands." Edwin's voice was cold.

Sun bared his teeth humorlessly, a mockery of a smile, but didn't speak. Silence stretched in the hold, and I quieted my chasing thoughts and found my voice. If finding the guns, probably meant to help Brazil revolt, was the one bargaining chip we had, we had to use it.

"You'll never find those guns without his help." My voice was rough, like I'd been talking or yelling for hours. "You want them, you'll let us go."

Martio made a fist, and his knuckles cracked. Edwin didn't look at him, but I almost felt his thoughts. Captain James was weighing if he could control the men long enough to search the island against his desire to have his cargo and be underway. He was trying to guess how badly Martio wanted Sun, and if he could get away with making deals.

"Very well." Edwin handed a ring of keys to Martio. "Release the prisoners."

The tension in the room increased. Martio took the keys slowly and looked at them. He stepped forward, toward us. He glared down at the tangle of keys, then swore. Apparently the desire to have the guns outweighed his desire to keep Sun.

"Throw me the keys," I said. I was pleased to note my voice wasn't shaking, though the bars behind me were the only thing holding me up as Martio advanced on us. I pressed against the iron so hard I thought I might push backward through them.

Martio grinned at me. He relished that I was afraid of him.

"Then again"—Edwin interrupted Martio as he took another step—"I have heard of this savage's fame in the fighting pits. Throw in shackles first, Martio, and see he puts them on before we release him."

Sun and Martio both glared at him. I could see Martio wanted to be the one to shackle Sun just as much as Sun wanted Martio to get within reach. If I'd seen murder in Sun's eyes before, it was nothing to the chilling depth of his eyes now.

A tense moment hung in the balance, and then Martio bent to retrieve my discarded leg irons. He threw them at me, and I caught them clumsily. I looked at them for a moment before passing them in to Sun. I resisted the mental image of the chain around Martio's neck, throttling him while the crew shot me.

Now was not the time for a last stand. I'd save that for the island.

Chapter 22.
Back on the Island

I'D NEVER felt sunshine on my skin more keenly than I did that day. I vowed I was never going back into that hole. They'd have to kill me first.

Martio held Sun's upper arm. Sun moved so gracefully the leg irons were more like ugly jewelry than an inconvenience. Edwin had sent Weasel for a pair of wrist shackles, and Sun was now bound by those as well. He still looked so liquid and dangerous that everyone, save Martio, stayed well clear of him.

Every time Martio moved, Sun made minute adjustments to his own stance. He was ready for a fight. I think probably the only thing keeping him from attacking Martio then was the improbability of our survival.

I heard the sailors whispering superstitious oaths as we walked by, protecting themselves from the killer. Nobody paid much mind to me at all. I wasn't chained, and I felt lucky about that until I thought about it long enough to feel insulted. I quietly told my pride it could be ruffled all it wanted, so long as I was free.

They'd reconsider my harmlessness if I could get my hands on a gun.

The landing party filled two long boats. Edwin, Martio, Sun, me, and two nervous sailors who kept their guns at ready climbed aboard the first boat while Weasel, Vasco, and four others I didn't know loaded themselves on the second. Butcher watched us leave from the *Fury*'s deck, and the way the others jumped to his bellowed orders, it appeared he was in command while both captain and first mate were away. I hadn't forgotten his kindness to us, and watching his tall, dark shadow recede behind us felt like taking ourselves out from under the umbrella of his scant protection.

"Well, then, lead the way." Edwin set Martio on the rudder and took up a position in the bow with Sun, who called back directions to his former master, his voice empty of emotion. I continually gauged the distance between the boat and the shore and the depth of the water, but a look over my shoulder at the armed men watching us depart from the ship's deck dashed my hopes. We'd make easy targets swimming.

If we were to escape, it'd have to be under cover of the trees.

"We must walk through the forest," Sun said as we landed. He jumped lightly to the shore, again unfairly agile despite the heavy chains. Martio plunged over the side and noisily crashed through the water, but Sun waited for him as though escape was the furthest thing from his mind. In a moment, the full complement of both long boats was on the shore.

I felt better. Two against ten were fairer odds than we'd had on the ship.

The six armed sailors watched Sun like lion tamers watch a new acquisition. Weasel and Vasco passed the water jug around before we started our hike. Nobody offered water to either Sun or me.

"Well, then, let us get underway." Edwin adjusted his belt. "If the slave runs, shoot him." He nodded, and Martio stepped forward and latched one meaty paw onto Sun's elbow. "Mr. Swift will accompany me," he said, and he prodded me with his gun.

Two by two we walked into the shadow of the trees.

I knew the way Sun could move if he wanted to. Martio held tightly to his arm, but Sun ignored the larger man as though he were a fly or a mosquito. He led us along one of the trails the pigs had beaten into the turf. I recognized it. If we took it south by west, we'd get to the watering hole and home.

A sudden longing to see the tree house again overwhelmed me. I hadn't realized how important it had become, but I suddenly and passionately wished I'd been a boring and honest merchant rather than a smuggler. Timber or cotton no one would have bothered to come looking for, and I'd still be living a happy life as a savage. Were the comforts of civilization no longer of any interest to me? When did that happen? Actually, I did know when—it was after I felt Sun's touch, and he mine. After I, like so many before me, and would again after me, fell in love.

"Be careful," Sun called back to us. He'd led us northwest, through the grasping bean trees, and we'd come to the canyon where Ernest had nearly unmanned me. There was no sign of the pigs—perhaps they had learned to fear men and guns during the pirates' visit. Sun left the path, scrambling up the steep eastern slope that would lead us across the top of the escarpment. Martio had to let go of him to follow.

"After you, Mr. Swift." Edwin waved his pistol. I scrambled after them, alert for any possibilities of escape, but Edwin kept back far enough it'd be hard to rush him and get the gun. He was, however, still close enough to put a lead ball in my back with reasonable certainty.

Neither Martio nor Sun were waiting for us when we reached the top.

"Martio," Edwin called out, not taking his eyes from me as we reached the summit.

There was no answer.

"Call him," Edwin ordered me. He kept his weapon ready. The others slowly joined us on the rise.

I knew who he meant. I called Sun's name. The forest was silent in the bright sun.

"Louder, please, Mr. Swift." Edwin's barrel didn't waiver.

"Sun!" I yelled. We waited in nervous silence.

"Where are Mendoza and Dupree?" Vasco asked. Long moments passed, but no one else joined us.

"I don't see them." Weasel, last man up, peered over the crest. "They were right behind me."

Others went to the ledge to look, but the missing men failed to appear. The remaining sailors gathered around their captain, each trying to look in every direction at once.

"Sóli." Vasco's voice was low, scared.

"There's no need for alarm." Edwin's words were confident and wavered even less than the weapon he kept steadily pointed at me. "Not while we have him." He glanced at my expression, indicating with his gun that I should walk forward. "Lead on, Mr. Swift."

I walked forward, deeper into the trees and up the slope of the mountain. I was keenly aware of the gun at my back as I strained my ears for any sounds in the dark forest around us. I had no idea where we were going, but I thought if Sun had hidden anything on the island, it would have been in the caves. He had hidden the bodies there, after all.

We were halfway up the steep slope, struggling through thick undergrowth, when we heard screams.

"What was that?" Vasco spun wildly with his long gun, attempting to point it in every direction at once. He was close to us, as if trying to find safety by being near the most important people.

Weasel burst through a shrub behind us, Edwin only just managed to point Vasco's gun down before it went off. The shot echoed eerily, and when it faded, I thought I heard an anguished cry in the distance. A bird? A man? My anxiety for Sun doubled, but my anxiety for myself was closer and more immediate. Of the two of us, Sun, at least, could take care of himself.

Weasel panted, his eyes rolling. Bloody speckles decorated his boots. "Something got them. Snatched them from right beside me." He fell to his knees.

The remaining two men huddled near Edwin with Vasco. The odds were improving. With Martio missing, that left five. Still too many for me by myself, even if I could trust Weasel not to cut me down if I ran. I needed to even the odds.

"There are things on this island worse than the boars," I improvised.

"What do you mean?" Edwin tightened his grip on my elbow, but I thought I heard a quaver in his voice that hadn't been there before.

"Sometimes we'll find a dead boar, partially eaten," I lied. I've always been able to spin a good yarn. Maybe I had learned something useful from my preacher father, after all. "We hear things in the night. It's not safe to travel without fire."

My words affected the two nameless sailors, who looked from the forest to each other and their captain in a series of glances that left little to the imagination. They'd desert in a heartbeat, if given the chance. Lying was a sin, but I thought God might forgive me, considering the circumstances.

"I won't listen to lies." Edwin pushed me forward. "It's your friend who has taken these men." He raised his voice and yelled into the woods. "If one more man is attacked, I will kill Mr. Swift. Do you hear me?"

Nothing but silence answered him.

We were now in such a tight group together, we moved through the underbrush at a snail's pace, pushing through vegetation by sheer force. Edwin used my body to break the waves, as it were, and I was covered with scratches. Many times I thought of turning on him to struggle for the gun, but Vasco had taken to watching me as though I were his saving grace. My desire to remain alive fought a short war with the satisfaction I would feel punching my old partner, the man who had betrayed me. Survival won.

"How much farther?" Edwin was winded. I wasn't. I'd scarcely stopped moving from the day I woke in Sun's cave. As captain, Edwin had no doubt spent his time aboard as I'd found him—at a desk signing papers.

"Not far," I answered. It was true; we were very near the caves, and we soon broke through the tree line. Everyone looked worse for wear. Sailors are not jungle men. Only high excitement had driven them this far, and they looked relieved to have escaped the darkness of the woods. Their eyes darted back to the trees—forbidding for them, salvation and home for me.

It was now past time for the midday meal, and the heat of the sun beat down on us. The men took quick bites of the food they had brought, looking around nervously as they chewed sea biscuit, cheese, and pig jerk. Weasel dropped some of his in the dirt and kicked it to me, then laughed as I lunged for it. The others chuckled, an edge of hysteria in the sound. However, I took it for what it was—Weasel trying to help me—and I wiped off the dirt and ate it. The cheese was heavy and crumbled, but I tried to eat slowly and enjoy it. The taste was so fine I nearly cried.

After he caught his breath, Edwin was hot to set forth again, and he dragged me to my feet. As we walked, Weasel talked about the last time he'd been in the caves, describing the abattoir in Sun's oubliette to the sailors. His voice was soft and haunted by the horrors within. By the time his story was done, we were there.

Entering the tunnels was the last thing any of my companions wanted to do. The stench rode the heat of the day, a physical presence at the cave mouth that left me gagging.

"Captain, we saw no crates the other night." Vasco stood several feet back from the opening, shaking his head and clutching his gun. "There's nothing in there but death."

Edwin pulled himself even straighter than before, glaring at Vasco and the two men who cowered behind him. He tightened his grip on me and pulled me close.

"Get in there."

Vasco shook his head and stepped farther back. Weasel started forward, tentatively climbing onto the ledge before the black opening. He kept low to the ground, squinting inside.

"I don't see anything, Captain."

"Prepare torches." Edwin pushed me up onto the ledge.

CHAPTER 23.
THE CAVE

THE SMELL at the cave mouth was physical, palpable—a great hand that pressed against my chest and kept me from entering even when I felt Edwin's gun dig into my side.

"Walk." He shoved me forward. I held my breath as I stumbled. I heard the rough oaths of the men as he ordered them to follow us. They tied cloth over their noses and mouths, more an attempt to keep the oily stench from their skin than to keep it from their lungs. There was no escaping it.

Time to act the man. My eyes watered as I forced myself to breathe, but I didn't retch. My stomach loved cheese that much, refusing to give it up so easily. I tried damned hard to do my stomach proud. I made it look as though the burning fingers of stench didn't bother me, even as they stole my breath and gouged my lungs.

After only a few steps, Vasco's torch was the only thing lighting the way. The cave walls were frozen waves, undulating like the huge stone intestine they were. Last time I'd gone in from one of the cracks. The main tunnel was far more impressive—an ancient lava pathway.

The cave was wet as a mouth, water dripping from the ceiling. I tried to remember if mold had been growing on the bodies when I'd fallen into the pit. My stomach stayed strong despite the memory. It vaguely occurred to me I should be shivering in horror, but I wasn't. Something in my brain was clearly broken. Had been broken.

As if the thought summoned him, Martio appeared out of the depths of the cave.

"Where is Sólmundur?" Edwin yanked me close to him, eyes wide. Everyone's eyes showed whites around the edges. The torches couldn't cast enough light into this place, and every man stared as though looking harder would make the cave brighter.

"Here." The big Brazilian was breathless, streaked with dirt and scratches, and looked angry enough to crack stone.

"Eyes to the sides." Edwin's order was entirely unnecessary. There wasn't a man who wasn't already jumping out of his skin. The group bristled with guns like a porcupine.

There was a killer on the loose. My killer. My love. I laughed.

"Shut up, you." Vasco hit me on the back of the knee, and I went down. Abruptly a terror came over me, lying on the ground in front of Martio, and I scrambled to the side of the cave away from him. I yelled, made unintelligible by my fear.

"Shut up! Shut up!" Vasco screamed.

A series of events happened too quickly for me to take them in. Weasel dropped to the ground, sliding a knife across Vasco's heel. The diminutive spy struck again, unstoppably fast. The last two sailors fell, one with a slit throat yawning wide and spurting, the other clutching his chest—Weasel jumped and slashed. Sun leaped from a large crack above us and took Martio to the ground, his irons around Martio's neck.

Vasco writhed in the dirt, screaming, bleeding. But he'd dropped his long gun, and somehow I'd picked it up. Smoke curled up from the barrel and my hands tingled from the force of the discharge. At my feet lay Edwin, surprise on his dying face, a black wound welling blood in his chest.

I'd shot him. I'd killed a man.

Weasel leaped on Vasco and stabbed him in the chest, once, twice, three times. His yells gurgled.

Martio turned purple as Sun choked him. Sun met my eyes. I picked up Edwin's pistol with my other hand. It was loaded and ready— he hadn't had a chance to fire it.

Martio rose to his knees before me, struggled to his feet, Sun hanging from his neck, and he slammed Sun into the wall.

I screamed again, but couldn't hear myself. My ears rang from the gunshot. My bullet, angled to keep Sun safe, took Martio in the chest. He crumpled, hands still clawing at the chains around his neck, despite the bleeding bullet wound.

Sun didn't let him go. He knelt on the big man's back, choking him, twisting the chain long after Martio went limp.

Weasel gently took the gun from my hand. The small man was covered in blood. He nodded in Sun's direction. I went to him.

Sun's face was expressionless, staring down into Martio's bulging eyes. The chains wound around his fists so tight the skin around his knuckles had mottled blue and white.

"Sun, let him go." He didn't respond, so I put my hands over his. I was surprised mine weren't shaking. They still looked like my hands had always looked, despite what they'd done. "He's dead. Let him go."

He looked at me at last, his eyes wide and lost, his mouth slack.

"It's over, Sun." I pulled on his wrists, and he let go of the chains and came into my arms. We held each other a long time then, and I wasn't afraid. I didn't care that Weasel saw. What mattered was Sun in my arms, we were safe, and our enemies were dead, no matter how it had happened.

We were alive.

CHAPTER 24.
MUTINY

THE AIR was sweet and clean after we left the cave. I still held Sun's hand, and I all but ran for the cool comfort of the forest's shade. Weasel followed with a black leather billfold of papers he'd taken from Edwin's coat while I freed Sun from his chains with the keys from Martio's belt.

Weasel said his real name was Marisol, and he was a French spy. As we ran through the forest, he spoke in whispers—things my mind wouldn't absorb—something about needing proof of the British Empire inciting uprisings in New World colonies. I tried to listen, but I couldn't focus. All around me were the familiar sounds and sights of our forest, the feel of Sun's hand in mine as we clung to each other, and we moved around trees and bushes together so we wouldn't have to break our grasp.

I followed mindlessly until Sun pulled on me. We were crossing the path that led back to his cave and our tree house beyond. Marisol the Weasel ran down the path the other way, toward the beach but stopped when he realized we weren't following.

"What are you doing?"

Wordlessly I looked at Sun, who tugged my hand toward the cave, but wasn't making much headway because I'd stopped on the path, staring between the spy and Sun without seeing them. In my mind's eye, I saw Edwin and Martio on the ground, smoking holes in their chests.

"Benjamin. Come." Sun pulled.

"What are you two doing?" Marisol demanded. "We have to go and help Swift."

I dimly realized, with Edwin and Martio dead, we were free. Free to regroup, at least, and keep ourselves away from the rest of the pirates for as long as possible. Perhaps free to allow Sun to neutralize their threat forever, one by one. The bloodthirsty thought disturbed my rational mind, even as my emotional response considered recent events and told my rational mind to go *fukka* itself.

"We can help ourselves, thank you. Swift and I are free," Sun fired back in rapid Portuguese.

"What?" Marisol wrinkled his nose. "Weren't you listening? This isn't Swift. He's back on the ship."

"What?" Sun asked. I was as confused as he sounded.

"His name is not Swift," Marisol said, pointing at me. "He's the famous smuggler Benji Swift as much as I'm a man."

And that was when I saw Marisol for what she was. Blood-drenched, spindly limbed, weasel-faced—a spy, a killer, and… a woman.

I goggled at her. So did Sun.

"So thick. *S'il y avait une taxe sur ton cerveau, tu n'aurais plus un rond!*" Then she swore at us in French so creatively, even I was impressed, and I'd learned no small amount of choice phrases from the Marquis de Sade before Mother confiscated that particular book and burned it. I thought I knew every French malediction there was, rounding out my collection with phrases from my too-brief stay in the New Orleans gin palaces. But Marisol was… imaginative and ruthless. And now I knew the exact phrase for licking the Devil's *couilles*. "You want off this island, we go help the real Benji Swift and his mutiny on the *Fury*, which by now is well underway," she said.

"Why would we want to go back *there*?" Sun yelled at her. I stared at him—tears flowed down his cheeks. My brave, strong Sun was coming apart. He needed me. It took heroic effort to pull myself together. I squeezed his hand to let him know I was back from the dark place shock and pain and death had taken me.

"What's going on? Tell us everything," I demanded of Marisol, in what I hoped was a tone that brooked no argument. I do not know if I spoke in French, Portuguese, English, or a mix of all three.

She rolled her eyes. "We do not have time to stand here discussing. You need to pick a side. Stay here on your island that other people won for you, killing everyone who comes here, even the innocent, and see how long until someone kills you and takes everything away from you. Or come with me to the *Fury*, help the real Benji Swift take that ship, and go somewhere safe."

Did such a place exist for Sun and me? I looked into his storm-dark eyes and gripped his fingers in mine. He glared at Marisol, but he didn't pull me toward the cave.

I made a decision. "What we do right now does not mean that we must leave our home, Sun. We can come back."

"Unless you are shot, or stabbed, or drowned." Sun tensed, as though he might attack Marisol. "I won't lose you. I won't. Never again." And I guessed he was thinking of that night at the mass grave when he thought I'd taken a bullet.

"Why should we help this Swift person? What's he ever done for us?" I challenged her.

Now it was Marisol's turn to gape at us. "Only saved your lives. He told Edwin to spare you, both of you—convinced him he might still find his guns. Swift boarded the *Fury* back in New Orleans because he'd heard talk in the taverns that the famous Captain Benji Swift was hiring sailors for a smuggling run. He discovered someone had assumed his identity, and came aboard the *Fury* as the ship's cook to learn the whos and whys of the false *Sea Swift* setting sail. When he found out who Edwin James was and his purpose, he alerted me, so I came aboard as a sailor. We've done our best to keep you alive and whole, despite Edwin and Martio's depredations. Have you forgotten how Swift nursed your wounds? Did you not wonder why you look as brothers?"

I stared at her. The Butcher was the one who had helped us… a tall mulatto. Benji Swift, the man I was impersonating. I pictured him without his bushy, black beard, and realized the similarity. We were of a height, the same dark brown hair—I glanced down at my sun-dark arm—and the same shade of mixed.

I looked at Sun. I had never seen him so surprised. I sympathized completely.

Marisol swore again so vehemently that I silently apologized to God for her under my breath—while taking mental note of the declension of that particular verb when concerning multiple goats. "Did his help mean nothing to you? He needs us now. He's the key to this whole enterprise."

Sun and I exchanged a look.

"Why did I bother saving your lives? Cowards. *Vous n'êtes que des petits branleurs bons à rien.*" Marisol turned and ran down the path toward the beach, having either given up on us or grown so anxious about Swift she would no longer wait.

I took a step toward the beach, stopped, and looked at Sun. He glowered, but he nodded. We ran after her.

GUNSHOTS RANG from the distant *Fury*, a chaos of men on deck, striving with cutlass and pistol. A sailor in the crow's nest picked off fighters using a long gun. We'd have to be careful he didn't see us coming. Marisol struggled, slowly pushing a long boat back into the water when Sun and I joined her, and in one fluid shove, we three sent it out into the lagoon. Sun and Marisol leaped aboard, and I scrambled up over the side gracelessly. Sun and I quickly gained the benches and pulled powerfully on the oars so we shot backward through the water. She nodded at us, wordlessly accepting our company and help, "worthless lazy good-for-nothings" that we were. Marisol primed and readied her flintlock, then put a knife on the bench next to Sun, who thanked her.

"What are you best at?" she asked me.

The real answer was reading, praying, playing the fiddle and flute, and getting other people in trouble, but since she probably meant the deadly arts instead, I said, "I'm a fair shot." That was true, at least. I made somewhat of a reputation for myself as a marksman with the other lads in the village and engaged in a few hunts. I knew my way around any flintlock. Marisol reached forward and pulled Edwin's pistol from the back of my britches, where I'd shoved the discharged weapon without thinking about it.

She primed and readied the flintlock with quick, skilled movements, despite the motion of our boat gliding through the water. It seemed Marisol was yet another person who excelled at everything. I decided spending my time with spies and knife fighters was probably not the best for my manly self-esteem. Then decided I didn't care about the status of my manhood if Sun and I got out of this in one piece. I wondered for a moment why we hadn't run back to our cave and tree house when we had the chance, then reefed the sail on those thoughts. We'd made our choice. *Alea iacta est*—the die was cast. Now hopefully we lived through the consequences.

"Keep down," I said, telling them both about the swab with a long gun I'd seen atop the mast. But Marisol said, "He's one of ours."

"How can you tell?"

"I know the men loyal to Swift."

"That doesn't really help us," I said, breathless from the strain of rowing and the burn of the lash mark across my chest with every stroke. "How will we know?"

She considered that a moment, then pulled open her shirt, showing a brace of short throwing knives strapped across her chest—her breasts were bound flat, but she definitely was physically female.

"I'll prick 'zem. If they're still standing, you kill 'zem."

"So be it," I said. She talked like no woman I'd ever known.

We reached the *Fury*. Marisol unsheathed one of her throwing knives, clamped it between her teeth, and climbed a rope ladder up the side of the ship.

Bodies floated in the gentle sea around the *Fury*, gunfire overhead. Sun stood to follow Marisol, but I grabbed his bicep, pulling him to me, and kissed him on the lips. He blinked.

"For luck," I said, a bit lamely. It was really because I couldn't face sending him into danger without one more kiss. He smiled, then put the knife Marisol had given him between his teeth and was on her heels. I shoved the flintlock she'd readied for me back in my britches, hoping I didn't accidentally shoot myself in a buttock, and followed them both aboard.

They were twins—the blond golden-skinned savage and the dark-haired, pasty spy—light and darkness, whirlwinds of death. Men fell screaming, clutching hamstrings or fountaining throats. Marisol paused, threw three knives into various combatants, who were nicked, hampered, or killed by her strikes.

I took a steadying breath and pulled out the flintlock, remembering the sneers and jokes of these men when I was forced across the deck to see Edwin. *No. Not for revenge.* I watched Sun strike down one of the men Marisol had marked, while another circled behind him, drawing back to slice him with a falchion. *For Sun*, I told myself. For him I could, and would, kill again.

I pulled the trigger, and my bullet dropped Sun's would-be attacker like a stone, with Sun off and slashing at another man Marisol had marked before the last one slumped to the deck. A shadow loomed over me, a man with a cutlass bearing down. I dropped the spent gun, jumping back, and picked up another pistol from the boards at my feet. It was discharged. The man lunged at me with his cutlass, and I dodged, but tripped over a body. My hand closed on the stock of a flintlock—I got the gun up and fired, taking the man in the shoulder, and he fell back. The sharpshooter in the crow's nest finished him with a bullet to the heart, and I was glad that, whoever he was, the swab was on our side. I thanked God the gun I'd pulled off the dead man had still been primed.

Then I found myself without a gun, facing a man armed with a rapier. He jabbed forward, and I fell back, slipping on blood. Sun was there, and with three savage, quick jabs to the lung, the man was down.

I was in a lull—no one attacking me, no one within reach to attack— while gunfire thundered and men screamed and died. Butcher was engaged in a swordfight on the quarterdeck, an impressive display of skill and footwork. I saw now that he did look like me—a deadly, thickly bearded me, who skillfully deflected the blows of his opponent. His attacker lunged, and he dodged the thrust and kicked the man in the knee so he fell forward and his rapier and sword hand lodged in the ship's wheel, which Butcher spun, trapping the man between the spokes. Against all odds, the man managed to keep ahold of his blade.

"Yield," my double thundered in a commanding tone.

The man dropped the sword. Marisol was there on lithe feet, dancing with her knives around the real Captain Benji, with Sun at her back, having dispatched the men remaining on the quarterdeck.

Faced with such incomparable bladework, their opponents threw down their weapons and surrendered.

"Tie them up," Butcher commanded. Marisol and Sun followed the order, tying fast the prisoners, while I covered the men with a pair of pistols they didn't know had already been discharged. The gunman climbed down from the crow's nest, and a few more came up from the hold. Six sailors, myself, Sun, and Marisol had survived the battle on Swift's side, taking five living prisoners from Edwin's.

The bound men glared at their captors. Marisol, whom they knew as Weasel, addressed them.

"Your captain is dead. Edwin James and Martio de Fortaliza are no more. You have two choices. Either swear your service to Captain Swift, or be marooned on Dread Island." She indicated the volcano with a tilt of her chin.

The survivors stared at the aspect of a skull formed by the partially collapsed cone, then each other, superstition warring with the desire to be free.

Sun turned on Marisol. "This is my island. Not theirs." The knife she had given him dripped blood. He was splattered from head to toe in red freckles from the men he'd killed.

The sailors looked at him, then swore themselves, every one, to join Captain Benji Swift's crew. No doubt they remembered the gruesome number of bodies Sun had amassed in the caves.

"Well chosen. You'll be treated fairly and have no reason to complain of your earnings," the new captain said, then turned to me. "I'll be taking my name back now, if it's all the same to you."

I nodded. "Of course."

He scratched his beard. "What do we call you, then?"

"Lector. My, uh, my family name is Lector. Benjamin Lector."

He laughed. "What are the odds? I suppose you were named for—"

"Benjamin Franklin, yes."

He smiled and shook his head. "As was I. Born the day he died. You?"

I shook my head. "Mother appreciated his treatise on abolition. Though we are close enough in age that you could be my elder brother, sir."

"Captain will do." He turned from me to address his new crew. "Listen up, you dogs! Anyone here troubles Mr. Lector or his friend Mr....?" He looked at Sun and then me, questioningly.

"Thorvaldson." I awkwardly pronounced the last name Edwin had mentioned. "Sólmundur Thorvaldson."

"There's a mouthful."

"Call me Sun." Sun spoke for himself as he cleaned the blood off his knife and glared around at the men, as if daring them to object to the name I had given him.

"Anyone causing them trouble will face quick justice—a hand raised against them is a hand raised against me."

It was a reasonably impressive speech. No doubt it made more of an impression because Sun and Marisol, dripping with blood, glowered like deadly bookends on either side of the captain.

The men muttered among themselves as Marisol cut the newly sworn sailors' rope bonds away.

"Now, then," the captain continued, "Benji Swift took this shipment of guns out of New Orleans. It's Benji Swift who is going to turn them over to the French Navy."

"They'll hang the lot of us!" one man burst out—the redhead who'd almost shot Sun back in the cave. I was slightly disappointed he'd survived. Then I prayed God forgive me the evil thought.

"They won't. We'll be flying *le drapeau francais*. Look around, gents. You're all French corsairs with a letter of marque from King Louis XVIII and Prime Minister Jean-Baptiste de Villèle."

"Prove it—" the redhead started, and Marisol advanced on him with her knife out. "Captain," the man added hastily.

"Go on, then," Captain Benji told Marisol.

"I am Marisol Soult, niece of Duke Jean-de-Dieu Soult of Dalmatia, Marshal of France. You will know him formerly as King Nicholas, Plunderer of Portugal and Master of Oporto." She opened her coat, revealing her brace of daggers and bound breasts, and produced the leather wallet she'd pulled from Edwin's body.

One of the men crossed himself. The rest, including the sailors I knew were Captain Benji's loyal men, looked too stunned to move as their fellow sailor was revealed to be a relative of a French general famous for sacking Oporto and declaring himself rightful heir to the Portuguese throne, then was deposed. Well, and also revealed as a woman, which was a double sort of shock, considering the lack of care most had with cussing and nudity aboard ship.

"This," she said, allowing the wallet to fall open, displaying official papers with loopy signatures, wax, and a ribbon, "says Captain Benji Swift, and everyone sailing with him, is in service to the French Crown and may plunder on her behalf."

The men exchanged glances.

"This here"—she tapped a familiar-looking signature with the tip of her bloody knife—"is King Louis's own mark."

"What do you say to that, corsairs?" Captain Benji asked.

"Long live King Louis?" offered one English sailor.

Captain Benji laughed, and his loyal men broke into cheers, which the former prisoners joined somewhat less lustily. "Now clap to, me hardies! We've enemies of the French Empire to plunder! Weigh anchor and ready the mainsail." The men scrambled to obey. The caravel had a lateen sail for tacking against the wind and close to shore, which the captain ordered run up and readied.

I sidled over to Marisol as she folded the wallet.

"You took an awful chance there," I said softly, holding out my shaking hand for the papers featuring my signature selling Sun and me to Edwin.

"You ever meet a sailor who could read? *Vous avez le cerveau comme une meule de fromage*," she challenged quietly, tucking the wallet into her coat.

"I'd like those, if you don't mind," I said through clenched teeth, reaching for her coat and thinking her comparison of my brain to a wheel of cheese unfair. She slapped my hand.

"I think I'll hold on to these a bit longer—at least until we can collect the real letters of marque from my colleagues at Tortuga." She stalked away to help ready the ship, the men wary of her but jumping fast enough as she relayed the captain's orders.

I would have prayed for God to forgive her lies to the men, except I knew she had much larger sins that needed to be addressed first. I wondered if she really was the niece of the Marshall of France, and realized I'd finally gained the wisdom to doubt others since leaving New Orleans with Edwin and Black Miguel. Second, I wondered why she was rendezvousing with her French colleagues at a famous pirate port recently taken over by revolutionaries of the Republic of Haiti, who had no love for Frenchmen after Napoleon overturned abolition and re-enslaved them all. Hispaniola had been the largest, most prosperous French colony, and subsequently the sight of the largest, most violent slave revolt known to modern man. Losing Hispaniola had cost Napoleon so much he sold Louisiana to the United States and effectively ended France's status as an empire in the New World.

"Benjamin," Sun said softly, next to me. It was a low, anxious sound. I gave him my full attention. He looked a mess—spotted with blood like a Carolina speckled trout. I reached up to wipe clean his cheek, but let my hand drop. There were too many other men around us, and, despite Captain Benji's orders protecting us, I didn't want to gamble with our safety. I was taking no risks where Sun was concerned.

His blue-gray eyes were dark with anxiety.

"What is it?"

He turned from me to look back at our island. I took his meaning. "You want to go back ashore."

He nodded.

I looked around the *Fury*, so like the *Sea Swift* I'd lost, and took in the welcome sights and sounds of the sailors in the rigging. I realized with a sudden pang that, while I loved Sun and I loved our island home, I had missed the society of other men and being underway to parts unknown, sharing tales, adventures, and songs. My stomach gave a grumble. And, cheese for brains or not, I missed a nice flakey cheddar.

"Sun, I—"

"Ready, Sun?" Captain Benji strode toward us with a purpose.

Sun sidestepped away from the captain, toward the gunnel.

Captain Benji held up both hands to show he held no weapon. "Easy, Sun. I'm not going to hurt you or Benjamin. You're free to choose. Stay or go, whichever you like."

Sun stopped moving but remained tense, as though waiting to see if Benji's promise could possibly be true.

"Tell me where the guns are. We'll tack over to them, my lads will load them, and you won't have the French or Portuguese or British mucking up your island looking for them. All neat and tidy and no one's the wiser to your paradise."

I looked at Sun, capturing his blue eyes with mine, and nodded encouragingly, hoping he would agree and therefore buy me more time to talk over with him the future that was newly forming in my mind— especially if the French paid me for the weapons that were technically still mine.

"I will show you and Benjamin only," he said finally, glowering.

"That's all a man can ask," Captain Benji said.

In short order, the deck was cleared of bodies and weapons, a brief Christian ceremony was held to honor the fallen laid to rest at sea, and the surviving sailors swabbed it of blood. The anchor was aweigh, and the *Fury* was readied to set sail.

CHAPTER 25.
THE MIRROR

BEFORE TACKING for the northern end of the island under Sun's direction, Captain Benji offered us the use of Edwin's cabin to wash the grime of battle away.

As soon as I shut the door, Sun pulled me close and held me tight.

"I saw the one with the cutlass," he murmured from under my chin. "But I couldn't come to you. There were too many."

"Hey-ho, now." I wanted to say I'd taken care of myself quite well, thank you, but bragging about killing a man didn't feel right. While I was offended Sun felt the need to protect me, it was damn hard to hold on to my indignation while feeling the press of his body against mine, even though we were both sprinkled with blood and gunpowder.

"*Allt* good, Sun. I'm all right." I stroked his muscled shoulders, as careful of the whip marks still livid across his skin as he was of the one I had on my chest. We were whole, yes, but we were worse for the wear. I traced my fingers up his neck and tilted his head back so I could capture his mouth with mine. The kiss started soft and gentle, then turned into something hard and demanding. Sun flinched, and I pulled back with a wince. Our faces were still bruised—I could scarce breathe through my swollen nose, and Sun still had a lump on his jaw and a bloom of purple across one cheek. Sun lifted on his tiptoes and kissed me again, carefully, so carefully, and we explored each other, discovering how we could avoid hurting ourselves.

Despite everything we'd gone through, desire for him throbbed up my legs, tingled down my arms, and I was hard and ready. One of the books I'd read about the War of 1812 said what a man wanted after a battle was a stiff drink and an intoxicating woman. What I wanted was a stiff man and high-proof rum. It was all in the wording, which I promptly stopped thinking about as Sun pushed me against the door, stroked his hands down my sides, tugged open my britches, and wrapped his warm, sucking mouth around me.

I moaned and had to bite my knuckle to keep quiet. He kept working me over, so I gave up and let loose some of Big Swede's favorite words. I swore so loudly and creatively in each language I knew that Sun stopped, laughing. Then I cussed myself for distracting him and him for stopping, so soon we were both laughing and cussing, switching between languages, pausing to apologize to God, and in general babbling in what would have been incoherence to anyone listening.

When the hysteria passed, we held each other tenderly, careful of our wounds, gifting gentle touches with hands and mouths. Afterward, I washed clean every inch of him, and him me. I found a shaving knife and worked up a thick cream and rid myself of six weeks of brown-and-black beard. I even forced a comb through my wavy hair, but we left Sun's braids alone for the sake of time.

It was a good thing too, because Sun decided to explore my now extra-sensitive face with his lips. He wanted to compare what kissing me without a beard was like. I didn't object.

We left the water in Edwin's washbasin pink and gray, but I felt nearly civilized. Captain Benji had bid us plunder Edwin's belongings as we would. Though I washed them in the ewer, I was dismayed I had to keep my own ragged britches, because I was a bigger man than Edwin, but I did put on one of the dead man's white ruffle shirts that only gaped across my chest a little. I tried very hard not to think about the fact I was wearing a dead man's shirt—a man I'd killed—and, with Sun beside me, doing his best to shave off his own almost nonexistent blond mustache, I nearly managed.

I examined my countenance in the mirror. I had two black eyes and my nose was swollen from the beating I'd taken, but the captain had set it straight and true. I was still a handsome man, for all my other shortcomings, and even I had to admit God had been kind in that regard. I wondered if Captain Benji really looked like me under his bushy black tangles.

Sun selected a pair of drawstring britches that weren't too baggy, a white shirt, and a blue coat I insisted he wear because it made his eyes positively striking. He wanted to carry his knife by hand, but I found him a belt and sheath to keep it in. It was quite strange to see him clothed. It seemed wrong somehow, as if he were meant to show off his wiry, muscled body to the world. Or perhaps it was because, now that he was dressed, I wanted to take his clothes off again myself.

However, we'd already dallied overlong. Much refreshed, we went above decks.

THE *FURY* had sailed from the lagoon and heaved to hard by the sheer faces of the mountain on the western side of the island—the places I remembered having to swim during my exploration, because there were no beaches.

"Ah, good." Captain Benji greeted and threw us each an apple—a lunch of cheese, pork, and hardtack had been laid by for us, and it was clear everyone else had eaten while we were refreshing ourselves. A few men tied fast the lateen sail. We were at anchor, awaiting Sun's pleasure and further direction. "If you'll pardon me, I've a mind to dress in a fashion more befitting a captain." And Captain Benji disappeared below decks.

Sun and I sat next to each other on the gunnel. I closed my eyes in pleasure as we ate, enjoying each morsel of cheese, still without the faintest idea of how to convince Sun to set sail on the *Fury* instead of returning to our tree house. The apples tasted very strange indeed after all this time eating *aldin* on the island. I looked around for Marisol but didn't see her. The sailors going about their duties looked away as soon as I looked at them, avoiding my gaze. Any that needed to pass by us gave us, or perhaps only Sun, a wide berth. In particular, Edwin's redhead watched with mistrust from his perch manning the rudder. I supposed it would take some time to forget Sun's prowess in battle. Also, the men he'd killed on the island. My men.

I couldn't help but remember them—Carlos and Joaquim, Black Miguel and Big Swede Erik—as I looked around the sister vessel. I remembered nameless bodies in the hole, rotting with no Christian burial. I put down the apple I'd been eating. I no longer had an appetite.

"What is it?" Sun asked, chucking his apple core over the side of the ship.

"Nothing." I didn't meet his gaze. What right had I to judge him, when I myself had taken the lives of three men?

"We can trade for cheese, Benjamin," Sun said, misinterpreting my silence.

I smiled weakly for him. "It's not that. It's... I'd like to... I feel I must bury Edwin." I met his gaze then—clear, guiltless, wondering. Of course killing was everyday to a man like him, a dangerous knife fighter. "And the others. I want to bury all of them properly," I added in a rush.

His eyes hardened, and I guessed he was probably thinking Martio didn't deserve a Christian burial, but he nodded nevertheless and said, "We will."

I wanted to take his hand in gratitude, but I dared not with the men watching. I thought of the state of some of those bodies, and nearly lost the meal we'd eaten. It wasn't going to be pleasant, but it had to be done. I hoped Captain Benji and Marisol were willing to wait for us to bury them before making their Tortuga rendezvous.

"A good repast?"

I turned at the sound of Captain Benji's voice. It was as though I had brought the mirror above decks with me, without the black eyes and swollen nose. He was older than me, yes, but without the beard, we were more alike than brothers. Closer to twins.

"By all the gods above and below, it feels good to be rid of that tangled mass." Captain Benji stroked his shorn jaw. "Close your mouth, lad, before a sea bird roosts in it."

I shut my mouth. He wore a pair of tailored britches, a long captain's coat with shiny brass buttons, and a cocked hat with a bushy feather, which he swept off and flourished with a courtly bow. He looked quite fine in such clothing, and it was very strange to be admiring the figure he cut, when it was so similar to mine. Did my narcissism know no end? I glanced at Sun, who was looking between me and Captain Benji as if trying to find the source of a trick. Benji's hair was presently a bit shorter, but once my wounds healed, my own parents would have had trouble telling us one from the other.

"*Inquiétant.*" Marisol stood by the captain, looking from his face to mine, but I hadn't noticed her over the distraction of seeing Benji in piratical dress. She, by contrast, wore white britches and a double-breasted dark blue coat, short in the front with many buttons, and long tails in the back, her scalp-short hair concealed under a black stocking cap. If she'd worn a bicorn instead, she would have looked like Napoleon's ghost, though there was no denying the aspect of a weasel in her features. However, despite her rough ways, I knew she'd saved Sun and me when Edwin was leading us away to die, and that softened my attitude toward her considerably.

"Ma'am," I said, rising with a bow as was our custom in North Carolina. Mother and Father had both seen to my manners.

"Stop that," she hissed. "There's no need to remind the men there's a woman aboard—they'll wonder why we're still afloat."

Sailors were the same, *Sea Swift* or *Fury*, to hold such superstitions.

"Yes, curtail that tongue, Mr. Lector," Captain Benji said to me. "She might mistake you for me and decide I'm polite and mannerly, and we can't have that."

"No danger of such, Captain." Marisol's mouth twitched.

"Well." He cleared his throat. "See you don't wander into the wrong cabin."

Marisol gave me an appraising look, toes to forelock. It was the same sort of glance I'd been getting from the fairer sex since I'd shot up in height and my shoulders had broadened. Like every other time before, I felt no call to fall all over myself impressing her, no stir in my loins, nothing other than a faint and unsettled anxiety, likely because I knew what she could do with a knife.

"No. He's not for me," she said, and I let a breath go I didn't know I was holding. "I don't like men like him."

My double put a hand to his chest. "Then there's no hope for the likes of me?"

"I wouldn't say that," Marisol said coyly.

"He's got everything I have—and greater youth besides. What else do you require of a man?" Captain Benji asked.

"That he be willing." And she stalked off to yell the long boat down into the water.

The captain took his hat off and held it to his chest. "She's a fiery one, eh, lads? Be still my lonely heart." And he followed after her.

I squeezed Sun's hand. "Now don't *you* go wandering into the wrong cabin," I said as he watched Captain Benji saunter away. He smiled back at me, then hopped down from the gunnel. He didn't answer, only gave me a playful glance over his shoulder, and ran after the captain to the long boat.

Sun was teasing me, even after all the horrors we'd been through. I laughed so loud, men stared, but I could give them no explanation for my sudden mirth, so I joined the boarding party in haste.

CHAPTER 26.
OLD FRIENDS

THE SHEER sides of the mountain looked like the black skirts of a washer woman dipping her hem into the sea. Fissures parted the rock here and there, wet tongues of the sea invading the mountain's interior. Sun stood in the prow, directing the rowers into a large opening, then raised his hand.

"Let go the anchor," Captain Benji ordered. "We'll go on alone—myself, Sun, and my little brother here."

Marisol scowled. So did some of the rowers—Marisol frowned probably because she was being left behind; the men likely weren't happy we were abandoning them with Marisol and her deadly blade. They were half Edwin's former men, half Captain Benji's. I pictured Sun's chess-like *tafl* game and realized Captain Benji wasn't taking any chances by keeping only his loyal men by his side and thus putting the *Fury* at risk of another mutiny. There were enough of his loyal men back aboard to prevent another change in captaincy while we were gone.

"We swim," Sun said and stripped off his blue coat and shirt.

Captain Benji and I followed his example, and I felt curiously like I was going back in time as I reverted to nothing but my worse-for-wear britches. Sun performed a graceful shallow dive into the dark waters of the cave. I remembered the strength of the undertow here, but he came up again and beckoned us into the water. I looked at Benji, who now, in nothing but britches himself, was so like me in build and color and appearance even I found it disorienting. The men, and even unflappable Marisol, stared at us in silence. Benji nodded at me, then jumped into the water, and I followed behind. I yelped in pain and got a mouthful of sea water.

The salt fiercely stung in the lash wound across my chest. I gritted my teeth and mastered myself, thinking of the half-dozen-odd whip marks Sun had on his back and how he hadn't even flinched. Soon we bobbed on either side of Sun, who looked at each of us, then slyly at me and grinned, raising his eyebrows. I pressed my lips in a thin line to hide my laughter and shook my head, gathering the gist of the sinful thought on his mind. I'd heard enough jokes about twin lovers from the salties I'd come here with, but I said nothing that might offend Captain Benji. He was, after all, our way out of here. Provided I could convince Sun he wanted to leave.

"Lead on," I said before Benji could puzzle out Sun's teasing, and Sun stroked powerfully through the water, leading us into the cave's depths. As darkness closed around us, I felt my old irrational fear of Dread Island resurface, especially as Sun's form disappeared into the gloom, but I soldiered on, swimming side by side with Benji, a fine swimmer, and I was pleased to note I kept abreast of him. Soon, however, there was naught but blackness and the sounds of water against stone.

"Stop," Sun's voice echoed ahead. I saw a glimmering ember, and then a torch flickered slowly to life in Sun's hand. He stood on a small rock overhang next to a raft made of thick boards and barrels. The interior of the cave looked very like the tunnels where he'd hidden the bodies, except coated with sea salt and lichen. In fact, I could smell the corpse stench faintly even here, though we must have been on the other side of the mountain. The wavering torchlight revealed Sun's wet body, muscles of his arms and chest glimmering, and again I was struck by how like some pagan god he was. If we had been here alone, there might have been a long interlude before any searching for boxes was attempted, but as we weren't alone, I decided to be polite to lonely Benji, promising myself a long interlude indeed when we were back aboard ship.

"*Ratljóst.* Enough to see by." Sun wedged the torch in the raft and pushed it out onto the water, then climbed aboard with a pole under his arm. He helped each of us aboard as well. The raft shifted under the weight of three men but did not capsize and, in fact, seemed quite sound. I mentally added shipwright to Sun's many talents. He used the pole to move us forward and shadows banished before the torchlight as we pushed through the darkness. Ahead, the cave roof sloped down, low over the water.

"Keep your heads down, Benjamins," Sun said, lowering to one knee and pushing us under the rock formation. Benji and I ducked. The tunnel widened considerably beyond that point, Sun's torchlight failing to illuminate the space, which, from the soft echoes of waves around us, was quite large. He poled across a shallow lagoon, where pale fish swam in the clear water below us, and then he said *fukka* very softly.

"What is it?" I asked in a whisper.

"The guns are gone."

WE BEACHED the raft at the other end of the lagoon, and it was clear now that many crates had once rested in the white sand rimming the cavern. I did some mental calculations—fifteen or so of the twenty crates the *Swift* had carried must have once sat side by side here on the lagoon's shore.

"Where in the—" Benji started.

Sun drew his knife. "There." He pointed out drag marks from the shore up and sand tracks dusting the gradual rock slope. The flickering torchlight revealed that the uneven cavern extended into the mountain. Benji drew his knife also. I wasn't wearing one, and I sent a quick prayer above apologizing for the choice words I said because I hadn't thought to arm myself. If one of Martio's or Edwin's scouting parties had explored the caves, found and moved the guns, why hadn't they returned to tell their masters? And why drag them farther into the caves rather than using Sun's raft? I was thoroughly perplexed.

"Take the torch," Benji said, following Sun as he prowled gracefully up the rock slope, tracking the sand trail. I wrenched free the torch from the raft and stalked behind them, annoyed by my lack of a weapon. They quickly drew ahead, despite the fact they couldn't see where they were going without me, because I was the slower climber, trying not to slip and scorch myself or drop our only source of light. Needless to say, it was with ill grace and humor I reached the tunnel above.

I was relieved to gain the smaller opening leading out of the cavern, because the torch lit the walls, ceiling, and floor of the circular tunnel and made it feel less like anyone could be waiting in the dark to attack us. Benji turned and motioned me to stop, waving his knife hand down as if he wanted me to put the torch on the floor, a finger of his other hand pressed to his lips. I did as he bid and lowered the torch slowly to the ground. Sun crouched beyond him, glowering down a turn in the passage.

I crept softly forward, and Benji and I joined Sun. A light glowed down the tunnel, which branched in twain. Down the right passage, flickering light revealed another cavern. In a breath's time, I glanced in to see some thirty-odd chests piled within, and no small number of barrels, casks, kegs, and canisters. A lantern burned atop one large barrel, blankets and sailcloth framing a crude sleeping area beside it. Piled along the wall were more chests and what looked like forty small two-foot keg barrels of powder. It wasn't the powder magazine of one ship. It looked like the full complement of several, plus metal canisters for restocking during cannonade. I'd never seen that much ordnance in one place in my short life.

I glanced at Benji, expecting him to admonish me for my mouth hanging open, but saw he was staring at the explosives, similarly agape. I glanced at Sun—he glared at the pile of chests, eyes scanning the cavern for whoever put them there.

Then appeared the architect of our troubles—a handsome, black-haired, clean-shaven man emerged from a side tunnel, carrying a small gunpowder keg leaving a trail of black grains.

He was thinner, and his clothes more ragged, but there was no doubt in my mind I was looking at a ghost.

Relief raced through my body, toes to scalp. I hadn't doomed the crew of the *Swift* to a man, after all. "Miguel!" I shouted.

He turned, and in one fluid motion, shifted the gunpowder keg and pulled a flintlock from the holster strapped to his thigh and pointed it at Sun and me and Benji, the point wavering between us as though he could not decide his target. I remembered suddenly that Black Miguel had orders to kill me. But, then, why had he tied me to that barrel in the storm?

"*Meu Deus*," he exclaimed in Portuguese, then continued in English. "You are still alive." He squinted at me as if not believing his eyes.

"Thanks to you," I said uncertainly. Whatever his ultimate goal had been aboard the *Swift*, he had saved my life when nearly all else was lost.

He looked hard at my bruised face, then Captain Benji's.

"Yes, thank you for saving me," Benji said. I turned and stared at him.

"One of you is the real Captain Benjamin Swift, I presume?" The gun remained pointed at us. I saw the muscles in Sun's back bunch together as he readied himself to leap and take Miguel down.

"Yes," I said, to buy time and keep Miguel talking.

Miguel raised an eyebrow. "What was the name of the famous capital you burned? Speak rightly, or I shoot the spare." The gun settled on Sun.

Fear and anger boiled in my gut. "I'm a smuggler, not a pirate," I answered him sharply, hoping I was right and he was bluffing. "I don't burn towns." I needed him to put down either the powder or the gun so I could watch for his gambling tells.

"What are you doing with our guns, Miguel?" Benji asked. The flintlock tracked back to him.

"They are not our guns. They are now my guns. And I won't allow them to fall into Pedro's hands. I'll sink them before I allow that rat Martio to take them to him."

"Oi! I paid for those guns fair and square—" I began, but Benji talked over me.

"You think I'm Pedro's man?" Benji said. "I work for myself, or none."

Miguel gritted his teeth. "You work for me. Or one of you worked for me. Or once did." The gun tracked between us, then pointed at Sun. He nodded at Sun respectfully. "Though, I should shoot this one now," he said to us, then spoke to Sun. "I saw what you did with the survivors in the darkness. I saw you harvest their bodies. Then the guns. When you got distracted"—he waved the gun back toward me and Benji—"I took my chance and moved them all. And I found your hoard here."

Sun wore a murderous expression I felt no amount of talking was going to forestall for much longer.

"They are both quite handsome, though. I cannot fault you there."

Sun's knuckles whitened around the hilt of his knife, but Miguel's gun was pointed directly at his chest now. Not even Sun was fast enough to dodge a bullet, and we all knew it.

"Stop," I said. Desperation and bile rose in the back of my throat. I had to do something, anything, before Sun got hurt. And Miguel had saved my life, for whatever reason. I owed him that. "We've—I killed Martio. No one here is working for him. Edwin is dead too. I shot him." The words burned. I had done those things, committed those vile sins.

Miguel raised an eyebrow again. He looked at me from the corner of his eye, and I could tell his gambling instincts told him holding the gun on Sun was the smart choice, because it did not waver. "Then you must be the real Benji Swift, because the preacher's son wouldn't have had the courage, though he did often *ouviu o galo cantar e não saber onde*, which is to say, hear the rooster crow without knowing where."

I'd heard this before. It was a favorite phrase of the Portuguese, which meant in essence, success from sheer luck, not skill. It was an apt description of the boy I had been.

"We're not here to take the guns to this Pedro person," I said.

"Pedro...." Benji's voice was soft. "What's this Miguel's full name?"

"Black Miguel—uh, Miguel Maria," I said, while Miguel and Sun exchanged glares, each clearly measuring the other's deadliness and reflexes.

"*Lagniappe*," Benji said and then swore in Louisiana Creole. I'd heard the first term before; it meant getting more than what was paid for. "Dom Miguel Maria do Patrocínio de Bragança e Bourbon...." Benji's powerful voice rang throughout the cave. "We are not working for your brother, Dom Pedro, and we're not working for Martio or Edwin's mercenaries. I am the smuggler Captain Benji Swift, to whom so much is owed by the Portuguese Crown, and you already know Lector here. Sólmundur Thorvaldson is now a free man and under my protection. No one need shoot anyone."

"Dom Pedro?" I asked. *Dom* was the honorific added before the names of the princes of Portugal. Dom Pedro was currently the regent of Brazil, while his father, King João, ruled the homeland.

Black Miguel was a prince—Dom Pedro's younger brother, whom many said was also *desgraçado*, a degenerate and bastard. My former first mate was royalty. I was glad I wasn't still holding the torch, because I would have dropped it.

Miguel's gun barrel hovered over Benji but then lowered.

"Very well, smuggler. We owe you a great debt, and we are not without honor. Whom you choose to protect is your business, but be warned, that man is a killer. If he kills again, I will act in the name of my father, the king, on whom the burden of justice weighs."

"You have not yet begun to understand what you owe me, Dom Miguel." Benji laughed. "There is a certain lady awaiting you outside the caves."

Miguel's eyes narrowed without comprehension, but he holstered the flintlock and slowly put down the keg, keeping his eyes on Sun. Then he held up both hands to show he was not armed. "It is a relief not to have to shoot you. I rather like both of you."

"*Obrigado.*" I let out a breath I hadn't known I'd been holding and climbed down to clasp hands with him, Sun a lethal shadow behind me. Benji joined us. I was quite surprised when Miguel pulled me into a one-armed hug, slapped my back, and kissed my cheek in the Portuguese fashion of greeting an old, staunch companion. "Be careful, preacher's son," he said softly in my ear. "If I had but known your tastes then, those nights in the captain's cabin aboard the *Swift* would have run a different course."

The heat burning my cheeks of a sudden seemed dangerous close to this much powder. Miguel released me, and he and Sun exchanged suspicious glares, until I held my hand out to Sun. He looked down at it like it had emerged quite surprisingly from a tree stump, but then he took it, and I pulled him gently to my side.

"I love Sólmundur Thorvaldson," I said, liking the way the words sounded out loud. "And the sailors told me stories of your legendary whoring, Miguel. Dom Miguel, my apologies. I thought you... well, uh... wouldn't have... er...." If my face were any hotter, it would have ignited.

He laughed. "The accomplished sailor voyages more than one sea, Lector."

"Any port in a storm, eh?" Benji said. "You're not the first sailor to enjoy the charms of both men and women. Not the first prince either." After the nonstop adventure of the day, it felt surpassingly odd to be standing in an underground cave, discussing the sexual proclivities of my friend, whom I had believed dead and now found alive, and who was also in line to inherit the throne of Portugal.

"I see you've had a shave but are perhaps in need of a good meal?" I asked, with no idea whatsoever what one said during such an occasion.

"*Sim*, but firstly, if I understand correctly, you've killed the Englishman and the rebel leader. What, then, is the fate you have planned for these guns, Swift? Or shall we eliminate them from the equation?" He addressed Benji and nodded at the powder.

"Ah, and that is why we must introduce you to madam without. Milady awaits."

Miguel pinched his chin.

"It's all right, Miguel," I reassured him. "She killed most of Martio's men."

Miguel's eyebrows shot up. "Well, then, this is someone to meet indeed. Who, ah—" He passed his hand over his face.

I realized he referred to my battered visage. "Martio. And this as well." I indicated the livid cut through my damp chest hair. "I'm alive, though, and give thanks for that. It's more than Martio and Edwin have." I did not mention the other harm Martio did to me, and would not. Not ever.

CHAPTER 27.
ALLIANCES

MIGUEL RETRIEVED a leather wallet of papers from his camp and tucked it into his coat, very carefully snuffed his lantern, and followed us back to the raft, which Sun poled out to where Marisol waited with the sailors. I worried about Sun the entire journey through the dark and kept my hand on his leg—I'm not sure why, only that I wanted him to know I was thinking of him and that he was more important to me than anything else, but I wasn't able to say the words with men like Benji and Miguel nearby. Yes, I could publicly tell Sun I loved him, but confessions of my undying convictions seemed awkward. So I touched him instead, likely trying to reassure myself more than him after this odd day. I strangely felt as if, once we returned to the sunlight, he would melt away, and none of this would have ever happened. I could not have borne that. So I held on to his ankle, and I prayed to Jesu, Joy of Man's Desiring, that all would be well.

Sun poled all four of us back out to the raft, where Marisol awaited with the men.

"*Meu Deus*," Miguel said as the dark shapes in the boat ahead of us became recognizable as human beings. "It's not…. It cannot be…."

Marisol—whom I had seen very calmly disembowel a sailor, clean her knife on her britches, then disembowel a second one—gaped at Miguel, her eyes like saucers.

"The Princess of Oporto!" Miguel got to his feet, his balance so superb he barely rocked the raft, and executed a mocking bow. "Will I find your uncle aboard ship? Has anyone bothered to tell him Napoleon is dead? Or you, for that matter?" He examined her matter-of-factly in the exact same way she'd examined me earlier. I didn't like him doing it to her any more than I liked her doing it to me. However, I kept my mouth shut, because she was more than capable of defending herself.

She did so explosively, in French, using epithets as creative in the extreme as they were unbecoming of a lady, and unsheathed her knife. Miguel twitched, his hand going to his gun.

"Stop it!" I said. Before I knew what I was doing, I leaped to my feet, rocking the raft in an ungainly manner, so Miguel and Benji clapped on to each other's forearms to keep their balance. "Miguel saved my life. Marisol, you've saved my life too. As has Sun, and you too, Captain Benji. While I can't understand why any of you have done so for a wretch like me, I'll not stand by and watch you kill each other. I owe each of you a debt, and from what I understand, you all owe each other debts as well. Can we not discuss this tangle over grog and a fine meal? It is a savage world, and so we must act as men—and women—rather than beasts. Let peace prevail for now, I implore you."

Marisol regarded us with narrowed eyes but sheathed her knife. Sun stopped gripping the pole as if he were about to brain someone with it. Miguel's hand dropped from his flintlock. Benji relaxed his fists. And six sailors took hands from the hilts of their blades.

"Good. Now, let's get back to the ship and get the rum flowing. There's no problem in this world that can't be solved over grog and a game of chance," I said, hoping I was right.

PROPERLY DRESSED and aboard ship, sitting at table in the captain's cabin, wearing Captain Benji's spare black coat and britches, which fit me much better than Edwin's ever would, I felt almost civilized again. The *Fury*'s sailors had spent the afternoon rafting back and forth, relieving the cavern of chest after chest, which were piled in the hold under guard by two of Captain Benji's most trusted sailors. Sun had disappeared ashore and returned with an iron tangle of differently sized skeleton keys. There were several chests Sun checked privately and guarded himself personally while they were being transferred, and I did not recognize the sigils wood-burned into the sides. They were not from the *Swift*, but from at least two other vessels. The *Fury* now carried cargo from four different ships and her draft was very low in the water indeed. Puzzling over their mystery, but not having the private occasion to ask Sun about them, was most annoying, and reminded me of another mystery that needed answering, so I asked about it as soon as we were all seated at dinner.

"If I may ask, Dom Miguel," I said respectfully as Captain Benji pushed in Marisol's chair as he would any lady, although she was still dressed in the fashion of a French naval officer. "What was in that leather wallet you tucked into your coat?"

The prince had taken his time preparing himself and wore Edwin's clothing well, also being of smaller stature, and he looked as well-groomed as any of us. It had not been easy to convince Sun to sit at table with such illustrious company, and we'd had quite the argument until I gave up and told him I was going to eat with my friends and he could do as he wished. What he said in response was "Where you go, I go," and patted his knife hilt. I pointedly reminded him we were safely having dinner with three people who had saved my life, and furthermore we were under the captain's protection, but he only glowered and insisted on wearing his knife to sup.

Dom Miguel produced the wallet with a flourish, and I realized he'd been waiting for me to ask this question. Marisol's eyes tracked it as though it were a mouse and she a falcon. He patted it and said, "First, we eat. Tell me, Mademoiselle Soult, what brings you out to sea in such company? When last we met, 'twas in Rio de Janeiro, yes?"

She regarded him with narrowed eyes. A few sea hands brought in our first course—pork roasted sweetly with *aldin*, which Captain Benji said was called *quenepa* or *quenette* by other islanders, and dry, oblong nuts that crumbled in the mouth, which I could not name.

Marisol took her time chewing before she answered. "*Oui.* At your departure ball."

"Ah, of course, that was it. Nice of you to see us off as Father and I returned to Portugal. But what has happened to your *cabelo castanho,* your beautiful brown hair? It looked ever so fetching."

She glowered at him, and I thought how alike she and Sun were in temperament.

"How did you come to be in New Orleans at that gin palace with Edwin, Dom Miguel?" I asked, trying to avoid an argument over our second course of potatoes sautéed in honey.

"Not long after we set sail, I left Father's side on a fast ship of my own. You see, my brother, Pedro, is not as wise as he believes. I knew once we returned to Portugal, Father and I could expect trouble here in Brazil. My brother has always been weak. The citizens clamor, crying out for a free Brazil. I knew while Father and I were home in Portugal, repairing the damage left by Napoleon—" He paused to glance meaningfully at Marisol, then continued. "—Pedro would be easily overthrown. And he knows it also, which is why he's been working to secure political alliances with revolutionaries like Martio. With Father and me out of the way, there is little to keep Pedro from declaring something ridiculous, such as the Empire of Brazil. I know how his small mind works. Never to the benefit of family or country, but rather to his own comforts."

"Personally I also find not being beheaded by an angry mob quite comfortable," Captain Benji said.

"France is interested in Brazil remaining Portuguese, because it is near our Guiana colony. The British have a settlement nearby as well," Marisol said. "Which is why Edwin—"

"He was a British spy, yes. I was able to convince him I was Pedro's emissary, a man I, in truth, had waylaid and clapped in irons on my ship. However, I was unable to take Edwin also, because he already had revolutionaries mixed in with his crew. So I found myself up to my earlobes in intrigue, privy to a plot orchestrated by my brother and the British government to supply guns to Brazilian revolutionaries for independence. I managed to get a message to the real Captain Benji—a man I knew operated in New Orleans and had undertaken missions for Father before, but had not yet met—but that was my last act before we set sail." He opened the leather wallet. I recognized official papers written in a flowing hand that was not Edwin's, though I recognized Edwin's signature at the bottom. "This confirms every one of these weapons was forged in England. With the information here, we can root out his contacts and stop any future shipments, and also prove to the rest of Europe the treachery of the English."

"And you're planning to swim to Portugal with that wallet in your teeth, are you?" Marisol asked sweetly.

Dom Miguel cleared his throat. "Well, as my ship took the prisoner I captured back to my father at Lisbon, I was going to ask if Captain Swift might—"

"No," Benji said. "I'm a French corsair now, and I have some missions given me by the Crown. I've no business in Portugal, but perhaps my new employer would see fit to take you there?" He nodded at Marisol.

"You have your orders, Captain, as do I," Marisol said. "But I suppose delivering a favored son with news of a conspiracy back to his doting father would be an excellent way to begin an alliance between

Portugal and France. The Navy is not far, Dom Miguel—Tortuga—and after we have shown them those documents and revealed we share a common enemy, I am certain the *capitaine* of my acquaintance will escort us both to Lisbon."

"Tortuga? You have *bolas*, Princess." Dom Miguel pinched his chin. "And what would I owe in return for such a favor?"

"I'm certain I will think of something," Marisol said, and she grinned, which was much more intimidating than her scowl.

CHAPTER 28.
ALL THAT GLITTERS

SUN SAID nothing at all during dinner, watching everyone with those storm-dark eyes of his and looking as though he wished he were anywhere else. Though Dom Miguel and Marisol did most of the talking, Benji and I added our own quips and kept the conversation moving, if a bit strained around the edges. After Sun resisted my many attempts to draw him into the conversation, I made an announcement over a nice egg custard boiled in rum.

"Sun, I'm hoping you'll join me in showing these gentlemen and lady the fine game of *tafl*." He looked at me as though I'd grown a third eye in my forehead. "Unless our guests feel they might not understand the rules? It is somewhat like chess, except you have a king who must escape odds against him. Considering your recent histories, I find it apt."

To a man, including Marisol, they insisted that *tafl* would not present them any difficulties, and, as propriety required, they prevailed upon Sun to teach them. Glowering, speaking haltingly at first, Sun began instructing them in the basics while I retrieved iron bullets to represent the attacking soldiers and silver coins to represent the king's men. A saltcellar made an adequate king.

As I'd hoped, before long, as the grog flowed and we all relaxed into the game, Sun's natural personality surfaced, and I was able draw out a smile or two with a few well-placed jokes. When Dom Miguel laughed and patted Sun's arm after the two of them got a king out from right under Marisol and Benji's soldiers, and, instead of tensing for a fight, Sun smiled back at him, I knew my plan was working.

I rotated the teams so everyone could learn each other's strategies for play and then begged off for some fresh air. "I'm sorry to steal your partner, Dom Miguel," I apologized. "But I hope Sun will join me above decks?" For my plan to work, I needed Sun to mingle with more than just the upper class.

Sun reluctantly looked up from the engrossing strategy he'd been contemplating with Dom Miguel, and Marisol and Benji looked markedly more cheerful when Sun left him to come to my side. Their pile of betting coins was the smallest, but from the way Dom Miguel rubbed his chin, I suspected it would grow larger before the evening was through.

Sun and I stepped around several groups of dicing sailors enjoying their ration of grog, and then I led him above decks, where night rested gently on the ship as it rocked at anchor next to the large black shape of the mountain. Men, both Benji's loyal ones and Edwin's former crew, kept their turn at watch while a few others told tales in small groups, diced, played at cards, or sang and danced. They quieted as we passed, giving Sun dark glances.

We leaned against the gunnel and took in the fresh night air, watching the ripples on the water glide between reflected moonlight and the lights from the ship's lanterns.

"There's the sodomite," a rough voice sounded from behind us— Edwin's redhead. I stiffened and turned around slowly. He stood behind us, feet apart, chin thrust high, fists clenched. Behind him were three more of Edwin's former crew—all four of them smelled strongly of the grog Captain Benji had generously distributed. "Martio plumbed his hawsehole but good."

Shame burned through me like a flash fire that left my earlobes tingling. Sun made a violent movement next to me, but I had the presence of mind to throw an arm across his chest. The very last thing I wanted was for Sun to turn his deadly arts on any of the crew, even ones such as these. The captain had threatened them all not to raise a hand against us, but as Black Miguel had once told me, threats mean nothing to some until they see a man act on his words.

And words were all these were, I told my shaking hands and arms. They couldn't hurt me.

Sun fired off in Portuguese too quickly for me to understand, drew his knife, and licked the blade. Two of the three men, both Portuguese, laughed.

"What did he call me?"

Still laughing, his companion translated. "He said because you're jealous, Artur, he'll *fode* your bunghole with that and then make some new holes for everyone else to have a turn."

Blood rushed to Artur's face, but he didn't say anything else, only coughed a gob of spit and snot at Sun's feet. One of his companions pushed him, saying he wanted more grog, and then they were gone as suddenly as they'd appeared. I looked at Sun in surprise—even Marisol would have been impressed by that reply.

"You shouldn't have stopped me," Sun said as I dropped my arm. "He needs to be shown."

"No, Sun. No more killing. There's been enough of that."

"I wouldn't kill him." Sun's eyes glinted in the darkness. "Only make him wish I had."

"Sun, no. I don't want that. Let it go." My whole plan for convincing Sun to set sail hinged on him integrating with the crew. A fight was the last thing I wanted. Well, other than a death.

"As you wish, my Benjamin." Sun put away his knife, but he glared over at the small knot of men laughing around Artur on the forecastle.

Pushing down the emotions rising from Artur's words, I rested on my heels to throw a few rounds of dice with other sailors here and there, drawing Sun in, and paying our debts with Edwin's silvers when we lost, until the small supply I'd found in his quarters was gone.

"Ah well," I said, turning back to the gunnel and looking up at Dread Island's peak.

Sun leaned next to me. "We can get more."

"Likely, I haven't really properly searched Edwin's—"

"No, Benjamin. I mean that I have some." He pulled on my sleeve and then walked back below decks. I noticed the sailors he'd lost silvers to were much more accepting of him as we passed, some calling out to him to roll the dice again. I caught up to him as he went below and stepped around more sailors as he took me down into the hold where the guards and chests were.

"Leave us," he ordered the guards.

"Please," I added politely. "Wait outside for a moment? I'll fetch you when we're finished."

They exchanged a look but then, to my surprise, obeyed, perhaps because of our connection with and my striking resemblance to their captain.

"There are more than guns here, Benjamin," Sun said softly. He pulled out the skeleton keys and started opening the group of chests branded differently from the guns. One was full of fine silks from the orient. Another, spices from the Pacific isles. Another, stacked full with hats, but under them were socks of gold and silver coins. Another contained beautiful tooled-leather shoe blanks a skilled cobbler could custom to any foot. There were more besides. I looked around at all these riches, then back at Sun in wonder. "I wasted nothing. Everything that washed up on my shores, I collected," he said.

It was a princely sum indeed. "Sun, do you realize you could near buy your own ship with this much?"

"*Þetta er ekki upp í nös á ketti*. This wouldn't fill a cat's nostril, Benjamin. When I first explored the caves, I found a cask half-buried in the sand. It's full of colored stones—*gimsteinar*. They are enough to buy every slave who ever fought with me or against me, with more left over."

I stared at him, at the treasure before me, slowly realizing what he'd said.

"Is that what you would like to do? Free slaves?"

"I...." He paused, and I realized he hadn't meant that was what he wanted to do, but was only making a comparison. He thought a moment and nodded. "*Já*. I do," he said firmly. "That would be... the proper use for riches."

Hope rose in my chest. "You do know it would be hard to do that if we stay on the island?"

He nodded again, solemnly.

I brushed my knuckles gently under his chin and traced his jaw with my fingertips. "You're not saying this because you know I want to sail away, are you?"

He shook his head and, his voice very small and quiet, said, "I've seen how you are with the others on this ship. How you make them... happy. Like you make me happy. I did not think I would ever be happy again, nor that anyone would wish for me to be with them, but.... Benjamin. You make people belong. You make me want... to belong again." He drew a breath to say more but then shook his head instead.

I kissed the place where his dimple hid in his cheek. "You belong with me, and I belong with you, Sólmundur," I murmured into his ear, then leaned back and returned his gaze steadily. "I miss the companionship of others, but if you need to stay on the island longer, we can do that. However, when the *Fury* sails, people will start to hear the truth of Dread Island. And, anyway, our cargo is already aboard, and I'd very much like to get at least my investment back for these guns. But, if afterward, you want to come back and stay here awhile, we can do that. If you want to sail to Georgetown and beyond and free every slave we find, I'm with you. If you want to go home and find the family that lost you, I'm with you." I kissed him, then borrowed his words. "Where you go, I go."

He lowered his eyes, head bowed, and I thought I must have said something wrong or hurtful, but then he hugged me tight, as he had done during those first nights. And I rested my chin on his head, and held him gently, as I had done before, and would gladly do again.

MANY SAILORS greeted us with bleary, bloodshot eyes but warm hellos in the morning mists as we made our way back up to the foredeck. After a long interlude in the hold together the night before, sealing our convictions to each other with rather more than a kiss, Sun and I had made more rounds about the ship, playing games and sharing stories with the men. We avoided Artur for now. I wasn't sure what to do with him. As for the others, Sun was awkward at first but trying hard to be friendly, and his natural skill at strategy games quickly made him friends who would moan when he approached and suggest wildly we play games of chance rather than strategy so they could win. He had no talent for song and dance, but my encyclopedic knowledge of bawdy tavern songs made up for it when sore feelings threatened to turn a loser against him, which wasn't often.

It seemed Captain Benji selected his men carefully for not only skill, but temperament. From hearing their stories, not a one among them had been crimped, but served Captain Benji willingly. The lot who had worked for Edwin James, all except Artur, in a time-honored sailor tradition of holding the captain of the ship somewhere above kings and just below God, seemed to have completely forgotten their old allegiances and were integrating almost seamlessly with men they'd been trying to kill the day before, united under the autocratic rule of Captain Benji Swift.

We found Benji amidships, calling soft orders to the men whose heads weren't hurting too much to obey them. "We'll be ready to sail by midmorning," he said, taking our measure. "Are we putting you ashore? Or are you setting sail with us?"

I looked at Sun, giving him pause to speak for both of us. He glanced at me, then said, "We're going with you. But I want to collect a few more things. And Benjamin wants a Christian burial for—" He paused. Was he feeling remorse? Perhaps he did not want to say Martio's name. "—the men who died," he ended quietly.

Benji nodded. "I thought you might want something like that, Lector. I have an idea from Dom Miguel, though he doesn't know it. I'll have a few trusty lads with no sense of smell set to it shortly."

"We, uh... I want to help," Sun said.

"Me too." I clasped his shoulder. He wasn't the only killer. Two of those bodies were my responsibility.

"As you wish," Benji said as Dom Miguel and Marisol joined us amidships. They both looked clean and fresh, despite the fact that they had continued to play *tafl* long after the rest of us went to bed. I had listened to the low murmur of their voices through the wall in the cabin next door for a long time as Sun fell asleep in my arms.

"Who won the most sets?" I asked, thinking Miguel looked far too pleased with himself.

"Oh, she did. Most definitely." He executed a courtly bow to her. "To my shame, I must admit we reached a point where she won every set until I had no course but to surrender completely."

Her cheeks and the tip of her nose pinked ever so slightly, and I wondered if her winning streak had ended the same way mine had when Sun first showed me how to play on the beach what felt like a hundred years ago.

"I suspect the two of you have made some progress on relations between France and Portugal?" Captain Benji suggested, rather bluntly, I thought.

Marisol pursed her lips, raised her eyebrow, and avoided his innuendo. "Perhaps. When do we set sail?"

He gave her a hard, measuring look but answered her question rather than press his own. "Soon. These two wish to collect their personal effects. And I'm told there's a burial to be had."

"Captain, we need to get underway if we're going to rendezvous with the Navy at Tortuga. Unless you agree to forego your orders and take us to Lisbon?"

He glowered.

"Then I suggest we let the dead lie where they are."

"We will be sailing by noon," he said.

"But—" I started, and he interrupted me.

"There will be a burial. And we will be underway by noon. Mademoiselle will pay for the speed she requires, yes?"

"Whatever it takes, Captain."

"Excellent. Forty kegs of powder should just about do it. I'll draw up the receipt."

And I understood Captain Benji's plan at once.

CHAPTER 29.
RETURN TO THE MOUNTAIN

SUN AND I took the long boat with two of Benji's men named Hardanguer
and Quinn, the oldest pair of sea dogs I'd ever clapped eyes on. They
were content to leave the rowing to Sun and me, and even though the
exertion made the lash on my chest burn, I gritted my teeth through the
pain and made no comment. The pain felt like penance for the deaths I'd
caused.

Miguel's powder stockpile didn't quite fit in the long boat with the
four of us—twenty kegs crowded around us, the others in two ten-keg
water-tight flotilla that Hardanguer and Quinn kept a sharp eye on as we
made our way back to the white beaches.

It was strange indeed to step back on our shores in the shadow of
the mountain. We'd rowed to the south beach because it was the shorter
way around, and I vividly remembered how Sun and I had passed the
morning here fishing and playing *tafl* before Martio and Edwin landed.
It felt like another lifetime as I stepped over the stones and shells we
had played with. Hardanguer and Quinn followed, each of us carrying
two kegs of powder. Sun led us up the path to the cave, and we trekked
in silence. I smelled the dead rotting in the tropical heat long before we
arrived at the cave mouth.

Edwin and Martio lay where we had left them. Hardanguer and
Quinn pulled both bodies farther into the cave so they were deep within
the tunnel.

I felt dizzy watching their heels leave furrows in the dirt and had
to stop awhile with my arms braced on my knees, breathing slowly. Sun
placed his keg between Martio's bloated, darkening legs. Hardanguer
and Quinn stacked theirs next to his. I could not move to Edwin's side
and the swollen face I knew so well. Hardanguer and Quinn went back to
fetch more kegs, and Sun joined me, rubbing small circles on my back,
but not speaking. After a time, I felt a bit better and straightened, but I

did not remark when Sun picked up the two kegs I had put down and set them on either side of Edwin so I did not have to move closer.

They had done wrong, Edwin and Martio, hurt us and tortured us and planned worse. I felt both fear and rage because of what Martio did to me—so much anger and darkness within—and I had killed them both. And in doing so, I had allowed that darkness to overtake and consume me. Was I still a man of Christ, who could do such things? Did it matter that they would have done the same to me? I didn't know, and without knowing, I could find no comfort.

My eyes burned as we returned with the second load, taking it deeper into the cave. And the third, deeper still. The fourth and final trip, no one could mistake that the tears trailing down my face were not sweat, but Hardanguer and Quinn didn't remark on them. They also didn't seem overly troubled by our gruesome task, as both Sun and I coughed and gagged with the stench. Perhaps they had no sense of smell, as Benji had said.

"Well, that's it, then," Hardanguer croaked. "Captain says you should be well away when it goes up, hear me?"

Sun nodded.

"Gather what you need, lads, and light them up. We'll meet you at the boat." And with that, the two elderly sailors left us.

Sun took my hand and led me down the path to the tree house, where he retrieved his favorite hunting spear, then to the meat-smoking cave, where he gathered his personal effects of any value into three leather bags and set a small chest decorated with hand-carved elephants on top of the barrel of hardtack. He took out his skeleton keys and opened it. It held enough uncut gemstones to buy a kingdom. I did not recognize the strange, looped language on it, but the art carved into the chest reminded me of etchings in my book of Alexander the Great's territory of the Indus.

"*Allt* good?" Sun asked when I didn't speak.

I nodded. Edwin's swollen face kept surfacing in my mind. Sun hugged me, kissed my cheek, then held out the chest. I tucked it under one arm so I could hold Sun's hand after he finished looping the bags across his chest. We carefully retrieved his kindling coal, and together we approached the burial site.

"We should run fast away, Benjamin. *Já?*"

I nodded and felt a shudder pass through my shoulders and down my spine. I had no idea what damage this much powder was going to do. I pulled out the small, black book one of the sailors, a man named Franqui, had given me. I tried to read from it, but couldn't see through my suddenly blurry eyes. So I said the Lord's Prayer, stumbling a bit over "Forgive us our trespasses," but hitting my stride in "Deliver us from evil," when Sun joined me with *"frelsa oss frá illu."* We said "Amen" together.

Sun carefully created a thick trail of powder leading outside the cave and ending in a small pyramid of grains that reminded me powerfully of a tiny volcano. Dread Island in miniature.

I shoved the small book into my pocket and picked up the chest again. Sun slung his three bags, then set his kindling coal on the powder cone. It fizzed and spat, and the two of us turned and ran down the mountain as fast as we could.

We were well into the trees when the first explosion sounded from behind us, followed by another, and another, and then the last—all four ten-keg stockpiles. I slowed, but Sun kept running all out, so I followed him. A fourth explosion sounded, then a great heave. The earth bucked beneath us, and Sun fell hard onto his knees. I stumbled head over heels, slammed my chest into the box of gems, and writhed in agony for a few breathless moments, but then Sun pulled me up. We looked behind us.

The side of the cone was staved in as though Odysseus's Cyclops had hit it with a club—a massive landslide moving down the mountain. A huge cloud of smoke rose above the cone. More quaking, and then running pigs parted the vegetation all around us, fleeing. I clutched the chest, and Sun and I ran with them. The rumbling and shuddering of the earth continued, and I didn't think that boded at all well.

Hardanguer and Quinn already had the long boat in the water, and we ran through knee-deep surf to get to it, pigs swimming all around us. Sun leaped in quick as lightning, then took the chest from me, and I vaulted in after him. Without speaking, we stretched oars as one and started rowing for all we were worth, trying to avoid hitting the pigs all around us.

Then the top of the mountain exploded, showering the sky with fire and brimstone.

"Row!" Hardanguer said, and he and Quinn unshipped the other pair of oars and bent their backs to business, Hardanguer calling out when to heave. "Row! Row! Row!"

No one acted as coxswain to face forward and guide us, so great was our haste as we shot back away from the island. I had an unobstructed view of the slabs of stone and rocks showering down the mountainside and across the beach, flinging small debris into and around our boat. So much smoke and dust rolled down the mountain and over the island that it was quickly obscured from view, though the pelting of small stones continued all around us, plunking into the water and pinging off our boat. A piglet swam frantically hard by, mostly failing to keep its nose above water. I have no real understanding why, but I pushed down my oars so they tilted up in the oarlocks, planted my feet, leaned over the side, and pulled the creature in among us. Then I lowered and set to sweeping my oars again and started coughing because of the ash in the air. Though my lungs burned, I didn't stop rowing for several minutes, not until we emerged back into daylight. A prevailing east wind pushed the smoke away from us and east by south.

"There she is!" Hardanguer called out, and I looked over my shoulder. The *Fury*, covered with sailors climbing the rigging, small as angry ants, was underway out to sea, making distance from the mountain as best she could while tacking against the wind. I counted tatters and rips in the sails where stones had shot through, but she seemed seaworthy.

"Row! Row!"

I bent my back to Hardanguer's commands, and we reached the *Fury* before she was out of the range of our strength. It took all four of us to attach the long boat while the *Fury* was so energetically underway, the squealing piglet stumbling back and forth between our legs, but the runner and tackle brought the long boat up quickly enough once we'd climbed aboard and clapped to the ropes. I helped the piglet aboard the *Fury*, where it lay on its side, panting.

"*Ansans ári*," Sun said softly. "Look, Benjamin."

I looked. The winds had peeled the spewing clouds away from Dread Island. White and gray still billowed from the blown cone of the mountain, which was now sending up gouts of flame crowned in black smoke. Red tongues of lava coursed down the sides, tracing zigzag paths. I remembered the number of fissures in the eroded mountainside and the erratic path the lava would have to follow. Captain Benji and I had been counting on the unstable fissures of the cave structure to collapse and create a burial, but not a landslide, quake, and eruption. More fire plumed and coiled from the lips of the cone. The stench was incredible. The men aboard the *Fury* looked like ghosts. Fine, gray ash coated everyone and stuck to Sun and me like mash, because we were still wet from the sea. Huge gouts of steam came up from the mountain's foot, seawater evaporating as it touched the infernal bowels of the mountain.

We watched in silence as the eruption calmed, but continued to belch forth lava. The mountain and the island and the eruption were small—this was no Mount Tambora, which had recently caused the Year without Summer and widespread famines—but impressive to us nevertheless. It may go forever unmarked by anyone but the men of the *Fury*, but it was a sight I will never forget.

The piglet cried plaintively at my feet, and I picked him up. He struggled a little in my arms, then calmed as Sun stroked his ears and snout. He was still breathing hard with a little wheeze, as was Hardanguer behind us.

"You boys certainly know how to make an exit," Captain Benji bellowed.

Reluctantly, I turned away from the volcano, which, with the flow of lava over the crown, now looked nothing like a skull at all, but rather, a glowing, fire-traced heart. The man I was quickly coming to regard as the brother I never had strode over to us and gave all three—me, the piglet, and Sun—a shameless hug. He looked a bit pale under the coating of ash. "How in the…?" He shook his head, apparently lost for words.

"It certainly was, uh, thorough," Dom Miguel said as he and Marisol joined us as well. They were both curiously clean of ash. They must have been below decks.

"*Porcelet adorable!* Who is your pink friend?" Marisol asked.

"His name is Ernest," I said.

Sun's grin was a sudden white crescent across his ash-coated face.

CHAPTER 30.
MATELOTS

MAKING READY to set sail took some time. Everyone, even Dom Miguel and Marisol, stripped to underclothes and helped scrub down the ship, mend rips in the canvas, and in other ways made the *Fury* ready. A small crew beat to windward with the lateen sail and tacked us away from the island and the falling ash, while the rest worked.

Sun and I had a short argument about Ernest. I wanted to keep him aboard with us as we sailed on, but Sun argued that he'd have a better life among his own kind on an island with plentiful food and no predators. Especially when contrasted with a ship full of human predators with a fondness for bacon. So, after Sun hid his small chest of *gimsteinn* deep in our quarters, which had been the first mate's—small with only one narrow bed, but Sun and I very much didn't mind sharing—we boarded and lowered the long boat again and rowed back as close to shore as we dared. Fortunately the wind held, blowing what remained of the ash and smoke east by south, and we got near enough to the south beach to find the rest of the sounder and set little Ernest in the cloudy water that had once been so clear as to show every shell and stone. I hoped it would be clean and clear again soon. Ernest didn't seem to have difficulty rejoining the sounder, which was, for the most part, watching the still-smoking mountain with suspicion, though some of the younger pigs were apparently enjoying swimming around and playing in the shallow water.

I rested my sore arms and shoulders, dropping the oars, and watched little Ernest touch noses with a sow. Then I reached for Sun and kissed him firmly on the mouth, careful of our bruises.

"Benjamin?"

I kissed him again, and his lips smiled under mine before I sat back and looked searchingly into his eyes. "Sun, there's still time to fetch our things from the ship and bring them back here, if you want to stay."

Sun regarded his smoking island. "We did blow it up somewhat. Though, when I was a boy, *Grímsvötn* blew up. It's probably still blowing up. Every ten years, *Afi* said." His brow creased as he watched the sow nuzzle Ernest. "I haven't thought about my *afi* and *amma* for years."

I smiled at him. "I'd like to see."

"Hum?"

"This Greemsvough."

"*Grímsvötn.*"

I grinned and shook my head. "Show it to me. Yes?"

Sun smiled. "Do you have any idea how cold it is where I am from?"

"No," I reported honestly. "But it's damn hot here."

"*Það er skammgóður vermir að pissa í skó sinn.* You'll like it for a little while, then not so much."

"I'm willing to take that chance." I added silently, *Are you?*

"We'll see." He kissed me back. "There are lots of ways to stay warm."

I laughed. Together, we bid farewell to the pigs, the sand, the jungle, and Dread Island.

THE SMOKE stack from Sun's island was visible for miles as the *Fury* tacked north and then started taking advantage of the strong easterly to move her out from shoals and toward open sea so we could get underway for Marisol's rendezvous at Tortuga. Sun and I bent our backs to helping aboard, and I watched him work silently with more of the crew—many of whom, no doubt egged on by Artur, still regarded him as a dangerous murderer and escaped slave, which was not helped by Sun keeping a blade on him at all times. He was so fast with it he could cut a fly in half on the rail. This seemed to intimidate more than impress. Though he was trying to use his skills to befriend others, I didn't think it was working as he intended. However, it fast became apparent that he had once been a very fine sailor—he knew more knots than I did and got the work done in half the time it took me. When there was a command, he hopped to, whoever was giving it. He climbed through the rigging like a monkey and made use of himself so much so that, before long, he had integrated seamlessly with the crew at work.

Social time in the evenings was another matter. Each night we were invited to sup with Captain Benji—who now frequently called me "little brother"—Dom Miguel, and Marisol. I, for one, didn't turn down the chance for the choice foods Cookie served to the captain's table, but after dinner and some polite conversation, I took the small coin Sun had shared with me, and we went to gamble with the men. I'm a fair enough player I can win often, but I was careful neither Sun nor I won too much. The relationships Sun had started building that first night grew, especially after I reminded him what we were doing and why—playing for friends, not for silvers. We won over a few more sailors each night. I knew not everyone would be comfortable with him, but it was enough to reduce tensions. I wished Marisol would join us too; it would help dispel the men's superstitions about there being a woman aboard, but she spent her evenings with Dom Miguel. In the mornings, their fingers were ink-stained and their eyes bleary, so I guessed they were working out finer details of the treaty between their two countries. Neither one was particularly pleased about whatever they were doing, so it must have been going well. In a good bargain, neither side is happy, my grandfather always said.

ALLIANCES WERE on my mind. Humanity seems to draw itself too easily into groups of *us* and *them*, and there was no better demonstration of that fact than the fissure I witnessed widening among the crew between Captain Benji's trusty lads and Artur's small group of followers. He did not miss an opportunity to whisper something that resulted in laughter from his companions whenever Sun or I were within earshot, and the day I'd been dreading, when it would finally come to blows, came upon me unsuspecting.

"Oi, plumb-bum!" Artur shouted to me one afternoon as Sun and I hoisted the lateen sail tacking the ship eastward from British Dominica. He made a very rude gesture with a belaying pin as he tied lines at the gunnel.

"Ignore him," I said to Sun as I hauled on my ropes, ashamed of the heat burning my cheeks.

Sun looked askance at me, then hauled hard on the swing line. The boom cantered out to take Artur squarely in the chest with a loud thunk, and sent him top over tail backward, right over the gunnel and into the drink.

"Goddamnit, Sun. Man overboard!" I shouted and ran to the gunnel, unshipping the ladder and readying the long overboard pole.

Captain Benji shouted commands to gybe over, and as the *Fury* turned and circled Artur, I reached out with the cork-tipped pole to where he splashed in the warm, blue Caribbean. Artur seized the cork, and with a nasty curse, punched it back. The butt took me hard in my healing nose, which sent me backward with a howl, clutching my face.

I saw stars, and when my vision cleared, it was to see Sun's anxious face over mine.

"I'm all right—" I started to choke out, but then Artur topped the ladder and came up over the gunnel, and Sun took him down to the deck with a flying tackle and a sodden smack as his back hit the wood.

Sun pummeled his face with both fists, Artur giving back what he got when he could, and I realized I was screaming, "Don't kill him!" as the captain's booming voice commanded, "Take them apart, lads!" The circle of men that had formed around the combatants stepped forward and pulled them off each other. At least one man caught a flying elbow in the face before four men restrained Sun, still kicking, and two men supported Artur on none-too-steady feet.

"The only knocks aboard this ship will be meted out by me," Captain Benji thundered, pointing at Sun and then Artur. "And no man shall pull a trick like that." He glared at Sun, and I felt a fear as strong as ever. We could not afford to lose our staunchest ally.

"He's sorry!" I said, leaping between Sun and Benji.

"I am not!" Sun shouted. "*Hlandbrenndu!*" he yelled at Artur, which sounded like a most vile curse, but no one seemed to understand, so he translated. "May your piss burn!"

"If you were men, I'd give you a dozen lashes of the cat-o'-nines, but since you insist on acting like boys, it's birching for you both. Bend 'em over, lads."

The crew hauled Artur over to one of the long-nines and bent him over the cannon, pulling down his britches. I held Sun's eyes with mine, begging him to submit to the punishment, and he allowed the same to be done to him. Captain Benji returned with a birch rod, and gave them a whipping my father would have been proud of.

"If this happens again, I'll keelhaul you both. Now get out of my sight. And you"—he pointed the rod at me—"come 'ere."

I stepped forward, and the captain gripped the back of my head with one hand and straightened my nose again with a sharp tug. I clenched my jaw to keep from cursing him as pain jagged up my forehead, and blinked away tears.

"Now get back on that lateen sail," he ordered. "And if any of you even think of going fist to fist, by God you'll answer for it, you hear?"

"Aye, aye, Captain," rang out from all the sailors around.

I got back on the lateen sail, but I watched Sun and Artur as they both walked gingerly to the hold, escorted below by some of Captain Benji's trusty lads.

AS SOON as my duty ended, I found Sun in our cabin, marching angrily back and forth.

"How is it?" I asked him once I'd shut the door. He scowled at me and looked daggers as he pulled down his britches and presented his livid cheeks.

"Oh, Sun." I wet a handkerchief and draped it lightly over the red skin as Sun hissed. "I'm sorry."

He swore for a few minutes in his native tongue while I pulled off his shirt—I was pleased to see the exertion hadn't reopened the healing lash marks Martio had given him. As I did so, I realized another of Captain Benji's kindnesses—if he'd used the traditional maritime punishment, and had given each man a dozen lashes with the cat-o'-nine-tails, Sun's back would have been laid open and weeping again. I had the good grace not to mention this to Sun as I guided him facedown onto the bed.

"My *sitjandi* is afire," he said miserably, his voice muffled by our mattress. "Is your nose...?"

"Captain Benji straightened it for me again." It throbbed like the dickens, but not as badly as before.

An awkward silence fell. "I'm sorry, Sun. Thank you for, uh, defending my virtue. But...."

He sighed into the mattress. "But I have to get along, even with goat dung like Artur. *Já*, I know."

He rolled onto his side and touched my cheek, turning my face side to side and inspecting my nose.

"How does it look?" I asked.

"Still handsome." He smiled. "Do I earn a kiss after battle?"

I smiled back and shook my head ruefully, noticing his staff hardening where it lay against his hip. "You are insatiable." But I leaned forward and kissed him, careful of my nose. He pulled off my shirt and kissed down my chest. "You realize you've just been punished for your impertinence?"

"Off with those britches, sailor," he commanded, and I complied. He cupped me gently and kissed the head of my staff, which was as eager as his was to be used.

"Come up here." He pulled on me gently, and I obeyed, joining him on the bed. "Down." He pushed me onto the mattress, wadding up our blanket and pushing it between my hands so I rested facedown, my forearms holding me up, the rest of me laid out flat.

His hands traveled up the backs of my legs, from ankle to *sitjandi*, and then I felt the heat of his mouth close around the soft skin of my bollocks as he pressed my thighs apart from behind. I lost myself to his hot, sucking mouth, the way his swirling tongue found first one stone, then the other, pulling each in turn between his lips, then switching, so carefully, so gently. I could not help but thrust against the mattress and moan his name. His hand found my staff and worked it.

The first tickle of fear came when I felt Sun's mouth leave my sac and his weight shifted so his thighs pressed against mine.

I turned sideways. "Sun...."

"I see your face when Artur says those things to you, my Benjamin." He massaged my buttocks as he spoke. "He owns that, he takes that from you. What Martio did—"

"I don't want to talk about that." Anger rushed up from the well within me that overflowed whenever Martio's name was spoken. I pulled away from Sun, trying to close my legs, but the bed was short and narrow and Sun's body was between them.

"Shh, my Benjamin. Do you trust me?" Sun stroked my thigh with one hand, and with the other, he took my wrist and placed my palm against his throat, rearranging me so I lay back on my buttocks, with him between my legs. I felt the throb of his pumping heart and it was quite difficult to feel threatened when I seemed to hold Sun's life in my hand.

"Yes...."

"Then touch yourself," he commanded.

I wrapped my other hand around my flagging staff. As I worked myself, Sun settled back on his heels, kneeling between my legs.

He pressed my palm to his throat more firmly. "Lower," he urged. As I slipped to my sac and cupped myself, he captured my staff with his hands and stroked me. My bollocks tightened as the pleasure from Sun's touch rolled through me.

"Bring your fingers to my lips." I did so, and he sucked my pointer and middle fingers until they were dripping. "Now touch yourself there."

I hesitated. I'd done naught but clean myself since that awful night, at first afraid I was badly hurt because of the clots of blood I found in my britches, but then slowly understanding that I was mending. It didn't hurt to empty myself on the seat of ease, and I certainly wasn't going to speak to Captain Benji about it, so I'd avoided thinking on it as much as possible once we set sail.

"Benjamin...." Sun squeezed my arousal with one hand, cupping my bollocks with the other, his throat pressing hard into my palm.

I was by turns disgusted, fascinated, afraid—but I lowered my fingers and touched myself, circling my rim.

"Go slowly." He pressed forward, and I eased back so he could come close and slip his lips over the head of my staff. I explored with my fingertips as he swallowed me. The strangest tingling pleasure began to build at the base of my spine as I circled my opening.

"Go inside, Benjamin." I did, the barest amount, because the angle was awkward. He worked my staff with one hand and sucked his finger. Then I felt his fingertip over my own, circling. I clenched and scooted back, the fear mastering me.

"Squeeze my throat." I did, and again felt the comforting throb of Sun's life in my hands. Vulnerable, like I was.

"My Benjamin.... Tell me yes or tell me no." I felt the tip of his finger press against my opening.

Frightened but curious, my heart burning in my chest with feeling for him, I said, "Yes."

He closed his mouth over my staff as his finger entered me slowly. It was a foreign sensation, a pressure, but also a growing heat built, and I surrendered to it as Sun pressed against me, sliding inside. He worked me with his mouth, then started moving his finger, until the sensations built into an eruption that rivaled Dread Island's. I made a mess of us both, and through it all, Sun spoke to me softly in his language, then gently withdrew his finger and lay on top of me.

I pulled Sun's face to mine and kissed him.

"The next time that *svin* says anything to you, I want you to think of us both touching you there, and how good what we did felt. You don't belong to Artur. You don't belong to Martio. You don't even belong to me, Benjamin. You belong to yourself." He kissed me. "Every part of you."

I held him in my arms and prayed to God that I had the strength to do as he said, and I thanked God for giving me Sun.

HOWEVER, MY resolve wasn't immediately tested, because Artur behaved himself, keeping his distance and shooting us the occasional filthy look, but no longer calling me names. I did note that either Captain Benji or some of his closest mates happened to be nearby whenever the three of us were on deck, keeping a weather eye on both Sun and Artur. I was grateful for their vigilance. Tensions eased over the next few days, and the crew settled into the rhythm of life at sea. The captain continued to invite us to dinner. One night after another of Cookie's sumptuous meals, Captain Benji joined me at the gunnel, where I was lounging, watching Sun dice with the boatswain—who had proved to be the excellent shot from the crow's nest during the mutiny—and a pair of riggers. Sun was losing and laughing about it.

"He looks all right, doesn't he, little brother? He'll be all right," Benji said.

I looked at Benji. His shrewd eyes watched Sun interacting with his corsairs, and I knew he meant more than healing from the birching. When Benji glanced at me, I held his gaze with my own. "Yes. He will." *We both will.*

He looked thoughtfully at Sun and nodded slowly. "Yes," he said, "but the law will want him, nevertheless."

"What do you mean?"

"He's a famous knife fighter. An escaped slave. Moreover, he's a self-confessed cold-blooded murderer."

"I've killed too."

"Self-defense. I'm sure of that. I knew what Edwin and Martio were after only a few days on the *Fury*." His voice deepened with some emotion I couldn't name. "But Sólmundur, he killed sailors, merchants, good men who did nothing wrong except landfall on the wrong island."

Benji was right, and I knew it. And there was nothing I could do about it. I ground my teeth in frustration. No safe place. No safe place in this world for us.

"There is something we can do," Benji continued. "If you be willing." Hope rose in my chest. "Such as?"

"You become his owner. His belongings would be yours. I saw those extra crates. I know they're not filled with anything the *Swift* was carrying. You pay reparations for the damages your slave incurred, if we get the right people to agree." He dusted his palms together. "Everyone's happy."

"Sun will never be a slave again. Never while I draw breath."

Benji nodded as if he had known that would be my answer. He handed me the leather wallet that had been Edwin's. How he'd bargained it from Marisol's grasp, I didn't know. Perhaps she no longer needed it now that she and Miguel were drawing up more papers. I opened it, flipped through the pages detailing what I owed Edwin and how many years I would have been an indentured servant, the arrangements that Sun would fight for them in the pits. I turned around and looked out to sea, watching the moonlight play on the water. I drew back my arm and threw the wallet as far as I could muster. It sank quickly below the waters and was left behind in our wake. Then I calmly turned back to watching Sun dice with the marksman boatswain and two riggers.

"There's another way. Again, if you be willing," Captain Benji said.

When he was silent for a while, I said, with some pique, "I'm not growing any younger, big brother."

He smiled. "My boatswain yonder. Have you seen him with Cookie?"

I thought about it. I had seen them together. Cookie was the name we all used for Angus MacCorquodale, the man who prepared our food. The boatswain often waited until Cookie was done preparing everyone else's food and then took his vittles with the man. I'd seen them chatting, dicing—clearly close friends, though they did not spend all their time together, considering their duties and other friendships.

"Yes, what of it?"

"Have you heard of the practice of matelot?"

"Can't say that I have."

"Well, Cookie and Abellard there"—he indicated the boatswain, whose name I'd forgotten—"are matelots. They're joined by a matelot. It's a pirate custom, and I saw no harm in adopting it as a smuggling ship. They split all earnings between them, take halves of each other's punishments, share a sea chest, inherit each other's property. Share a bed and a life, if you understand me."

I stared at Abellard the boatswain. The way Father had spoken about sodomites, I'd expected horns to grow out of one's forehead. He was the same balding, round-faced swab from New Orleans he'd been before I knew he shared a bed with Cookie. I clapped my hand to my own forehead—no horns there either.

"Sea birds, boy."

I shut my mouth.

"Thereby, if you take my meaning, you and Sólmundur Thorvaldson could sign on to my crew and join in a matelot. All his booty and punishments then be yours, and vice versa. It's a chance to take, but considering what we've done for France and Portugal, and with the three of us speaking for you, we may be able to get you both a pardon from the French *capitaines* and any law we run into, pay some reparations for what we'll say are misunderstandings, and be on our way."

"Does that sharing include taking a birching?" I tried not to let my anger show in my voice. I knew Captain Benji's intentions were good, but that hadn't made watching Sun whipped any easier.

"Lad, you know as well as I do that order must be kept aboard ship. I can't have sailors tossing each other overboard or we'll never make Marisol's rendezvous. But yes, you would have had six of those swats from me, and Sun the other half dozen. The contract says as much."

"And there would be documents to this effect?"

"Drawn up by me own hand, or Dom Miguel's, a bit from us each if you prefer. Free men, both of you, royally pardoned and lawful French corsairs under the command of Captain Benji Swift. I've seen you with the men—you chum along well. Furthermore, I lost my clerk in the mutiny, and you strike me as one who knows his letters and numbers."

I studied the man. "Why do you care? I am grateful, truly, but I don't understand why you're helping us. You're corsairs. It would not be a stretch to seize my guns and Sun's crates and kill us both. Why help?" I felt afraid saying such things, as if they might come to pass by speaking them. I'd spent too much time among superstitious sailors. I made the sign of the cross against evil.

"Corsairs aren't pirates, boy. We stand for the French Crown against her enemies. Laws about killing people apply. As I've always said, I'm a smuggler, not a pirate. I don't torture, and I don't kill unless there's call for it. In any case, you cut me to the quick. Haven't I proven I'm your friend?" He looked me in the eye, but smiled. "It's not often a man meets his own double. You look like me, boy, and no mistake. That'd be dead useful for some of the situations I find myself doing business in—if you can keep from getting knocked in the beak in future. I'd just as soon us remain friends, and good ones. We are friends, little brother?"

My lips twitched of their own accord. "You help Sun and I go free, and I'll be your friend forever."

"And a clerk for now, but perhaps a higher post once we've cleared up our business in Tortuga?"

It was a very generous offer. Captain Benji held out his hand, and I shook it.

CHAPTER 31.
CONTRACTS

THAT VERY night, as Sun and I went to bed, I asked him to be my matelot. He did not suffer from my ignorance of the term, having lived many years among pirates. He looked surprised that I knew the meaning enough to ask him but shook his head firmly, no.

"*Nei*, Benjamin. Then you would share my punishments. If I am taken, I will be hanged. I have killed helpless men. I will pay for that one day. I am a murderer and an escaped slave. Law will not suffer me to live, nor will the lawless."

"What was your plan once we met up with the *capitaine*? To leap overboard and swim away?"

"*Nei*. I believe that Captain Benji would hide me, for your sake. You would be useful to a man like him. Don't let him hold too much over you, Benjamin. He will expose you to dangers you would not otherwise suffer."

Apparently I was the only one who hadn't realized my value as the captain's double.

"Benji thinks that, with my guns and your crates, we'll have enough to pay for reparations to the families of the dead men."

"Material goods do not make up for taking away someone's son or brother. Someone's father," he said. I realized a trembling moved through his shoulders. His eyelashes glimmered. "I'm a killer. I deserve to be punished. I don't deserve someone so good, so full of light. I haven't earned someone like you, Benjamin. I am nothing. I am less than nothing."

"Sun...." I could not bear the pain in his voice. I took him gently into my arms, held our bodies close. "God forgives you, Sun, if you have remorse in your heart. Do you believe that God forgives you? Do you have remorse?"

He did not answer me for a long time, only held on to me, then said, "Yes. Even for the bad ones who were killers like me, Benjamin. I am so sorry. I cannot be sorry enough. Sorry will not bring back anyone."

I stroked his braids gently. "Neither will your death or punishment, Sun. Nor will your running away. By pooling our resources to give back what we can, we can do some good. And, if you can walk again proudly as Sólmundur Thorvaldson, with Benjamin Lector at your side, as your matelot, we can do a lot of good. We can free all those others you wanted to free. To stop them having to kill too. Free with papers signed by us to prove it. Isn't that still what you want?"

He was quiet, and I listened to him breathe awhile, letting him think about the idea.

"Be my matelot, Sun. Take me as your partner, and I will have you as mine. Say yes."

He said something into my chest that I couldn't hear, so I pulled back until I could see his face and he mine. His was puffy and streaked with tears. Runny nose and all, he was still the most beautiful person I'd ever seen.

"Will you have me, Sun?"

"*Já*, Benjamin. Where you go, I go."

There was nothing else to do in reply but tenderly kiss him and kiss him and kiss him until the candles burned out.

BENJI, BY the powers vested in a ship's captain, oversaw our matelot ceremony the next day. I'd wager we were the only matelots ever joined with a royal prince in attendance. Sun had risen before the dawn to make what he called "matelot knots," which were three intricately woven belts, cords linked in flat stripes that crossed both over and under each other in a way that reminded me of the engravings in a book I used to have about Irish and Scottish legends.

When Sun tied the one he'd made for me around my waist during the ceremony, it was the finest thing I'd ever seen. I lost my head completely and forgot what I was supposed to say when I put Sun's belt around his waist, and Captain Benji kindly guided me through it by whispering the words, "Do cleave to Sólmundur Thorvaldson as matelot from this day till my last day, come storm or sun, plenty or poverty, punishment and prize, through both illness and health, to share all, my sworn brethren-in-arms and bedmate, till death part us from this world." And I sheepishly repeated.

The captain bound our hands together by draping the third matelot knot over and around our clasped hands, and then Dom Miguel gave his royal blessing. Marisol, crisp and bright in her French military uniform, presented us with a leather wallet containing a matelot contract stating we shared all, a royal pardon from Dom Miguel for Sólmundur Thorvaldson, and an addendum from Captain Benjamin Swift that we were both free men and loyal crew of the *Sea Fury*, under his command, and corsairs for King Louis.

With a shaking hand, I signed the contract, and after me, Sun made his mark, which looked like a lightning bolt *S* with an upright arrow next to it. The crew cheered and passed around bottles of wine Sun had produced from one of his chests. Even Artur joined in the revelry, though he didn't congratulate us. I believe he was starting to notice some of the men were in pairs, like Cookie and Abelard, me and Sun. It didn't hurt that, when we had occasion to practice our flintlocks yesterday by shooting at refuse in the sea, I comported myself well and was a better marksman than anyone else, including Dom Miguel, Abellard, and the captain himself. Artur had occasion to be wary of us both now; nevertheless, he gave us flinty looks and did not seek our company.

However, he could not tarnish this day for me. The sun was bright, the sea calm, a gentle wind blowing puffy white clouds slowly across the sky, nudging us ever closer to Tortuga. I felt strongly that God watched us from above the open blue sky, and, though I knew not why, I had a distinct impression he was smiling. I went to my knees then and prayed with everything in my heart—thanking God for Sun and the fine friends we had found and made, whatever their strange origins and regretted sins.

Sun helped me to my feet, and the crew heartily celebrated our union with one of the best meals Cookie had ever produced—a deliciously hot dish he called curry, made with some of the spices in one of Sun's chests and served as a kind of porridge with tender bites of goat and the flat bread Cookie made only for special occasions. He and Abellard had been the first to congratulate us with hearty smacks on the back.

My head felt as though it were crammed with bits of fluff for the remainder of the day as the men sang and danced, drank wine, diced, played *tafl*, and made merry. Sun and I moved among them, as one with them, as one with each other.

We celebrated privately together that night—undressing each other slowly, touches lingering, allowing slow kissing to lead to more, exploring each other's bodies with a different, less urgent, but no less powerful passion and desire, becoming one together in our cabin, while the sounds of the crew still celebrating drifted down through the deck boards.

"Does it bother you?" Sun asked some time later as I traced his purple scar with my fingertips.

I shifted down and kissed the scar. "Only when I think of the pain it must have caused you."

He blinked his golden lashes slowly over his rain-cloud eyes, like a sated cat, watching me kiss his body. We'd exhausted ourselves by now—from the call of the watch echoing down from above decks, it was the middle of the night.

"Benjamin."

"Hmm?"

"Will you please untwine my hair?" There was a note of something young and vulnerable in his voice.

"Of course."

We rearranged ourselves—his back and my chest were healing nicely, so he fit quite comfortably in the cradle of my legs and leaned back against me. I rolled one of his blond braids between thumb and forefinger, then traced down to its tapered end to find a band of thread wound around it.

"Why do you wear your hair in braids, Sun? Why not cut it?"

He shrugged under my hands. "*Amma* always said you should not cut your own hair. Cutting your hair yourself tempts fate, she said, so I wove it instead. That kept it out of my face for fighting, and from tangles, and no one needed to come close to me with a knife or scissors."

"My Sampson." I kissed the braid and slipped off the thread band. The strands of white-blond hair were so fine beneath my fingers they felt delicate as spider's lines. It took a very long time indeed to untwine every braid, leaving a fluffy, white-blond mane behind. I reverently combed the soft, kinked hair that flowed over his shoulders like a golden raiment.

"I was wrong."

"*Ha?*"

"I've often thought you are some misplaced pagan god or lost angel. But now you appear divine—my golden angel in truth."

Sun grunted, and the sound vibrated up my chest. "A fallen angel."

"A vengeful one, perhaps, but ne'er fallen." I tilted his face to mine for a kiss, which he returned. We fell asleep in each other's arms, and I dreamed we were back on our island, in our tree house, safe and innocent of what dangers lurked before us.

CHAPTER 32.
THE END OF AN AGE

OUR JOURNEY to Tortuga was not as smooth as hoped. Though we flew the French flag, we were waylaid off the coast of Puerto Rico by a fleet bearing the Stars and Stripes, which cruised close with gunports open, and we were obliged to allow them to board the *Fury* and prove we were actually French corsairs guarding His Majesty's interests in lawful ways. Captain Benji produced the paperwork Dom Miguel and Marisol had worked so hard to create over the last few days and satisfied the commander of the *USS Grampus*, one Lieutenant Francis Gregory, who released us with a warning that any and all piratical acts would receive swift justice.

Fortunately we all had time to dress as sailors before we were boarded, including Marisol and Dom Miguel, and the good lieutenant did not inquire after each sailor, in part owing to the excellent forgeries, as well as Benji's convincing role as a French corsair out of Louisiana, complete with heavy accent. I could see why the men respected him—not only was he shrewd, straightforward, brave, and kind, the man was a consummate actor.

When the lieutenant paused for a more discerning look at my face, then Benji's, I realized enough time had passed that, with my bruises gone and my nose mostly healed, our similarity passed into twin-like status without my noticing. The oddity wasn't enough to waylay us, though. If Sun's fame as a fighter had reached so far, there was no one to recognize him. I'd captured his white-blond hair into a queue and tied it with a short, blue ribbon, but, like a playful afrit, it continued to escape and wisp about his head in the winsome sea breezes.

Captain Benji and Marisol joined me at the gunnel as we watched the distant, battle-scarred *USS Enterprise* follow us to Tortuga—for protection, they said, but more likely to ensure we were really going where we said we were.

"The American West Indies Squadron is going to make a smuggler's job harder, little brother, policing these waters so vigorously. The age of piracy, of slavery, and of the sailing ship are at an end, my friends. The *SS Savannah* has crossed the Atlantic using steam power. Soon there will be no more need for sailors at all, because there will be no need to harness the wind. Men will sail metal boxes over the sea, and machines will do all the work." Benji sounded melancholic.

"The world will always need sailors, *mon ami*." Marisol rose to her tiptoes and kissed the captain's cheek. "Who else will spread pox, clap, and pregnancy?"

"You do realize pregnancy is not the same as syphilis and gonorrhea?"

"*Oui.* There is no ointment for pregnancy."

I laughed so hard, I felt sure the sailors aboard the *Enterprise* could hear me over the bright blue water.

Sun tugged the ends of my matelot belt and gave me a sly look but didn't speak.

"Yes?" I urged him.

"I saw the way you looked at those men in uniform."

I sputtered, but I could not deny that Lieutenant Gregory and his men had cut very dashing figures in their blue jackets, red vests, and black hats all a' matching.

Sun crisply pulled the wrinkles from his jacket and then aped the posture of the military men, marching up and down the deck, swinging his arms. Catching sight of his performance, some of Captain Benji's trusties hollered encouragement, having no particular love for those enforcing the law. Abellard sang out, "Away-o! Oi-o! I'll go to join the Navy-o and set the lasses crying!" Other voices joined him, and I was delighted by a most inappropriate ballad about a young man who joined the Navy looking for adventure and found a "pinch and tickle" where he least expected it, and it wasn't from a lass. Scandalized, my face burning, I laughed and shook my head for sheer joy. I did not, however, miss a dark look from Artur manning the rudder. Whatever truce had been forged was a tenuous one, but I didn't let my concerns about him stop me from memorizing as many lines of the bawdy song as possible.

TORTUGA WAS a rocky island eight leagues in length and two in breadth, with tall palms, rust-red dirt, and, from a distance, the aspect of a great floating sea turtle, for which it was named. The small port held centuries of fortifications built by Spanish, English, and French settlers as well as navies, pirates, smugglers, and anyone else who had used the natural rocky cliffs of the sheltered southern bay as a refuge. The coastal town was packed with taverns, and Cookie said it was fed by a natural freshwater spring, which was another reason it had been used as a base so often by so many.

The narrow streets were filled with such a cacophony of dogs, sailors, horses, adventurers, pigs, whores, cats, soldiers, parrots, merchants, pet monkeys in tiny vests, and a great press of sights and sounds as to bewilder us after weeks of quiet sailing. Tortuga's governor required a payment of 10 percent of our cargo's value for the *Fury* to berth, but this custom, and the haggling thereof, Captain Benji handled with shrewdness and grace. He also bargained further repairs to the damages the *Fury* suffered from Dread Island's eruption.

After Marisol's reminder of the unpleasant diseases sailors contracted in such places and might be lingering on flea-bitten beds, Sun and I resolved to sleep aboard the *Fury* but went ashore with Marisol, Dom Miguel, Captain Benji, Abellard, Cookie, Hardanguer, Quinn, and four other hardies to guard us. We were each well outfitted with cutlass, flintlocks, knives, and personal weapons of choice, though with Sun's and Marisol's proclivities, I wasn't sure such a show of force was strictly required for our safety. We positively clanked with every step, but our display was probably a kindness and convenience to prevent the unnecessary deaths of rogues who might have attacked a smaller, less-provisioned force. Sun committing more murders was something I wanted to avoid when our fate had yet to be decided by the French *capitaine* we hoped to meet. Marisol made a few inquiries on the docks, paid some likely urchins to act as lookouts for her contact, and then led us into the town proper.

Sun stayed close to me, so tense that muscles corded on his neck and arms, jumping at every loud noise. He'd become quite comfortable among the men of the *Fury* and they around him, but after living alone on the island for so long, and surviving the horrors he experienced before escaping slavery, I could understand why being among such a press of humanity would challenge his nerves.

"Do you want to go back to the ship?"

"Where you go, I go, Benjamin," he said breathlessly.

I reached for his hand, then stopped, not wanting to make a public spectacle and endanger us.

"It's all right," Hardanguer's voice growled from behind us. "Look with the eyes in your head. We're headed for the Huîtres et Perle, and there's naught to object to such. Especially not on Tortuga, boy."

I looked around us in the press of animal and humanity coursing around our little party—indeed there were men arm-in-arm with women in a variety of scandalous states of ravishment, but also men holding hands companionably with men, and women likewise with women. I nearly tread off the boardwalk in my astonishment.

"There she be." Hardanguer pointed to a large wooden sign cut in the shape of an open oyster with a huge round pearl carved into it, sporting the gilded script Huîtres et Perle. The establishment behind was two-storied and bursting with light and song.

Marisol took Dom Miguel and Captain Benji's arms and led them inside, Abellard and Cookie behind them, and the rest of us filed in two by two. It was very different from the country taverns of my boyhood, but also from the opulence of New Orleans gin palaces and gambling establishments. The boards forming the walls of the Perle had been garishly painted in a variety of colors. However, what immediately caught the eye was the carved and decorated—gilding stripped, of course—sterns of decommissioned sailing ships forming a bank of private dining compartments on the north and south walls.

Two dark-skinned women—a mulatto and a mestizo—played a ferocious fiddle battle, accompanying each other in the center of the room, which was an open area strewn with rough-hewn tables and rougher clientele. Many were as armed to the teeth as we were, both men and women and people not easily identifiable as either gender, who all looked more or less able to defend themselves in a fight. At the moment, those who weren't heartily clapping along to the fiddlers or losing themselves in cups and loud conversation, were locking lips with a variety of colorfully dressed men and women and people I could only class as both or neither gender. The lack of specificity didn't seem to matter to anyone giving or receiving affection, so I decided not to worry about it either.

A flat bar of dark wood was a commanding presence along one wall, stacked towers of kegs of various spirits stamped with languages from around the world piled behind it, and through a rectangular widow, a kitchen full of steam and bustle. As I watched, a huge platter of boiled crabs passed through the window and was picked up by one of the brightly dressed servers, who brought it to a table of sailors. I recognized at least one couple wore a pair of matched matelot belts. I hadn't realized they were something Sun and I could wear on shore to show our commitments to each other, and I suddenly wished we'd brought them—we'd decided to remove and leave them aboard because I did not want to risk them getting muddied or frayed on land. I did capture his hand, and held it proudly in mine. The astonishment on his face at the location we presently found ourselves was much like mine. I wagered the fighting slaves were not brought out carousing with their masters, if slave masters ever went to a place such as this.

Marisol led us through the tumult, graciously avoiding disrupting the fiddle players, who, as a fellow player of no small skill myself, I must admit were possessed of most impressive talents. She approached a large African woman with a deep, friendly laugh, who spoke in a smooth Jamaican patois and guided us to one of the former ship sterns. Within, we still heard the fiddle players and the carousers quite clearly through the glass panes, but the illusion of privacy was welcome. We arranged ourselves around the table while Captain Benji ordered of one of every dish for the company to share.

"When should we expect this *capitaine* of yours?"

"As I did not see *Les Amoureux* in port, we must wait for her to finish a patrol. Captain Christophe LeFebvre will seek us here at the Perle. Until then, alas, we must find some way to amuse ourselves."

Neither she, Miguel, nor Benji looked at all dismayed by this prospect. I, on the other hand, preferred to have the matter resolved straightaway—Sun was tense as a cat with all these people around him, and I felt he'd be more comfortable out to sea. Furthermore, while we were formally members of Captain Benji's crew on board the *Fury*, which made us French corsairs under the contract created by Marisol, with a pardon for Sun from Miguel, Sun had still not been tried by an official court of law, and that was something I very much wanted as soon as possible. I prayed that our matelot contract and joint belongings were enough for reparations, and that the French governor of Tortuga, once we approached him with the official backing of the French Navy in addition to the Portuguese throne, would be swayed. If only Marisol had been born a man and could reveal herself as a royalist spy—I felt certain her connections to her powerful uncle would have been enough. Alas, as it stood, we needed this Captain LeFebvre, and I hoped he would listen.

CHAPTER 33.
L'INFANTERIE

WE PASSED the evening quite pleasantly. After eating near to bursting a variety of extremely spicy marine creatures, we discussed our plan, namely, to convince Captain LeFebvre to not only endorse Sun's pardon and give us letters of marque that had actually been signed by the king, but also to escort Dom Miguel and Marisol to Lisbon—and be royally rewarded for this service. The signed letters would allow Captain Benji and the *Fury* to immediately set sail in the name of King Louis. The paperwork from Marisol had duped the American captains, but if we had been waylaid by the French, it would not have passed muster. From the snippets of conversation I absorbed, it seemed Marisol had been in New Orleans for multiple reasons and had several other points of interest to investigate there, which would now be Captain Benji's mission, after the men had rested and reveled on Tortuga while the *Fury* was repaired and Marisol traveled with Dom Miguel.

A rolled parchment rested inside my coat—the names of the two ships that wrecked on the shoals of Dread Island, and the number and descriptions of the men Sun had killed, starting with the owners he slew to escape. He had a very clear memory and knew something distinctive about each of the deceased. How their faces must have haunted him. Creating the list had been difficult for him during our nights together in our cabin—he could neither read nor write—but since our matelot and decision to face punishment and provide reparations, Sun was determined to ensure no single family went without some recompense for these deaths. Dictating the list to me seemed to remove something heavy from him, some darkness that each name, or description when he did not know the name, drew out of him. Each remembering session exhausted him, which was why it had taken us most of the voyage, and yet his step was lighter and his laughter more frequent as he had worked and played with the crew of the *Fury*.

After dinner, and with our plans laid, the company joined the revelry continuing in the main room. Dogs, men, parrots, women, dancers, people of every sort had filled the common room full to bursting—including many men from the *Fury* who'd joined us here. Men sat on other men's laps, laughing and kissing with gusto, women doing the same, and every conceivable combination of couple, including no small number of belted matelots. Every now and then, a couple or triple or more climbed the staircase at the back to the second story, where there were beds for rent.

One fiddler was taking a rest while the other played a merry jig for the revelers, who were dancing with zest. The resting fiddler, a mulatto named Lovelie, for the loan of my flintlocks, let me borrow her instrument. It felt so good to hold the bow in my hands again—I promised myself I would acquire one as soon as we reached New Orleans—and I struck up a tune when the other fiddler paused to rest. I caught sight of Artur and two of his friends coming in late to join us, but didn't think anything of it. I had a fiddle in my hands, and I resolved not to allow his presence to trouble me. In any case, Sun kept a weather eye on him.

The fiddle was a fine one and needed very little adjustment. I played the opening bars of "The Pretty Ploughboy" and was very pleased when Black Miguel's sweet tenor rose to greet me. I nearly cried. I'd spent so much time thinking my friend had died, only to have him revealed as a royal son, which was another way of losing him. For me, Black Miguel was no more. Dom Miguel—no matter how easily he switched between nobleman and sailor—was not he, and the emotion that rose in me as I played and he sang made this the finest rendition of "Ploughboy" I'd ever performed. There were tears and laughter among our listeners, and Miguel and I clasped each other in a hug afterward. Lovelie complimented me handsomely and said I could have loan of her fiddle the rest of the evening, and Dom Miguel and I performed six more songs together, including the Portuguese "Song of the Sea," which I sang while dancing around Sun's table, before my hands started to cramp from overexertion. Dom Miguel likewise excused himself to wet his whistle and soon went upstairs together with Lovelie and a young man with large brown eyes, who'd cried during our performance.

Fortunately the other fiddler, whose name was Cuicatl, played some jolly music from the mainland that people either danced to, gambled to, or ignored while being lost in each other's eyes.

"How are you?" I sat down next to Sun with a satisfied sigh and a mug of ale.

Sun had removed his jacket. He was sweating profusely, which was strange, considering he hadn't been dancing. He glowered at the back door of the Perle and didn't answer me.

"Sun, are you all right?"

He started and stared at me. With a hand that tremored slightly, he pushed back the hair that had come free of his queue and stuck to his forehead. The white of his eyes all around his pupils was clearly visible, and his breathing was shallow, as though he were possessed by one of my father's devils.

"Let us go outside," I said, wanting nothing of the sort. "The air grows close in here." And I promptly took Sun's hand and pulled him out behind the Perle—he came along like a dog on a leash.

The relative cool of the night felt good against my face, and while the cacophony sounding from the Perle was but dimmed by our exit, the close sides of the alley felt like another world. A world that smelled of piss.

"That's better, yes?" I asked as I relieved myself into the gutter like so many others before me had done.

Sun freed his hair and pushed his hands through it, then tried to retie it, but his hands were shaking, and he lost hold of the ribbon, which drifted down onto his shoulder. He swore and stared at the strip of velvet as though it had betrayed him.

I finished and stuffed myself back in my britches. "Here, let me help you."

I finger-combed his hair, which I knew he liked, and he was tense at first, then relaxed as I moved behind him and pulled him into the circle of my arms. I continued to comb his hair until his panting quieted and the fine shaking I felt move through his body calmed.

"There," I said, pulling his fine blond hair back into a queue and tying it.

He was quiet for some time, leaning back against me.

"Sun, talk to me. *Allt* good?"

"*Nei*. There's too much…. I cannot…. I don't…."

I rubbed his back in small, soothing circles. "It's all right, Sun."

"*Nei*. It's not." He turned in my arms to look up at me, the moon lighting the planes of his face and silvering the fine, soft fuzz of his mustache-that-almost-wasn't. "I can't…. You deserve someone like Miguel. Someone who can sing and dance and…."

It was difficult to hold my tongue as he spoke, but I felt if I interrupted him, he would not be able to share all that was in his heart at this moment.

"Benjamin, I can't read or write or do sums. I can't abide a place like that… but you… you belong there, in the light, with all the people. You belong with someone like him."

"Do you remember when you brought me in from the storm?" I asked. "I was lost in the dark and the terrors, and you came for me."

"*Já*, but I'm not—"

"You took me into your cave but wouldn't come near me. I wanted you so badly. I, who barely knew anything about the joys two men could discover together."

"I…."

"Do you remember? I took off my shirt. I asked you to come and look at my wound from the boar hunt."

A small smile curved his lips. "I remember."

"I needed you so badly. I could scarce breathe for the wanting." I placed his hand on my britches, where I was hard from the memory of holding him those first nights. His breath left in a gasp as he gripped me through the cloth, and I gasped too, but kept talking. "You are the one I want, Sun. Not Dom Miguel. Not an American navy man. I want Sólmundur Thorvaldson."

"But you like…." He tilted his head toward the Perle. Dom Miguel's beautiful tenor echoed from within.

"Yes, I do like a good fiddle, to dance and sing. I'll sometimes want the sea and sometimes I'll want this." I nodded toward the Perle. "But there's one thing I'll always want." I traced my thumb over his lips. "Us being different only makes life more interesting."

He smiled and, with slow deliberation, sucked my thumb into his mouth.

I moaned, but our tryst was interrupted by a shout that echoed from around the corner of the Perle, followed by the dull, meaty thuds of fists hitting flesh. Sun and I exchanged a quick glance. He pulled his knife, and I swore as I patted my hips and realized my flintlocks were still with the fiddler. Sun gave me his pistol, and I readied the weapon as we ran down the alley behind the Perle and turned the corner into a narrow space between this tavern and the next.

Artur's red hair was unmistakable even by moonlight. A fellow held him by the kerchief and punched him in the eye while another yanked on something Artur wouldn't let go—his sailor's purse, bulging with coin.

"Oi! Leave off!" I shouted. The assailants looked up. The one punching Artur dropped his hand and came up with a knife, clearly intending to finish off Artur quickly so he and his partner could flee with the purse. I held up the pistol, sighted for the knife as best I could, making certain Sun wasn't in the way, and then I dropped the hammer. My shot flew true, the ball taking the man in the hand. He yelped and ran down the boardwalk. Meanwhile, Sun attacked the other man, slicing forward so viciously that the robber forgot all about the purse and Artur and ran after his companion. Sun started to give chase, but I called him back, because I had no ready weapon to defend myself.

Artur was a frightful mess—kneeling in a puddle of urine with his britches undone, clawing at his throat, blood running down his face from a cut over his eyebrow. His kerchief had been twisted into a garrote.

"Here now, mate," I said. "It's all right. Sun, cut this free."

My eyes met Sun's, and he seemed to question my request for the barest of moments before he joined me and sawed through the cloth. Artur sagged in my arms, breathing like a horse that had been pushed too far. I supported him over to the boardwalk so he wouldn't have to sit in the piss puddle he'd made. He leaned on all fours and heaved. Sun and I crouched in silence on either side.

As his senses returned, he buttoned up his britches and put his purse away. When he caught his breath, he croaked out, "Why?" His eyes burned darkly, and he looked at us with mingled astonishment and suspicion.

I didn't know what to say, because I didn't truly know. I'd acted without thinking.

Sun filled the silence. "You may be a goat turd, but you're our goat turd."

I could not help but laugh, and that set Sun off too, and even Artur joined us for a rasping chuckle. I gave him my kerchief to clean the blood from his face, and we helped him to his feet.

"You two should go back to the ship," he said with a shaky voice. "It's not safe around here."

I reloaded Sun's flintlock and passed it back to him. "I think we'll do all right."

Artur nodded, his eyes darting to the door of the Perle and back to us, then down at the boardwalk and back to the ship. He scowled, and his eyes were wide. "I think… I'll go back."

"All right, then. We'll walk you."

He waved his arm, staving us off, shoved his hands in his pockets, and all but ran down the boardwalk toward the bay and where the *Fury* was moored.

"That was odd," I remarked as Sun nodded his agreement. We watched his retreating back until he disappeared in the darkness.

"Do you want to go back now?" I asked Sun, hoping the answer was no. He smiled at me, took my hand, and led me back inside the Perle.

I CONVINCED Sun to join me in playing several games of chance with other matelots who seemed friendly and open for conversation. Naturally I was very curious about their stories, so I asked how they had come to be matelots. Each one was different—sailors who'd found each other in navies but left to become privateers so they could be matelots; buccaneers who'd first captured their matelot as a booty; a few of Chaucer's January/May captain-and-cabin-boy matelots also, but most were simply men who had met each other and fallen in love, like Sun and I had. It was both strange and wonderful to be able to tell them about us, hear their stories, and, for once in my life, feel as though I weren't a creature sprung unnaturally formed from nowhere and nothing.

We stayed very late indeed. Dom Miguel commenced on a second adventure upstairs, then a third, each with different partners or sets of partners, and then joined us for wine and sang several songs in a Portuguese so badly slurred I could barely recognize the curse words. His head was not going to be kind to him in the morning. When it was time to return to the ship, most of us were quite deep in our cups. I was rather unsteady, but Marisol and Sun had both forgone drink, by design I guessed.

I exchanged handshakes and quick embraces with several of the matelots we had met, and then Captain Benji led us, somewhat crookedly, back into the street as we shouted our loud compliments to the owner, who happened to be the Jamaican woman, and she laughed back at us and told us in her wonderful deep-voice patois to come again tomorrow.

The number of both people and animals was greatly reduced as our party made its way down the nighttime boardwalks. And if not for the loud, drunken singing that was heralding forth from some of the taverns we passed, Tortuga in moonlight shimmered peacefully, her riot of colors softened by the dark.

They were waiting for us at the *Fury*. Our sailors stood guard at the gangplank, but there was a crush of soldiers around them—Haitian *infanterie* all in black uniforms with red piping and gold chevrons, a few of them mulatto, the rest black Africans.

"Which of you is Captain Swift?" asked the lieutenant. I noticed the men with coloring like mine and Benji's were officers.

"He be I. I mean, I be he." Captain Benji stepped forward. "I'm Swift." His back was straight, but there was a weave in his step. He'd drunk rather more wine than me, and I was none too steady myself. "What be the meaning of this?"

"We've heard on authority you have a killer and escaped slave among you."

A hand of ice trailed down my spine and fisted in my gut. I glanced up to the deck of the *Fury*, suspicion crawling on the skin behind my ears. Artur and his too-fat purse was nowhere to be seen.

"Sirs. This is Tortuga. There's an escaped slave or killer on every corner. You'll have to be more shpashific. Pacific. Specific."

"A white. Sólmundur Thorvaldson, wanted for the murder of those who purchased him and others after his escape, I'm told. These men here are being less than helpful in locating him." He frowned at the *Fury* sailors blocking his way up the gangplank.

"I, sir, am a Portuguese pri—" Dom Miguel finished his sentence by vomiting over the edge of the dock. Nausea roiled in my stomach and saliva flooded my mouth. Captain Benji and Dom Miguel's wits were fuddled by wine, and mine weren't too sharp at the moment either. Of the present company, the three of us were best at talking our way out of a situation with the Haitian guard. But I became suddenly aware we were each too soaked to do so.

Sun stirred next to me. "Don't!" I threw both arms around him and held him tight to my body.

"What's that scuffling there?" My motion had drawn the attention of the soldiers, who shone their lantern on us both. I yanked Sun with me toward the water, intending to jump in and swim for freedom. Several soldiers brought their long guns to bear on us.

"Stop." Sun's voice was calm and clear. "I am Sólmundur Thorvaldson."

"What are you doing?" I asked desperately as the soldiers advanced on us.

"It's time to stop running from what I've done, Benjamin. It is time to pay."

"No, Sun. We need the *capitaine*'s support first."

"You will get it for us. I trust you." He held his arms out to the soldiers to be shackled.

I intercepted, slapping the shackles to the ground, and a soldier pushed me roughly away. Marisol pulled me back, or I would have gotten a rifle butt in the face. "Stop, Benjamin. It will be easier if we don't have to get you both from *la prison*."

"No! You are not taking him from me. He is my matelot!"

"Shut up, Benjamin." Marisol jabbed me in the back. "He's drunk," she told the lieutenant.

"Where he goes, I go. We have a contract. There was a ceremony."

"No, Benjamin. Go find the *capitaine*," Sun said.

The lieutenant in command narrowed his eyes at me. "Is this true? You own this white man?"

"He's not a slave. He's a free man and my matelot. His punishment is my punishment, his debt, mine. I will not suffer him to be parted from me. Till death part us from this world."

"You might get your wish. Take him."

"Oh, Benjamin." Sun's voice was sad.

They shackled us both and took us away. I looked over my shoulder at our companions—Dom Miguel still retching into the bay, Marisol looking very grave indeed, Hardanguer and the other sailors grumbling angrily among themselves, and Captain Benji waving.

"Don't worry, *cher*!" Benji, his words slurred, called after us. "We will sort this."

CHAPTER 34.
PRAYERS

THE SOLDIERS escorted us up a narrow channel through the rock to reach the fort on the hill overlooking the bay. Two twelve-pound cannons stood as sentinels atop the rock, ready to cannonade anyone rushing the fort. Men would have to pass up the cleft two by two if they made it past the twelve pounders and then could be easily picked off by musket fire.

Larger cannons, two hull-shattering twenty-four pounders and one thirty-two pounder, which must have been decommissioned from a warship, sat nestled against the fortification on the edge of the cliff, and would give any ship firing from the bay pause, assuming attacking forces were able to penetrate the bay, which housed Haitian warships also. I understood even more deeply what made Tortuga a desirable stronghold—defensible by sea and ground, with a natural source of clean spring water. Blockade and siege would be the only significant threat, and the amount of animals I'd seen in town would be enough to feed the fort for some time, not to mention the sounders of pigs I was sure had been husbanded in the interior jungle of the island.

"Benjamin, what are you doing?" Sun asked in a hushed voice as the soldiers thrust us through the postern gate and into the fort proper.

"Where you go, I go," I said stubbornly, though I was realizing it would have, perhaps, been more intelligent to stay with the others where I could be of some use to Sun on the outside. Inside, I was as useless as usual. Actually, being inside might be the best plan, because this would at least keep my ineptitude from slowing down the rest of our friends.

I stopped, then was pushed roughly forward down the last few stairs into a small eight-cell jail that smelled like piss and vomit. *Our friends.* When had I started thinking of Marisol and Benji as friends? Black Miguel had been a friend, but when had Dom Miguel become one? And Hardanguer and Cookie and the rest? I examined my feelings as the soldiers put Sun and I in a two-man cell with an empty bucket and some musty hay.

Perhaps because we'd put up no struggle at all, the soldiers removed our shackles, gave us a second bucket of water with a tin cup, and one wool blanket each. I used mine as a pad and sat against the wall. Compared to our previous accommodations aboard Edwin's *Fury*, I felt almost as though I should offer the soldiers coin for our stay. However, thinking of Sun and my first imprisonment together reminded me of Martio, and what he had done to me, and how I had killed him for it. Perhaps I did belong in a cell. I was a murderer too, and were my reasons so different from Sun's? We'd both defended ourselves in our own battles.

"You're so quiet, Benjamin. What are you thinking about?" Sun put his blanket down next to mine and joined me in leaning back against the stone wall.

I shook my head, thinking he didn't need to bear my burdens when he had his own, but then he put his hand over mine, I clasped it, and moonlight flooding in through the high, barred window left a stripe of light across our entwined fingers. We were matelots now. That meant sharing everything, including a troubled mind.

"I was thinking of the last time we were imprisoned together."

"And Martio."

I nodded. This was the first time I'd heard him say Martio's name with such little emotion. I studied him—the sharp angles of his face had softened somewhat from eating Cookie's meals, and his braids were now a white-blond cascade tied back by my ribbon. He looked older, civilized in his modern dress, calm and collected. The savage fire that had burned behind his eyes when I had met him was banked.

"You've changed," I said tactlessly. I realized I was still drunk and apologized. "I'm sorry. I didn't mean...."

"No. You are right, Benjamin. I have changed. You showed me something better than my island—your companionship, your love. And then you showed me something bigger than the two of us. The friendship of men. I had forgotten what it was like to be part of a crew. The *Fury* reminded me what it feels like to be one of many. And meeting those other matelots at the Perle... meeting all those people who are different, who are like us...."

He ran out of words and pressed my hand to his lips. I knew what he meant. Tonight had been beyond anything I'd yet experienced. I had been in public, honest about what and who I was, who I loved, with others living their true selves openly as well, doing what I did best—playing the fiddle, gambling, making friends. And, well, as present circumstances showed, getting others into trouble.

I moaned. "What are we going to do?"

Sun pulled me into his arms. I lay on my side and rested my head on his chest. The blue coat was scratchy against my cheek—I much preferred us both naked, but I dared not undress him when soldiers could come and take us away at any moment.

"This is God's will, Benjamin." Sun's voice was quiet and resolute. He rested his chin on the top of my head.

"What do you mean?" I decided not to tell him my suspicions that Artur's purse had been so fat because he had informed the government we were here, not if Sun finally wanted to talk of God and God's will.

"When I saw the soldiers and I felt calm, I knew it was time."

Was he talking about some kind of epiphany? "I still don't understand."

He stroked my hair, which was long enough now to be an unruly mess of curls but not long enough to be ribboned. "The time for answering for what I have done is here. This night is the test before the dawn. Tomorrow I will know how God has judged me."

"This is my fault, Sun."

"Why do you say this?"

"If I'd chosen the island, if I'd only gone back to the tree house with you, none of this would have happened. This is a poor way of thanking you for saving my life. I would be dead without you, and now because I've convinced you that God is a forgiving God, here we are. Perhaps facing our deaths." Would Tortuga's governor condemn us both? What did our contract mean for him?

Sun kissed my forehead. "You're wrong, Benjamin. I took you from the beach, gave you water, food, but you were the one who saved me. It was an animal, a murdering beast that took you into its cave because of a need for human touch. But you taught me so much—showed me so much that I was missing. Not simply another person to share my life with, but a whole world I had turned myself away from. A self I had locked away. You freed me. Saved me."

I sighed against his chest, then hugged him.

"Pray with me?" he asked, his voice rumbling against my ear.

I nodded and kissed him, and then we placed our folded blankets in the streaming moonlight and looked up into the barred, silver face of the moon, as though it were God's eye. We went through the Lord's Prayer together aloud, then each prayed silently, holding hands. Night deepened further, and I realized he was right—the governor must have already been abed when we'd been arrested. Our arraignment would wait until the dawn.

I prayed for God's forgiveness of my sins, of Sun's sins, and for acceptance of our love. I prayed for Dom Miguel and Marisol and Captain Benji. I prayed for Abellard and Cookie and Hardanguer and Quinn. I even prayed for Edwin's and Martio's souls. I prayed for the men Marisol had killed helping us, the men who died in the mutiny, all the men who had died coming to Sun's island. I prayed for Lovelie and Cuicatl and the patrons and the owner of the Perle, whose name I either never knew or had forgotten. I prayed for my father's soul and that he would understand I loved Sun, and even with all the other things we both were, we were good men with remorse and caring for our fellow man, deserving of happiness and life. And most of all, I prayed that last was true.

BRIGHT TROPICAL sunshine streaming in from our narrow window woke me, and I blinked, expecting a headache that wasn't there. Sun and I had drunk deeply from the cool spring water the soldiers left us, and it had not only worked to refresh and sober me somewhat during our late-night vigil, but it also must have been a tonic against pot verdugo, because I felt well, if a bit stiff as we roused ourselves.

Sun was curled under my arm, tight against my side, straw in his hair and a peaceful expression on his face as he blinked slowly awake. His eyes were the light gray-blue of a dawning sky when the sunlight touched them. Perfection. He was my cherub. I wanted to kiss him and never stop, but I heard the sound of approaching boots.

Ten soldiers marched into the jail, with one lieutenant, filling the narrow spaces between the cells as we got to our feet. I thought the number a bit excessive for only two prisoners. Their black uniforms were meticulously lint-free and pressed, brass and braid all in order—a clean-shaven, professional lot. I didn't recognize any of them from the night before. A duty change, perhaps.

"Benjamin Lector?" the lieutenant addressed us.

"Aye," I said.

"Sólmundur Thorvaldson?"

"*Já.*" Sun brushed the hay from his coat.

"You're to come with us to be seen before the governor."

"Well, no time like the present," I quipped.

"Do you wish to refresh yourselves?"

I said yes, and a soldier came forward with a pail of water and a shaving knife and cream. Another approached with a buffed tin that served as a mirror. Sun and I cleaned up. He didn't need a shave, but the shadow was dark on my cheeks, and I was glad of the chance to look my most respectable. I could do nothing about the wild state of my curls except wet my hands and comb them as flat as I could make them. We were both shipshape in short order. I thanked the soldiers with heartfelt gratitude. They shackled us again, nevertheless.

"Lead on," I said, and the twelve of us left the jail.

CHAPTER 35.
SUN'S STORY

THE FORT yard in the morning light was somewhat less striking and forbidding than the night before. The artillery was still impressive, but the cannons looked smaller and less intimidating in the sunshine. The fort itself was small, little more than the governor's two-story great house with a stone tower at the end from which we'd emerged. The fortifications were high enough to protect the cannonade and governor's manse, but no larger than that. A well-defensible fortress, but small.

We were marched along to the front of the house—where an old, wide bearded fig tree provided shade on the front lawn, which was more bare dirt than tufts of grass—to a white breakfast table. An elderly mulatto gentleman sat on a cushioned chair, a plate of croissants and butter before him and an equally elderly floppy-eared dog resting by his heels. Two servants, both mulatto, were nearby with tea service and folded, white hand towels.

He did not trouble himself to rise as we were brought, clanking softly, before him, though the dog lifted her head to regard us questioningly with her droopy eyes, one brow lifted, then the other, before she lost interest.

"Join me." The governor's voice belied his age—he sounded much older than he looked, the sound a thin, crackling parchment. His hair was much curlier than mine, the tight curls of our black ancestors, but his skin was paler, either from parentage, old age, lack of sunlight, or all three. I exchanged a look with Sun, and we both sat in the chairs soldiers pulled out for us, Sun more gracefully than myself in the shackles, but I managed not to embarrass us by pitching over.

"I am Jean-Gerard du'Martinique," he said, buttering a croissant and waving over one of the servants, who I now realized looked so like the old man they must be his sons or, more likely, grandsons. He motioned that we be unshackled and served tea. The lieutenant saw to the first with hesitation, the grandson the second with speed.

When we were unshackled and served croissants, du'Martinique spoke again. "I have the pleasure of being governor of this small outpost by grace of President Boyer of the new Republic of Haiti." He observed us with shrewd eyes. I felt as though his gaze penetrated both my past and my future. "Tell me, lads, why are we having breakfast together today?"

Sun and I exchanged another look. "Because of your kindness, good sir?" I asked.

He nodded and pursed his lips appreciatively. "Lieutenant Jean-Giselle tells me murderers sit before me. Is this so?"

I put down the croissant I had been about to eat. I knew there would be no dissembling with this old man. "I have killed men, yes. We were imprisoned and attacked by a Brazilian and an Englishman. I killed them both, and another man besides, in the mutiny that allowed us to come here."

"A man might defend himself with lethal force when beset by lethal foes," he said, considering his tea and taking a slow sip.

Silence stretched, and then Sun spoke. "I have killed men. The first were men I did not know, when I fought as a slave in the pits. My total was forty and three, before I took the wound that nearly killed me."

I realized I had never asked Sun to describe more about his terrible scar. I heard the soldiers shifting behind us and was certain if I looked at them, I would see hands to sabers and muskets. Unperturbed, Sun continued in his soft, even voice.

"Two Spaniards bought me for very little from Martio when no one else wanted me because it was certain I would die. They had a mulatto-mestizo *brujo* slave, who gently healed me. When I could fight again, the Spaniards set me to the pits every night for a week, where I killed seven more. When the *brujo* complained they should allow me to rest, they beat him. One Spaniard was drunk and beat him so badly his eye came forth from his face. The *brujo* bled out on the floor, cursing them and drawing signs in his blood. We left that place in a hurry, but after my cage was loaded aboard the ship, I discovered the door was not locked. In the dead of night, I crept out of the hold and onto the deck without being seen. We were out on the open water, but I could see the shadow of land in the moonlight, so I leaped in the water and swam. Better to drown than to go back to the pits."

The governor motioned that our teas should be refreshed, which both grandsons had neglected, being fully engaged in Sun's story. He then waved that Sun should continue.

"I came to shore and hid in the forest. The Spaniards followed me, sending men onto the island looking for me. I killed them, in ones and twos, until no one else would come ashore. Finally the two Spaniards came because, even injured, I won them many doubloons. They liked to fight me naked so those who were wagering could see my scars." He pointed to his crotch, where I knew the purple scar was. The soldiers shifted uncomfortably behind us again, though I thought for a rather different reason now.

"I killed them and the six men they brought with them. I hid the bodies in the caves and used their blood to paint the symbols the *brujo* used on the beach nearest the ship. I hid in the forest and watched. When the remaining men aboard at last sent a boat to check on their captain, they saw the symbols and left instead."

"Well, lad, that is quite a—"

"I'm not finished."

"Sun, don't you think you—"

"I will finish, Benjamin."

I closed my mouth and let him go on. The dog, who the old man called Belle, watched us with her expressive, droopy eyes. Governor du'Martinique gave her a croissant, which she snapped up with the agility of an alligator.

"I never saw the Spanish ship again. The island was part of a shoal. Two merchant ships foundered there, the Portuguese *Donzela* and the French *Gros Bourse*. When the survivors washed up on the beach, I hunted and killed them. When Benjamin's ship, the *Sea Swift*, foundered on the shoal, I hunted and killed the men who survived. This is a list of their names and descriptions." Sun produced the manuscript we had worked so hard on together. One of the governor's grandsons passed it to his grandfather, who looked over it carefully.

Silence fell again. No one spoke. The governor buttered another croissant.

"And this man here? Benjamin Lector. He survived the shipwreck. Why not kill him?"

"I...." Sun's voice faltered for the first time. A red blush rushed up his neck, across his cheeks, and tinged his forehead pink under his tan.

"He was—I... that is.... Well... he's very handsome." Sun determinedly did not look at me. "And he... was so helpless."

It was my turn to feel heat across my cheeks. Ah well, one battle would be enough to show these soldiers and this venerable old man the truth of Sun's words. I fiddled with my teacup and decided to have a talk later with Sun about his rather forthright honesty.

"I'd wager he reminded you of that *brujo* who healed you?" the governor asked kindly.

Sun nodded. "*Já*. When I first saw him on the beach, I was confused. I thought it was he, but as Benjamin searched the island for water, I recognized he was not the *brujo*. As I watched him, I felt—I could not kill him. I waited for him to die. But then I could not allow him to die either. So I saved him."

I couldn't repress searching out Sun's hand with my own and squeezing his fingers. He fell silent, and I elaborated on Sun's story, telling of Martio and my former business partner's arrival, their forced enslavement of us, then of the men aboard the ship mutinying and us coming to be here. I left out the guns, but told him we had trade goods, since the governor already knew some of our resources because of the tax we'd paid to berth here and the deals we'd made to repair the *Fury*. I didn't want him to know a ship loaded with a double cargo of weapons sat in his port, nor that a Portuguese prince, a French spy, and a famous American smuggler were aboard. I did, however, tell him about our matelot contract and that I would share all Sun's punishment, but I would not suffer him nor myself to be made a slave.

"You are in the territory of the new Republic of Haiti, lad. Slavery is outlawed here, but so is murder. Furthermore, though we say no man's status is determined by the color of his skin, a white man's life does not count for much here. Saving the life of a mulatto does. And a white man who was a slave adds another complexity. Nevertheless, you have many murders to answer for." He stood suddenly and stretched, and Belle got laboriously to her feet. "You've given me much and more to think on. It's a small and rough land I rule, but rule I must, and justice is my responsibility."

He told a grandson to set the trial for noon today and wandered off to the seawall with Belle following him. The boys, who must have doubled as clerks as well as tea service, picked up the breakfast trays and made for the house.

Our audience at an end, Sun and I were shackled and escorted back to the small jail. I thought the soldiers were a good deal more battle ready and cautious of Sun, but they were as courteous with us as they had been before. Our shackles were removed again, and we were given freshwater and put back in our cell to wait.

"Why didn't you tell me all this, about the Spaniards and the *brujo*?" I asked Sun after we'd washed the croissant crumbs from our hands and faces.

Sun flushed pink again. "I didn't want you to know that I, uh, had found him handsome, and that you reminded me of him. I didn't want you to feel—less."

I pursed my lips. "That's ridiculous." I hoped my jealousy didn't show on my face. "Why would I feel less?"

Sun shrugged and sat cross-legged on his blanket. I plunked down beside him. "Was he, er, very good at, ah, healing?" I imagined the man touching Sun in that area and felt myself frowning.

Sun took my hands, smiling and shaking his head. "Benjamin. We might be killed at noon today, and you want to know about my past lovers?"

I spluttered until Sun kissed me, a long, wet, and searching kiss.

When he let me come up for air, he said, "How do you say it in English? None of them are fit to hold the candle for you, my Benjamin."

He threaded his fingers through my hair and pulled my face down to his again. And we kissed, and I wanted our skin together, but I was afraid the soldiers would come and look in upon us, so I had to content myself with my hands under his shirt, in his britches, finding him hard and ready for my touch. I brought him to the edge of ecstasy with my hands, then quickly took him in my mouth. After I swallowed his seed, he pulled my face back to his and kissed me again, hard, and I had to force my own hands away from my britches, because I wanted my staff against my matelot's skin like nothing else in this world.

The strength in my hands and arms melted to nothing when Sun knelt and clasped my wrists and held my arms at my thighs. He unbuttoned each button of my britches with his teeth, holding me still, looking up at me between each tug. My fear that the soldiers would come at any moment made each unbuttoning a torture that stole my breath. When he swallowed my staff to the hilt, and I felt his throat close and grab around the head of me, I lasted not a moment, but exploded with pleasure in his mouth, biting my lip to keep from shouting his name. He looked up at me with lazy eyes, purring my name, and I came again, and he laughed and captured my staff with his hands until I was fully spent.

He buttoned me back together as I lay panting, then tenderly washed us both with a corner of the blanket. I was glad my suit was black, because if I'd been wearing white, I would have gone to our trial with the stains of our lovemaking visible to all. At the moment, however, I didn't really care. Sun curled against me, kissed my forehead, and held me in his arms.

"My Benjamin," he whispered, stroking my hair. We stayed like that until we heard the sounds of boots on the stairs. A distant bell rang out twelve strokes.

It was time.

CHAPTER 36.
THE TRIAL

SUN AND I emerged holding hands, squinting in the sudden bright light of tropical noon. The fort yard now held a large number of people—Captain Benji, who had shed his captain's coat and hat in the heat, was foremost, sweat stains down the sides of his shirt. Frowning, he looked rather worse for wear. Dom Miguel stood next to him, dressed in a cravat and black suit, looking every inch the prince, though he was rather pale, and I wagered his head hurt him mightily in addition to his boiling alive in the heat. Marisol was there in the blue tails and white pants of the French Navy, looking crisp. Beside her stood a tall, slender, long-faced French *capitaine*, whose short, dark blond hair stood up like so many sheaves of chopped wheat. His clean and pressed uniform marked him as Christophe Lefebvre of *Les Amoureux*, for whom we'd been waiting. Seeing them didn't surprise me, but what did surprise me was Abellard and Cookie, Hardanguer and Quinn, and the rest of the crew of the *Fury*, including Artur, who looked guilty enough for confession.

Moreover, behind them was the African Jamaican owner of the Perle, Lovelie, with Cuicatl beside her, both in pretty dresses and matching parasols. With them were many matelots we'd met yesterday, all the servers, and a whole collection of other people I hadn't remembered ever meeting. It was as though all the riot of Tortuga had tried to fit inside the fort yard, and only the animals—barring a few colorful parrots and playful monkeys who stayed near their owners—had been kept out. The press of humanity far outnumbered the soldiers, and I was uncomfortably reminded of how most of the population of the town I grew up in turned out for a hanging. Lack of public entertainment here must be similar, and no government had ever discouraged their subjects from seeing the punishment for crime being carried out.

Then I saw it, the gallows against the back wall, which I had not noticed until now. It was a repurposed mast and yardarm, and though no noose currently hung from it, I assumed one could be fitted with speed. My mouth went suddenly dry. I eyed the cannons, well-manned with soldiers, as if they expected trouble. The twenty soldiers in attendance, which must have been most of the small garrison, were armed and looked more than ready to defend themselves. I sent a few more prayers heavenward.

The governor's little white breakfast table had been placed next to the gallows, and the old man stood behind it, his hound, Belle, and grandsons in attendance. This time one of them sat at the table with pen and parchment, clearly our scribe for the proceedings.

"Today we try Benjamin Lector and Sólmundur Thorvaldson, confessed murderers, by the mantle of governorship and the burden of the duty of justice laid on me by President Jean-Pierre Boyer, first of his name, of the Republic of Haiti, also first of its name." The old man's voice, despite its rasping thinness, rang throughout the yard. No one spoke, not even a parrot.

"I have a list here of the slain." He produced the papers Sun and I had given him at breakfast. "Though there are at least fifty additional names to be laid before Mr. Thorvaldson when he was under the bonds of slavery. Do you deny these charges?"

Sun stepped forward, his back straight. "No, I do not deny having killed those men."

There was an angry murmuring among the crowd.

I hastened to follow Sun's example and also stepped forward. "I too, do not deny the deaths that are my responsibility and claim them before God and men."

Governor du'Martinique nodded. "Who will speak for the slain?"

No one stirred.

The governor stepped forward. "Then that burden falls to me. The fifty slain by Mr. Thorvaldson while under the bonds of slavery were slain in single combat in the fighting pits, yes?"

"Sometimes they would send two or three at me at a time, sir, but *já*. Many were in single combat."

The angry murmuring at the mention of slave fights hushed, and an appreciation of Sun's battle prowess seemed to settle on the crowd.

Governor du'Martinique cleared his throat. "Being slaves, they were compelled to fight, as you were. They did not deserve the cruel deaths they were given."

Though we were shackled again, I longed to take Sun's hand.

"No, sir," Sun said steadily.

"And the other names on this list—slave owners, but also the sailors and merchants of the Portuguese *Donzela* and the French *Gros Bourse* ships who found themselves on the island where you took up residence."

"I killed them too, sir."

More murmuring scattered through the crowd, and I heard the name "Dread Island" more than once.

"Did they deserve death?"

"No, sir."

No man deserved to die, but a man who plays with crocodiles should expect to be bit, my grandfather had said. I prayed that God might make me sorrier that Sun had killed his cruel owners, because I was having trouble doing it by myself.

"Who will speak for Benjamin Lector and Sólmundur Thorvaldson?"

Captain Benji, Dom Miguel, Marisol, and Captain LeFebvre stepped forward. The crew of the *Fury* shuffled behind them, as if they wanted to step forward too, but there wasn't room for all of them to fit.

Emotion rose as a lump in my throat and stung my eyes, but I managed to force it back down.

Captain Benji started. "I met these two while investigating someone tarnishing my good name." He paced back and forth. "An Englishman named Edwin James, who was a harsh captain, and a Brazilian slave master with brutal ways did imprison and torture both of these men, which, as ship's cook and surgeon, I was called upon to treat the wounds they suffered. Under duress, Captain James forced them to sign themselves into slavery. Their rising up and killing of these men was in defense of their very lives."

Marisol came forward. "I witnessed the deaths of Edwin James and Martio de Fortaliza. It was self-defense, as were the deaths of the other men of their crew."

The soldiers looked at both her and the *capitaine* with mistrust—bad blood from Haiti's revolution—and I hoped her testimony would help rather than hurt us. Also, she wasn't being strictly truthful. The men she'd slain freeing me and Sun hadn't had a chance to cry out, much less draw a weapon to defend themselves, but I didn't quibble.

"I led the mutiny to take the ship and my good name back," Captain Benji said, walking up and down the small space before the gallows.

"Is this man a relation of yours?" the governor asked what must have been foremost in the audience's mind, seeing how much Benji and I resembled each other.

Benji came close to me and stood by my side so everyone could get a good look at how alike we were. "Not as I know of, Gov'ner. I'd never seen him before, but there are stranger things that have happened. Many of us don't know the families from whence we came, nor the homelands where they were born. But I would claim this man as brother, no matter how he looked. He's a good man, righteous and true."

The knot rose in my throat again. Benji clapped me on the back.

"There's not a man nor woman of Tortuga who does not know you well, Captain Swift, and who does not know your word is good. Very well. By this testimony, Benjamin Lector was defending himself. However, the sailors and merchantmen not engaged in combat or mutiny who were slain by Mr. Thorvaldson still need answering with justice. What say any of you to that?"

Dom Miguel stepped forward. "As I attempted to say last night," he said, glaring around at the Haitian soldiers, "I am Miguel Maria do Patrocínio João Carlos—" He took a breath and continued. "—Francisco de Assis Xavier de Paula Pedro de Alcântara—" He took another breath. "—António Rafael Gabriel Joaquim José Gonzaga Evaristo."

Someone in the crowd giggled and was shushed.

"I am the son of Doña Carlota Joaquina of Spain and João Maria José Francisco Xavier de Paula Luís António Domingos Rafael de Bragança—" He took a breath. "—also known as King John IV, King of the United Kingdom of Portugal, Brazil, and the Algarves."

No one tittered at the Portuguese penchant for long royal names this time. Lovelie's eyes grew wide as saucers.

"As a prince of Portugal, it is within my happy power to pardon murderers. This I do, in the case of Sólmundur Thorvaldson, who, at the time, believed he was in danger for his life by suffering the shipwrecked to live. Therefore, and for service rendered to the Portuguese Crown, I grant him clemency."

"Have you proof of your lineage?" Governor du'Martinique asked.

Dom Miguel fished inside his shirt and produced a heavy gold signet ring on a chain. He pulled it over his neck and handed it to the governor for inspection.

"These are indeed the Portuguese royal arms."

The crowd murmured in astonishment, and the aged governor seemed nonplussed for a moment, then gave the ring back to Dom Miguel.

"This may be so, but you are on Tortuga now, Your Highness. The royalty of Europe no longer rules us here, but rather the President of the Republic of Haiti."

"Were those killed citizens of Haiti?" Dom Miguel asked.

The governor looked down at the list. "No."

"I submit that the lion's share of the dead are Portuguese and Brazilian. It is my duty to see to justice for them, and I am of a mind that paid reparations will be more of a boon to the families they left behind than this man's death. I require trade goods in the equivalence of one hundred Portuguese gold royals for each man."

There were gasps at the amount. Marisol swore in French. Only I knew that the number was equivalent to both shipments of guns and much of the chests of trade goods Sun had. We could pay it, but there would be, as Sun would say, not enough to plug a cat's nostril after.

"There are the French to consider as well."

"I am Captain Christophe LeFebvre of the French ship *Les Amoureux*. I speak for the men of the *Gros Bourse*. I will not have it said they are worth any less than the Portuguese, and I too think asking for the death of this man will not help their families. We require trade goods equivalent of one hundred gold francs for each Frenchman on the list." Captain LeFebvre's voice was a high tenor. If Marisol would consider the receipt Benji had drawn up for the powder we used to blow the volcano as another equivalency, we might be able to pay for those also, but it would require the remainder of Sun's chests.

"Very well. I rule the English and Spanish deaths were in self-defense. However, there remains a name unaccounted for here, one Erik Gunnarsson."

Sun spoke. "I am Eiríkur's killer. By old Norse law, *réttdræpur* means I am rightfully killable. Let he who would claim justice come forward and kill me. Whomever does so, I ask that he pay one hundred Danish kronur to Gunnar, father of Eiríkur."

Silence met these words. No one in the crowd seemed anxious to challenge Sun to a duel on Erik's behalf. The governor let the silence stretch for some time. I worried one of the young soldiers would want to try his hand, but no one spoke.

"Very well. In absence of Danish or Norse representation, this course accepts this *réttdræpur* as a ruling." The elderly gentleman pronounced the

Nordic term admirably. "Sólmundur Thorvaldson, do you have the funds with which to pay the reparations requested by Portugal and France?"

Sun and I exchanged a glance, and I spoke. "I am in a matelot contract with this man, which are recognized on Tortuga?"

"Indeed."

"Then together, we possess the goods to pay Captain LeFebvre and Dom Miguel and request that they see to it the proper amounts reach the families of the men on these lists. Mr. Thorvaldson and I will see the payment to Gunnar is made under the eye of Captain Swift."

Captain Benji winced at the prospect of sailing to Sun's home, which he'd shared with me was an inhospitable-sounding place called Iceland, but did not naysay us.

"Very well. By the mantle of governorship of Tortuga and the burden of the duty of justice laid upon me by President Jean-Pierre Boyer, first of his name, of the Republic of Haiti, also first of its name, I do sentence Sólmundur Thorvaldson to reparations to the families of the dead as we have discussed here and one hundred lashes."

The crowd grumbled at the pronouncement, and the men of the *Fury* and the friends we had made on Tortuga did so angrily—Artur included—and I hoped they murmured because Sun was going to be whipped, not because they didn't think it was fair we weren't being hanged.

"Tortuga is not a safe haven for murderers, and I will not have it said that it is." The governor spoke sternly. "He'll take his hundred lashes and count himself lucky to have his life. Anyone who murders on this soil will face swift justice, even with the history of this port as a pirate stronghold." The old man's parchment-thin voice held a note of iron hardness.

I stepped forward. "As matelot to this man, I gladly share his punishment and request that half of it be laid across my back."

"That is within the rights of your matelot contract."

I remembered the pain of the single lash I'd taken from Martio's whip across my chest and tried to convince my bowels not to turn to water at the prospect of fifty.

Captain Benji stepped forward. "I'll share some of that as well. These men are under contract with me as corsairs. As their captain, they are my responsibility."

The lump was back in my throat. I wanted to tell him no, that the lashes were for me and Sun alone, but I couldn't get words out around it.

"Aye. Benjamin and Sun are our shipmates. We'll share in that too." Hardanguer's gruff voice rang out, and he and Quinn stepped forward. Followed by Abellard, Cookie, and the rest of the crew of the *Fury*, including Artur, who held his head high. Curiously, the matelot couples we'd met the night before stepped forward also.

"*Nei*, you cannot!" Sun said.

"Aye, lad. We can and we will. Now shut your trap and take off your shirt. We're brothers now, in truth," Hardanguer said.

The lump welled up and forced tears from my eyes and down my cheeks. With everyone sharing the lashes, it would be two per man. I stood before God and men and cried like a child, until Sun hugged me, and then I bawled harder. There was no safe place in this world for Sun and me, but there were safe people, and we had found them, and they knew us, and we knew them, and together there was hope for something better for all of us.

CHAPTER 37.
LES AMOUREUX

GOVERNOR DU'MARTINIQUE commanded the lashings be delivered on the spot, and the men of the *Fury* and the matelots we had met stripped off their coats and shirts and lined up against the stone wall. I noticed from the scars that many of them had borne whippings before, as lashes were the common punishment aboard ship. None were as severe as Sun's, whose scarred back showed the savagery of his previous owners and the fighting pits, and caused the crowd to murmur again.

A large, dark-skinned soldier was given the whip, and he did due diligence to his assignment, delivering one lash to each man in order, then a second. In most cases the lash didn't break the skin, but the man did not shirk his duty. The whip bite stung like the dickens, and when it came time for the second, I tried not to flinch away from it and failed. But then it was over, and soldiers came forward to apply ointment to the few bleeding, helped us on with our shirts and coats, shared freshwater with us from the spring, and let us go.

While our punishment had been carried out, the governor's grandson wrote up in triplicate the decision of the court concerning the murders. All was ratified and signed by the governor, with signatures from Dom Miguel for Portugal and Captain LeFebvre for France, concerning their citizens. I took the ruling and folded it carefully into the leather wallet where our precious matelot agreement was kept, inside my jacket, next to my heart.

"There are opportunities for mulatto in the government of the Republic, Mr. Lector. I would be pleased to write a letter in support of your application," Governor du'Martinique said as the crowd filed out.

"I hold to my matelot contract, sir. Sólmundur would not find safety here."

The governor looked uncomfortable, but nodded. "I thought that might be your answer. If things change, the offer remains open."

"My thanks, sir." I bowed. I was grateful to him—the trial could have gone much, much worse. It was because of this man that Sun wasn't hanging from the yardarm. Therefore, I graciously took my leave, with nary a thought for my stinging back, and returned the sentiment to him that I did hope we would meet again.

In fact, I hoped the *Fury* came often to Tortuga, because there had never been a place in the world where I'd felt more safe. I laughed out loud at myself as we walked away from the well-defensible cliff. The place I felt most comfortable in the world was one of the most infamously lawless ports of all time. Sun looked up at me questioningly, but I only squeezed his hand and walked proudly through the streets with my matelot by my side.

THE WHOLE lot of us retired to the Perle, where the men of the *Fury* and the matelots were treated to drinks by Captain LeFebvre, who kept offering the men French commissions, saying the French Navy could use sturdy lads like them, which they declined, saying Captain Benji had already rounded out the crew of the *Fury* with their signing on. It seemed most of the population of the port of Tortuga was giving the Perle their custom for the afternoon, and every seat was filled with people discussing what had happened.

Artur sat at our table and paid for food for all three of us.

"I'm sorry," he said. "It was I who.... I told the Haitians you were with us and at the Perle and that they could arrest you when you came back to the ship."

"We know."

"I came and told them I'd lied, but—you know?" My words sank in while he was confessing, and the weight of guilt was replaced by surprise in his countenance.

"I saw it on your face."

He looked openmouthed from me to Sun and back again.

"We're men of the *Fury*," Sun said. "We saved you in the alley. You saved us from all but two lashes. We do as we should."

"And I would again, I promise you," Artur said fervently. "You're good sailors and true, and I was wrong about you."

I smiled slyly at Sun, then said to Artur, "And even if you are a bit of a goat turd from time to time, you're our goat turd."

Artur laughed and bought us three more plates of boiled crabs. "Well, I for one plan to never piss without you again. To the *Fury* and turds and men," he said, and he raised his mug in a toast, which we fervently joined.

"To the *Fury!*"

"Aye, aye!"

"To Captain Benji Swift!"

Agreement rang from our shipmates around us. I was still beset with emotion for all that had been done for us, so much so that, when Lovelie offered her fiddle, I declined because I was in no fit state to play it. Sun was safe. We were both safe, among friends, with a future ahead and adventure beckoning. We passed the afternoon coming to know our newest shipmates, who were a hardy and experienced lot. Captain Benji was quite pleased with his fortune of rounding out the crew of the *Fury*. His usual ship, the original *Sea Swift*, was undergoing an extensive refit in New Orleans and would be for some time, and he shared that he did not mind sailing the *Fury* until then.

"This ship needs a good name renewed by the right people," he said. "And I can complete the work we've been given aboard her as easily as another."

I pressed him to reveal more, but he only shook his head and said we were bound for New Orleans to look into a few things for King Louis, which might then send us back across the Atlantic, with a side journey north to Iceland, so Sun and I could pay recompense for Big Swede Erik, who it turned out was not Swedish at all but Icelandic, which was currently a colony of Denmark. Captain Benji said we might meet a Danish dignitary in New Orleans to whom we could pay Erik's recompense, but I still wanted to meet Sun's family and see what a volcano beset with ice and snow and glacier might look like.

Sun seemed more interested in New Orleans than Iceland, and when I pressed him on that point, he shrugged.

"What's in your thoughts?" I asked as we walked back to the *Fury* to start repaying our debts. "You seem troubled."

Sun fiddled with the bottom button on his coat as we walked down the boardwalk, dodging the various two- and four-legged population of Tortuga. "I… it's only…. I have not been home for a very long time. I do not think they would even know me…."

He fell silent, and I offered, "You feel like you've changed from who you were—so much so that even people you were once close to wouldn't recognize you?"

He nodded.

"I sometimes feel my own mother wouldn't recognize the man I've become." I had been through so much—shipwreck and falling in love and pirates and joining Captain Benji and all—I felt like the nymph that crawled up from the muck and became a dragonfly, completely transformed. And yet still the creature I was born to become.

I squeezed his hand, and he said, "I don't even know if *Afi* and *Amma* are still alive." In his voice lurked the boy he had once been—the fear and loss.

"If we go to Iceland, you'll know." When he didn't answer, I said, "And I'll be with you there, whomever we meet, whatever they think about you, and whatever we find there. I'll be with you, Sun. Always."

He brought my hand to his lips and kissed my knuckles and smiled. We walked hand in hand, in the open streets of Tortuga, stealing glances back and forth at each other, without worrying who saw us holding hands or what they thought. For me, there was only Sun, and freedom, and our future together.

AT THE docks, Captain LeFebvre gave Captain Benji the official corsair letters of marque actually signed by His Highness and the prime minister, and agreed to take Dom Miguel and Marisol, with promise of a reward, to Lisbon so they could do their best to foil Brazil's bid for independence. However, if it had the positive result for slaves and my fellow mulattos that the independence of the Republic of Haiti did, I wasn't sure I wanted it to fail. But I kept those thoughts to myself.

Captain Benji, Sun, and I oversaw the appraising, bartering, cataloging, and transfer of goods from the *Fury* to Captain LeFebvre's *Les Amoureux*, which, true to its name, had a most scandalous figurehead of two nudes, entwined. Their slender grace had a feminine quality, but one could not have truly named their gender. The question if Christophe LeFebvre had perhaps been born as Christophine rose in my mind, but I dismissed it. Did it matter? Not to me. LeFebvre was a kind soul and amusing—a joke ready here and there, but through and through a sailor, speaking with authority and grace. *Les Amoureux* would set sail in the morning with Dom Miguel and Marisol aboard, under a very capable commander.

I was so meticulous in the accounting and my clerk's duties that Captain Benji offered me the post of quartermaster on board the *Fury*. I gratefully accepted; the position of quartermaster was second only to the captain, just above the boatswain, and would give me a lot of authority. I was intimidated, but thought that was probably a good thing. And, anyway, I already knew I wasn't ready for my own captaincy. I'd been uncomfortable the entire voyage of the *Swift*, having to rely on Miguel to preserve me from my mistakes. When I earned my captaincy, I wanted it to be by my own merits.

The proceeds from Edwin's share of the guns, after an amount was taken out against repairs and provisioning the *Fury*, was split among all hands, old and new, and doled out to them before evening fell. Since we needed another night in Tortuga to see to the repairs on the *Fury*, we all returned to the Perle, where the men were not in the least shy about spending their coin—and celebrating their new quartermaster. The main part of the sailors from *Les Amoureux* joined us, as well as Dom Miguel and Marisol.

Having somewhat recovered from our ordeal, I accepted Lovelie's invitation to play her fiddle and managed to keep up with Cuicatl as we played our way through the more popular sailor's sea songs. I was pleasantly surprised Captain Benji joined in, his deep baritone barking out "*haul-in, haul-two, haul-belay*" as Captain LeFebvre's men sang "*un, deux, trois.*" Dom Miguel joined with his tenor, singing "*um, dois, três,*" and Sun, who had no fit singing voice whatsoever, joined in with a hearty "*einn, tveir, þrír!*" I laughed myself from my stool then and returned Lovelie's fiddle to her so I could pass some very pleasant time with Sun on my lap.

The evening and everyone's cups deepened, coin and wine flowed, and the stairs to the levels with the beds saw frequent use by the matelots who would soon set to sea with us, both crews of the ships, some of whom went up together—the sailors of *Les Amoureux* seemed to take the name of their ship as a personal duty—and the good folk of Tortuga. Through all of it, as he had the night before, Captain Benji stayed with the men and did not fondle the staff, made no invitations to accompany anyone upstairs, and none was offered by those who served under him, due to the status of a captain. It felt good to hold Sun on my lap, but I didn't want the captain to feel lonely. As I was about to stop exploring Sun's earlobe with my mouth to invite our captain to play a hand of cards with us, Captain LeFebvre and Marisol, her cheeks crimson, approached Captain Benji. He looked up at Marisol as though some unlooked-for angel had fallen from heaven.

"*Allons quelque part moins bruyant*," Captain LeFebvre said, inviting Benji to go somewhere more quiet. They both offered him their hands, which he took, and they drew him up the stairs among teasing shouts and lewd suggestions from both crews. Captain LeFebvre and Marisol glided with the indifference of circus performers before a crowd, a slight smile curving Marisol's lips, but Captain Benji walked like a man stupefied. The last three steps up, he seemed to come to himself, because his deep baritone sounded out "*un, deux*, ménage à trois" as he climbed and went through the door, accompanied by gales of laughter from all and sundry.

Sun showed our new friends the game of *tafl*, which all players had vigorous arguments about and enjoyed immensely. Dom Miguel sauntered by where we were playing with two young partners and invited both Sun and me to join them upstairs. I shared a glance with Sun, who had stilled the way an animal does when it senses a dangerous predator nearby.

"No, thank you. I barely have the wits to be in love with one person. More than that is beyond my ken. In fact, one is probably beyond my skill, but I have no other choice. I am his." I smiled at Sun to take any sting from my flippant words.

"Benjamin is mine," Sun told Miguel firmly. "And I am his."

"Ah! *A mal desesperado, remédio heróico*," he said, which was a Portuguese saying that meant a horrible disease required drastic measures.

I wanted to shout after him that love was not desperate, and monogamy not a heroic sacrifice, but reasoned it was a waste of breath.

We stayed far too late, drank a bit too much, gambled more than we should, ate heartily, and tearfully shared promises with the Frenchmen and Dom Miguel that we would most certainly see them off in the morning. When Captain Benji didn't return and seemed to be making rather a night of it, I inquired after him and was told Marisol had booked the room for the duration of the evening. So, in my duties as quartermaster, I joined with Abellard the boatswain in rounding up our drunken crew, who gave hugs to the crew of the *Les Amoureux*, whose quartermaster wobbled to his feet and followed my example. The whole lot of us tumbled out into the street without our captains, singing "*un, deux*, ménage à trois" and laughing uproariously.

There was another parting at the docks, the French kissing the cheeks of our men, who clapped them heartily on the back, and this time there weren't soldiers waiting at the gangplank to arrest us. I saw to the men getting settled—many of whom dropped off to sleep—set the less drunk ones to a half watch, sent the short watch who had been guarding the ship off to take their leave at the Perle with a little extra coin to spend and instructions to keep an eye out for our captain, and then Sun and I retired to our cabin.

I lowered myself to the bed and let out a long breath, my limbs falling limp and akimbo as I lay back, having drunk enough wine that I barely felt my lash marks.

Sun watched me settle in with that long, slow blink I'd learned meant he was about to do something lascivious. I could not help grinning, but he didn't let my enthusiasm break the mood. He disrobed slowly, deliberately, revealing the savage god I had fallen in love with one piece of clothing at a time. I was breathless with desire by the time he stood naked before me, but when I reached for him his soft "*nei, nei*" stopped me. Apparently, for this game, I was not allowed to move. The anticipation I'd felt in *la prison* returned, and I was powerfully hard and ready for him as he disrobed me slowly, then placed his body along mine, and touched me, withholding permission for me to touch him in return until I was panting with need. I begged him. I cussed him. He laughed at me and insisted on bringing me off, not once, but twice—which, I must admit, with the many hours I spent as a teen with only the images of the stableboy to amuse me, I had not been able to accomplish alone since I'd first discovered what my runner and tackle were for. Then, and only then, was I allowed to touch him. I worshiped his body with a fervor and devotion I had never given anything else in my life.

Spent, we rested in each other's arms, in our own bed, aboard our own ship, free men, members of a crew, servants of the French Crown. Sun was going to get to see his family again, if we could find them. All was well, except....

"Sun, I'm sorry."

"Hmm?" He blinked sleepily up at me from where he was nestled across my chest.

"All your booty, my guns. It's all gone. We could have lived quite handsomely off the proceeds, but now we will have to earn our keep. Sailor's wages and a share of what we capture as corsairs. It won't be much, and it won't be glamorous."

"Remember what I said? *Þetta er ekki upp í nös á ketti.*"

"Yes, but now we really don't have enough to fill a cat's nostril."

"You forget, Benjamin." He got fluidly up off the narrow bed, his bronzed muscles glimmering in the lamplight, and shuffled around at the foot of the bed under our sea chest. Then he lifted a small, ash-scarred box decorated with elephants onto the bed.

The *gimsteinar*. With everything that had happened, I'd forgotten completely about them.

"We can use this when we need to," he said, inserting his key and opening it so the gemstones sparkled in the lamplight. "And still free everyone we can. I would like to do that, Benjamin."

"We will," I promised, gathering him into my arms and kissing the top of his head. We'd started by freeing ourselves, and now we could pass that gift on to others.

CHAPTER 38.
AU REVOIR, POUR LE MOMENT

MOST OF the town came to see us off. As usual the sun shone with tropical intensity, but it wasn't yet hot. A light breeze blew in from the sea, and it played with Sun's white-blond hair and caressed us where we stood on the docks. The night watch had escorted the two captains, Marisol, and the last of our sailors back just after dawn.

Captain Benji's eyelids were at half-mast, a wistful smile on his lips that looked like it might never, ever fade. I assumed that was what I looked like after an energetic session with Sun, and resolved not to show that to the men I was supposed to be commanding. Both Captain LeFebvre and Marisol looked, as usual, fresh as a new sail, and they retired to *Les Amoureux* for a few hours of sleep before we left port. Sun and I saw to bedding down Captain Benji, who said he didn't want us to talk to him because he was trying to remember everything that had happened to him that night.

We let him be until all the men were mustered on the docks with the men of *Les Amoureux* to bid them farewell, then fetched him. The governor had come to the docks with much of the garrison, and I again thanked him heartily for our deliverance. Most of Tortuga came as well. Lovelie pressed her fiddle on me—I was speechless at her kindness. Sun excused himself and returned, then gifted her a little box with our thanks, but made her promise not to open it until after we set sail. I guessed it held one of his gemstones, and silently approved.

Dom Miguel had found some princely attire somewhere in Tortuga and looked very dashing in a high-collared black coat with gold embroidery on the cuffs and collar, gold epaulettes draping delicately over the shoulders, and gold buttons from neck to sword belt, complete with horseman's saber. Long tails trailed gracefully over black britches and high black leather boots. My tailor grandfather would have wept, it fit him so beautifully. He embraced both me and Sun and kissed our cheeks, then Captain Benji as well, who still looked thunderstruck by his good fortune of the night before.

Marisol, dressed as before in the manner of a French naval officer, kissed us on each cheek, as did Captain LeFebvre. Among the men, there was a great deal of clapping one another on the back and kissing one another's cheeks and wishing *au revoir*. Then Miguel was wringing my hand and a promise from me that if I were ever in Portugal, I would visit him, then an *"au revoir, pour le moment"* from Marisol, with a promise that she would seek us out after her business in Lisbon was complete. Finally the crew and their illustrious passengers boarded *Les Amoureux*.

I had been nervous about Captain LeFebvre's ship being allowed to leave without trouble, considering the current relations between France and Haiti, but I'd been told that *Les Amoureux* had earned a perpetual welcome in Tortuga. Considering the disposition of captain and crew, I wasn't surprised. They glided gracefully out to sea, and we watched them, waving, until they were a speck on the horizon. The men had time for one last lunch from the cook at the Perle, and then our repairs were complete, and it was time for the *Fury* to get underway.

Captain Benji had returned to himself by degrees throughout the day and was shouting orders as usual by afternoon—except this time, as quartermaster I was relaying those orders and finalizing the payment for repairs and a hundred other duties so much so that I had not a moment to catch my breath until the *Fury* was pulling away from the dock. I waved farewell to Tortuga as vigorously as Tortuga waved farewell to us, our now-full complement of crew working half as hard as we had getting underway from Dread Island. Our heading was west, sailing for New Orleans and our mysterious business for King Louis.

As Tortuga dwindled behind us in the late afternoon light, Sun joined me where I watched from the quarterdeck and rested his head on my shoulder. I put my arm around him, no longer afraid to express my feelings now that I knew half the ship was matelots. The sunlight was bright in Sun's pale hair, and the wind played with the strands. He turned to me and smiled, revealing his beloved dimple. He was so beautiful he no longer looked human. The years and scars faded away until he was something greater than all we had survived—he was my light, mine to protect and be protected by. He was my love and my life. I pulled him into my arms and kissed the top of his amazing head.

We stood on the deck and watched the light sparkle on the sea, and I thanked God for storms and darkness, because the sunshine after was so sweet.

"Benjamin?"

"Yes?"

"I love you," Sun said calmly, inexorably. A fact, like "It is raining."

"I love you too," I echoed him.

And then the wind changed, and Captain Benji's baritone rang out "Haul-in, haul-two, haul-belay," and we all, to a man, answered him, unfurling the lateen sail and tacking our way windward into the setting sun. Losing ourselves in the work, in each other, in our joy, and in our safe place. A trusty ship in a big world made smaller by the right people, the right place, the right time.

GLOSSARY OF FOREIGN TERMS
AND PROVERBS

A mal desesperado, remédio heróico: *Portuguese.* A desperate disease
    calls for drastic medicine.

Afi: *Icelandic.* Grandfather.

Aldin: *Icelandic.* Fruit.

Alea iacta est: *Latin.* The die is cast.

Allons quelque part moins bruyant: *French.* Let's go someplace quieter.

Allt: *Icelandic.* All.

Allt í lagi: *Icelandic.* All right.

Ameaça de carinhosas marés: *Portuguese.* Threat of loving seas.

Amma: *Icelandic.* Grandmother.

Annað folk: *Icelandic.* Other people.

Ansans ári: *Icelandic.* Devil's demon.

Api: *Icelandic.* Ape.

Au revoir: *French.* Good-bye.

Au revoir, pour le moment: *French.* Good-bye, for now.

Bolas: *Portuguese.* Balls.

Brauð: *Icelandic.* Bread.

Brujo: *Spanish.* Sorcerer.

Bursti: *Icelandic.* Brush.

Cabelo castanho: *Portuguese.* Brown hair.

Canibales: *Spanish.* Cannibals.

Capitaine(s): *French.* Captain(s).

Caraca: *Portuguese.* Whoa.

Castrati: *Italian.* Castrated.

Cher: *Louisiana Creole.* Dear.

Couilles: *French.* Balls.

Desgraçado: *Portuguese.* Bastard.

Donzela: *Portuguese.* Damsel.

Einn—tveir—þrír: *Icelandic.* One, two, three.

Encontrei onde estava o sinal de fogo: *Portuguese.* I found where the
    signal fire was.

Erfitt: *Icelandic*. Difficult.

Facón: *Spanish*. A fighting and utility knife used widely in South America.

Farðu að sofa: *Icelandic*. Go to sleep.

Fiskur: *Icelandic*. Fish.

Fode: *Portuguese*. Fuck.

Frelsa oss frá illu: *Icelandic*. Deliver us from evil.

Fukka: *Pidgin*. Fuck (as Big Swede Erik used it).

Gaucho: *Spanish*. Cowboy.

Gimstein(n)(ar): *Icelandic*. Gem(s).

Grímsvötn: *Icelandic*. The proper name of a volcano in Iceland.

Gros Bourse: *French*. Fat purse.

Ha?: *Icelandic*. Huh?

Harðfiskur: *Icelandic*. Dried fish.

Hlandbrenndu: *Icelandic*. May your urine burn.

Hnífur: *Icelandic*. Knife.

Inquiétant: *French*. Disquieting.

Já: *Icelandic*. Yes.

Komdu: *Icelandic*. Come.

La prison: *French*. Prison.

Ladro: *Portuguese*. Thief.

Ladrões do mar: *Portuguese*. Pirates.

Lagniappe: *Louisiana Creole*. Something given as a bonus or extra gift.

Lauf: *Icelandic*. Leaf.

Le drapeau francais: *French*. The French flag.

Les Amoureux: *French*. The Lovers.

L'infanterie: *French*. Infantry.

Marujo Português: *Portuguese*. Portuguese Sailor.

Ménage à trois: *French*. Threesome.

Meu Deus: *Portuguese*. My God.

Mon ami: *French*. My friend.

Morðingi: *Icelandic*. Murderer.

Nei: *Icelandic*. No.

Obrigado: *Portuguese*. Thank you.

Onde estão os homens: *Portuguese*. Where are the men?

Oui: *French*. Yes.

Ouviu o galo cantar e não saber onde: *Portuguese*. He heard the rooster crowing without knowing where; to succeed by sheer luck.

Það er skammgóður vermir að pissa í skó sinn: *Icelandic*. It is only a temporary respite to urinate in his shoe; something that fixes a problem for a while, but ends up making it worse in the long run.

Þetta er ekki upp í nös á ketti: *Icelandic*. Not enough to fill a cat's nostril; not very much.

Plátanos: *Spanish*. Plantains.

Porcelet adorable: *French*. Adorable pig.

Quenepa (*Spanish*) or quenette (*French islander*): Spanish lime.

Ratljóst: *Icelandic*. Enough light to find your way by.

Réttdræpur: *Icelandic*. Rightfully killable.

S'il y avait une taxe sur ton cerveau, tu n'aurais plus un rond: *French*. If there was a tax on your brain, you wouldn't have any money left.

Sim: *Portuguese*. Yes.

Saltfiskur: *Icelandic*. Salted fish.

Sitjandi: *Icelandic*. Bum; behind.

Strönd: *Icelandic*. Beach.

Svín: *Icelandic*. Swine.

Tafl: *Icelandic*. Short for *Hnefatafl*, an early Scandinavian board game.

Tire-au-flanc: *French*. Shirker; someone who evades obligations.

Tveir: *Icelandic*. Two.

Um—dois—três: *Portuguese*. One, two, three.

Un—deux—trois: *French*. One, two, three.

Você fala Português: *Portuguese*. Do you speak Portuguese?

Vous avez le cerveau comme une meule de fromage: *French*. Your brain is a cheese wheel.

Vous n'êtes que des petits branleurs bons à rien: *French*. You are nothing but little wasters, good for nothing.

KAREN BOVENMYER was born and raised in Iowa, where she teaches and mentors new writers at Iowa State University. She triple-majored in anthropology, English, and history so she could take college courses about cave people, zombie astronauts, and medieval warfare to prepare for her writing career. After earning her BS, she completed a master's degree with a double specialization in literature and creative writing with a focus in speculative fiction, also from Iowa State University. Although trained to offer "Paper? Or plastic?" in a variety of pleasant tones, she landed an administrative job at the college shortly after graduation. Working full-time, getting married, setting up a household, and learning how to be an adult with responsibilities (i.e. bills to pay) absorbed her full attentions for nearly a decade during which time she primarily only wrote extremely detailed roleplaying character histories and participated in National Novel Writing Month. However, in 2010, Karen lost a parent. With that loss, she realized becoming a published author had a nonnegotiable mortal time limit. She was accepted to the University of Southern Maine's Stonecoast MFA program with a specialization in Popular Fiction and immediately started publishing, selling her first story just before starting the program and three more while in the extremely nurturing environment provided by the Stonecoast community, from which she graduated in 2013. Her science fiction, fantasy, and horror novellas, short stories, and poems now appear in more than twenty publications. She is the Horror Writers Association 2016 recipient of the Mary Wollstonecraft Shelley Scholarship. She serves as the nonfiction editor for Escape Artist's *Mothership Zeta Magazine* and narrates stories for *Pseudopod*, *Strange Horizons*, *Far Fetched Fables*, *Star Ship Sofa*, and the *Gallery of Curiosities* Podcasts.

Website: karenbovenmyer.com
LinkedIn: www.linkedin.com/in/karenbovenmyer
Facebook: www.facebook.com/karen.bovenmyer
Twitter: @karenbovenmyer

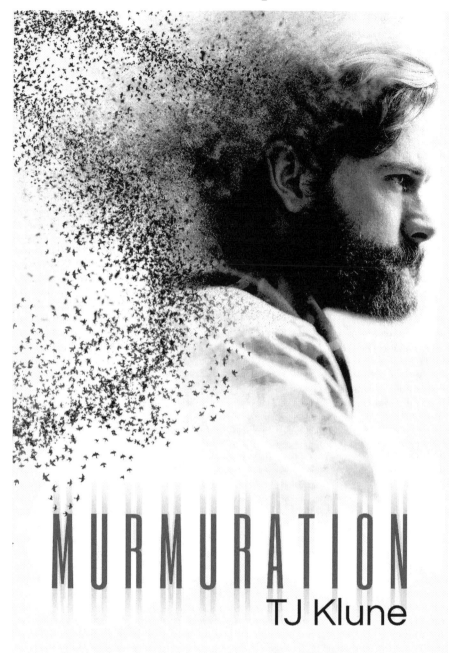

Also from Dreamspinner Press

www.dreamspinnerpress.com

Also from Dreamspinner Press

STRONGHOLD

Nicki Bennett
and
Ariel Tachna

www.dreamspinnerpress.com

Also from Dreamspinner Press

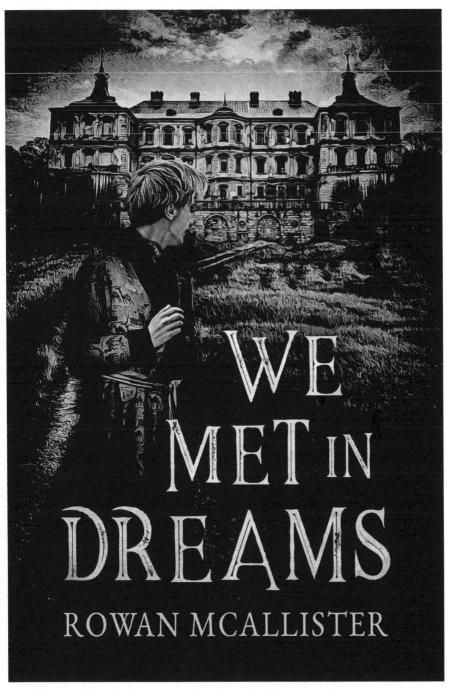

www.dreamspinnerpress.com

Made in the USA
San Bernardino, CA
18 August 2019